Truck Stop

John L. Thompson

Truck Stop

John L. Thompson

A Dusty Desert Press Publication

To Renee,

For being the patient and enduring wife during this voyage…

Also to Wayne Stanton,
One of the reasons for going back into diesel mechanics as a profession
…gone but never forgotten…

"And, above the packed and pestilential town,
Death looked down…
-Rudyard Kipling, A Tale of Two Cities

"There is a looming shortage of skilled diesel technicians, but we don't want to pay
any more than necessary for those skills…."

-Upper management at most trucking companies

"This truck stop is a miniature city within a city."

-Shop manager at a New Mexico truck stop, 2005

ONE

It was a week before Thanksgiving when the El Camino blew its guts out somewhere between Albuquerque and nowhere. Blue and white smoke rolled out from under the hood, rising to the heavens like some sick sacrifice smoldering on the altar of some pagan god of old.

"Fuck! Fuck! Shit! Fuck!" I howled, kicking the ground, shaking clenched fists to the cloudy heavens above like a banshee whore on bad crack. The gods, amused by the outburst, pissed a little cold rain down on my face.

I stared long and hard at the billowing plume of burning anti-freeze mixed with a hint of oil. Like getting pissed off and going on a rant and rave was going to fix anything. A cracked block, head, spun bearing, or a rod; it was any combination of things, but the motor was shot. I was sure of it. I started back off into a tirade of obscenities and danced around kicking the gravel lot and punching the empty air with angry fists.

So close, yet so far. *"Ahhh…damn it."*

Midland, Texas. *Be there Tuesday morning* the recruiter said. *We need diesel mechanics ASAP.*

I was glad to be a diesel mechanic, elated in fact but today was Monday. *One God-damned day, just one damned day is all I needed!*

Oilfield jobs in Texas were an up and coming thing for as far as one could see. They were cropping up all over and a fair number of companies were looking for diesel mechanics. You had to be Johnny-on-the-spot in the hopes of landing those jobs.

Having worn out my welcome and options in Las Vegas, I made a few phone calls, searched the internet, and tossed my resume out into the vast voids of the ether land. A recruiter from Dawson Petroleum called a day later, and after a series of questions, offered a conditional hire status. I needed to get there by Tuesday for orientation and drug testing.

I had high hopes that by blowing Nevada, I would've left the bad mojo behind, but that bad bitch karma was waiting for me. Divorce, the lack of high paying jobs in my field, financial debt, *everything*…she had kicked my ass good on this one. I'd hoped the El Camino would've made the trip, but when the motor started knocking and banging coming up the hill, the Midland dream of milk and honey evaporated like cow piss on a hot rock.

The whispered sound of passing cars on the freeway cutting through the air taunted me with my failure. The green exit sign off I-40 stated I was at some place called Sedillo. I took off my sunglasses and looked around. I was lucky to have coasted off the freeway into a large dirt lot by a frontage road. But looking around, there were limited options.

The good times passed by this place years ago. The few residents left lived in dilapidated houses of broken foundations, peeled paint, and sagging roofs. I guess no one had the heart to explain to them they were clinging to a wheezing, dead corpse. Surrounding the living were the scattered tombstones of the dead, abandoned homes slowly being reclaimed by Mother Nature. Other buildings and rusted cars melted back into a large swath of tangled trees and thick undergrowth. The only building close to living was a lone gas station perched on the edge of Route 66. The modern gas pumps stood abandoned waiting for customers who would never come. The owners probably realized it was a mistake to have opened a business in the middle of a ghost town.

The middle of bum-fuck New Mexico.

This is it, Logan Pierce, dead in the water, nowhere to go… homeless…and about broke. I knelt down, put my sunglasses back on and leaned back against the El Camino. Looking up, the clouds that had showered the dusty earth moments before had drifted eastward, leaving bright blue skies in their wake. I fought to contain my rage and disappointment. The early winter sun had crested its zenith and hung in the skies like an angry eye of God casting judgment.

I did a mental tally of what money I had left. The cash pile was down to thirteen hundred. A rebuild would cost an easy three thousand, maybe more since this was a 396 big block. I might be able to scrape by with finding a used one, but where in hell could I even begin looking for one around here? The motors were hard to find and commanded a premium. If I bought another vehicle, I sure wasn't going to get anything for the El Camino in trade and there was no way I could part with it. The beast had traveled many years with me on the road to life. It had survived high school in Connecticut, survived the Vegas elements, the countless trips to California to visit the in-laws and damned if it hadn't just survived the rock-strewn shores of divorce.

The pearl-white paint glared in the sun. I envied putting money into the bodywork instead of the engine. Just before being laid off at the union gig, I got the wild hair and reworked the body and replaced the interior. I should've used the money to rebuild the engine but I wanted it to look good first.

Well, it did look good though…sitting there dead and spewing its guts all over the ground.

I took out my cell phone and confirmed the time. The El Camino had blown a heart valve at just before noon. Waylon Jennings was singing '*Lonesome, O'nery and Mean.*' At least the radio still worked. Nothing like a bit of Waylon to keep you company when you're down and out. All that was needed was the Crown and beer. I looked around, pulled down my sunglasses, peering over the edges.

A black and white Ford Expedition drove by. The brake lights suddenly lit up. The large gold star on the driver's door screamed Johnny Law.

I muttered a curse. Was this friend or foe? Some cops loved to screw with out-of-staters knowing full well they're not going to court to contest a ticket.

The Expedition flipped a bitch, rolled into the parking lot, the gravel crunching and popping under the tires. The SUV rolled up next to the El Camino, and the window slid down. The driver hung a hand out the window. The first thing I noticed was the tattoo. It was a skull, with bright, glowing red eyes, tearing through the inked skin and bones. Under the torn flesh, the words '*Dead*', were scrawled in large, elegant cursive. His Spanish features were typical, long face, well-trimmed mustache, thin lips women found attractive, but the tattoo commanded attention. He lowered his sunglasses, revealing soft, light brown eyes. He looked the El Camino over. "Nice car. What's the problem?"

I was still focused on the tattoo before realizing he was talking "Blew the motor I think." I wondered how he managed to get on the police force with that kind of a tattoo.

"*Aww*, no shit?" he sounded genuinely concerned. He popped open the driver's door and stepped out. He stood a half head taller, and his build was stocky. His name tag said *A. Fernandez*. He slid his left hand, the one with the skull tattoo, down to adjust his duty belt that held a Glock .40.

"Yeah, coming up the hill here. I was lucky to coast off the freeway."

He walked down the side of the El Camino, brushing his fingertips along the pearl paint. "It happens a lot, coming up the hill can be a bitch. What year?"

"'69."

He whistled. "Damned hard to find those these days in decent shape, nice looking car."

"Thanks."

He pointed to the trailer hitched to the El Camino. "I think maybe a bit much weight on the old gal."

The trailer held my triple bay toolbox, a side cart full of tools and a few personal belongings. "I think so."

"How much?"

"I'm sorry?"

He looked back at the El Camino. "How much would you sell it for?"

"It's not for sale."

He stood silent for a moment. I didn't think he liked to take 'no' for an answer. His face became unreadable. "Where you headed? Or I should say *were* headed."

I took a look east. "Was going to Texas."

He lowered the sunglasses. "Don't look like it now."

"Nope, we ain't."

"So..." He pulled out his wallet and shuffled through one of the dividers. "I'm guessing you need a tow." I then saw the large rose tattoo on the back of his right hand with the words 'Life', written in the same cursive lettering

"Right you are, sir," I tried to stay focused away from the tattoos. There was something I didn't like about the guy, not just because he was a cop, but something else. I couldn't put a finger on it. Maybe it was the way he brushed the El Camino, much like he was caressing the skin of a lover he was about to murder. Maybe it was his demeanor or maybe the fact he was a cop. I didn't particularly care for cops. Not that I hated them or anything, I just felt uneasy around them. The only upside in this was I wasn't getting a ticket or my shit ruffled through.

"You can't leave your El Camino out here. Someone will end up stealing or stripping parts off it before too long," he handed over a business card. "I got a '70 Mustang Fastback. I understand how it is with these old cars. We get attached to them for some reason. This here is a tow service out of Moriarty, just up the road."

I took hold of the card. *Pleasant Tow Service.* Below was the phone number. I'm sure it was going to be pleasant for them getting my hard-earned cash.

"They're pretty good people and will come out pretty quick," he flashed a smile then slid back in the Expedition and snapped his seat belt in place.

"How far up the road?"

He looked out through his windshield. "Oh, I'm guessing something like ten, fifteen miles."

I sighed and shook my head.

He smiled. "You ever change your mind about selling, look me up in Moriarty, it's where I'm stationed for the moment."

I smiled and told him, "Thanks, but no thanks."

He took another long look at the El Camino, placed the Expedition in gear and pulled back out to the frontage road, gunned the engine and dropped out of sight over the small hill. I envied the Expedition but was glad to see him go. There was something about him that didn't feel right, but then again, maybe I was reading too much into it.

I was feeling lonesome, ornery and damned mean. I hammered

the keys on my cell phone with a heavy thumb, calling the tow company to get the El Camino and trailer towed to a town called Moriarty. Just the name alone sounded too close to 'mortuary' but I was holding out hope it was a bigger town as compared to Sedillo. With so few dollars in the pocket, I might have to take a local job to scrape together enough money for either another vehicle or repairing the El Camino. I knew it was going to be the later.

The thing that was going to hurt was making the call to Dawson Petroleum. I hated to explain my dilemma and hoped they would understand and hold the job opening for me. Maybe call in some favors to a few people and hope they could help out on the financial end. Maybe rent a truck, put the El Camino in storage and haul my toolbox to Texas.

The phone rang and I took another look around at Sedillo.

Down and out in the middle of nowhere.

TWO

I downed a shot of Crown Royal and held up the empty tumbler for another refill. There's nothing like drowning one's sorrows in an ocean of alcohol kind of positive. This day was at least going to end on a positive note. The old Vietnamese bartender kept the chambers loaded with shots of Crown and replaced the empty bottles of Heineken as the vapors began to take hold.

The lounge was empty with the exception of a couple employees and a single patron who were all busy dozing away while watching a baseball game on a giant flat screen. Music from the Rolling Stones drifted from the overhead speakers. I downed a swallow on my third round of Heineken brew while pondering my next move.

The call to my sister had done jack-shit nothing. I was hoping she would've tossed me a few bones to limp into Texas but there was no answer. We hadn't spoken for years. Our father, who had passed away eight years ago, had split everything between us equally in his will. I had given up my portion of the house to her. I hated seeing her struggle to make rent every month and she had a daughter to care for. Giving her the house was the right thing to do at the time. I was married then. The ex-wife was a nurse and I had a good union gig as a diesel mechanic. We could afford such luxuries. I had hoped my sister would've remembered what I had done and helped me out this time.

She didn't.

I figured it had something to do with her belief in Scientology. The last I heard anything from her, she had married a big shot in the local Church. She told me I had a *'reactive'* mind and I needed to get my *'thetan'* squared away before we could ever speak to each other again.

Whatever the hell that meant.

Then there was the call to Dawson Petroleum to explain my predicament. They couldn't hold the position and they were moving on to other applicants. The line went dead before I could say anything further and so did the hopes and dreams of big money and a new life.

I finished off the Heineken and held up the empty bottle. The old Viet replaced it with a fresh bottle and went back to wiping down the granite counter.

I took a couple of twenties from my pocket and tossed them down on the bar top. More alcohol was needed. Even though I needed every penny to get out of here, the alcohol helped lubricate the neurons into formulating a plan. It was needed in fact. I downed the shot of Crown and held up the tumbler. The alcohol held a firm, massaging grip on the cortex of my brain.

The old Viet took an interest in my plight. Or maybe it was the fact I was the only customer buying shots and he wanted tip money. He eyed the money on the counter. He poured a shot of Crown and smiled. "You look so down in dumps. What problem could make you so down?"

I smiled. "Too many problems."

"Where there is a problem, there is a solution," he flashed a toothy smile.

Bartenders love to listen to people's problems. It's a cliché but if you're a paying customer you get a built-in shrink for your dollar. "You think so huh?"

He listened to me bitch for the next several minutes and stopped me a couple times to ply a question until he came up with his own conclusion on the matters of the heart. "Duggan's, they may be looking for mechanics."

"He's right, try Duggan's."

The voice grabbed my attention. At the end of the bar stood a man somewhere between his late thirties to early forties. He had crow feet lines at the corners of hazel colored eyes. He stood an even six-foot but his most striking feature was his black hair streaked with grey. Some broads find that attractive in a man but I had the impression he could've cared less. His dark blue uniform was grease stained and the name patch was worn and stained to the point I couldn't make out the lettering. He motioned for the bartender and held up his glass with hard hands. "Another shot of liquid courage, Lee."

Lee moved to refill the glass with a combination of Jack Daniels and coke. "You working?" Lee asked.

He nodded. "In about an hour," he took out his wallet and tossed a few bills on the counter. "I *should* be sober enough to survive."

"Duggan's? Sounds like some sort of fruity drink," I said.

"Oh, it can be sometimes, I assure you," he flashed a smile and took a swallow off his glass.

"Who are you again?" I motioned for another shot.

Lee topped off my own glass. "This shot on me," he whispered before scooping up the two twenties, but I was too drunk to care.

He pointed to his name patch. "Hendricks, just plain old Hendricks," he took another sip. "You?"

"Logan," I sipped on the amber fluid. "So, what's Duggan's?"

"I couldn't help overhear you saying you're a mechanic, we're always looking for mechanics," Hendricks twisted, pointing a thin finger behind him.

"Yeah?" I followed his finger, across the lounge and through the tinted pane glass. Across the main street, trucks moved in and out of a truck stop. I had seen it coming into Moriarty when the El Camino got towed here but never gave it much thought.

The truck stop was a throwback to another era and those times had passed by decades ago. The main complex, with its rows of dark tinted windows, chalky white painted siding and red-tinned roof, looked like a leering sun-bleached skull under the New Mexico skies. I could imagine the world beyond those nicotine-stained windows, where layers of painted walls peeled and faded under the harsh suns of the seasons. It would be a place where truck drivers conjugated in smoke-filled hallways and lounge areas looking for the dealer with the magic pill that would carry them to their next destination a dozen states away. There would be runaways lurking in dark corners trying to hitch rides across the US in exchange for sex. An army of unconcerned employees would be mopping and scrubbing away at pools of stale vomit and old sex stains.

Most modern truck stops were corporate owned paradises, strategically positioned along the nation's highways to generate maximum profit and focused on driver comforts for dollars. They were sanitized, cleaned and well cared for facilities that offered anything from fuel to a wide range of chain restaurants, showers, laundry services and anything in between. This truck stop that Hendricks pointed to looked like it got stuck in time somewhere around the middle of the nineteen-eighties. This one was a virtual time machine you see on those sun-faded vintage postcards. The exception was you didn't want to send it to family or friends letting them know you had visited such a place.

A dust devil kicked up amidst a line of trucks. Discarded trash bags and papers danced and swirled high above the lot in a dusty brown cloud mixture, before vaporizing into the clear blue skies. The trash then floated back to the broken asphalt and waited for the next winds.

Off behind the main complex, I could see part of the shop at the far end of the lot. A mechanic knows where a shop is located on any trucking property. From my vantage point, the placed looked busy. Trucks and trailers were lined up waiting to get inside for whatever ailed the machines.

"It looks like a shit hole," I slurred. Maybe a whole new complex would be in order.

"It is but if you need money you can get a job there. We got jobs for days rolling in at all hours. Hell, they'll hire anyone," he said with some disdain before downing the last of his drink.

Lee stopped wiping the counter long enough to refill his shot glass before focusing back on some stubborn stain only he could see.

"You know what they're paying?" I asked.

He shook his head, "Everyone negotiates their own wages."

"I'll look into it."

"Sure, but one thing," he tapped out a cigarette from a crumpled pack of Marlboros. "Don't mention me."

"Don't mention you, got it."

"Nothing personal, but management won't hire you if you tell them I recommended you to them."

Swallowing the shot of Crown, I looked back through the window. Maybe it was an option. Albuquerque would've been a better choice but with no transportation, that idea was in the toilet. This might get things started until something better rolled around. Once I had the money, the next goal was to fix the El Camino and head to

Texas. I hadn't lost all hope on finding employment with either Dawson Petroleum or some other oil outfit.

"I'll head on over tomorrow, thanks."

He lifted his glass and nodded. "Good luck," he slipped away from the bar with his drink and back to the ball game.

I stood up, dug out a couple tattered twenties from my pocket, placed them on the bar, and got the bottle of Crown and a couple Heinekens. I wasn't sure if I got screwed in the deal. Eighty bucks seemed high but I had drunk a lot. I thanked the old Viet anyway and limped out to the main lobby and stumbled back up to my room.

I placed the bottle on the nightstand, took a piss and lit up a smoke. Smoking was another leftover curse from a bad divorce. Tendrils of smoke rose up from my fingertips like a summoned genie with no face but I could hear the bitch laughing.

I slid the balcony door open and felt the chill of the winter air wash over me. I didn't even want to think about the ex. The wounds of deceit were still etched across my heart and mind. I still hated...missed...and loved her. I took another hit off the Crown bottle to drown the memories.

Duggan's was busy as hell. I continued taking shots and lighting up one smoke after another as the sun faded from a bright blue clear to the late shades of dusk. The light poles scattered across the lot flickered to life like matchsticks being struck. Shadows moved in and out of the main complex. The worn yellow headlights from the truck traffic poked through the thick, ever-present exhaust haze. A steady flow of trucks lumbered off the highway. They lined up at the fifteen diesel pump stations behind the complex like a group of eager sailors on shore leave sauntering up to the bar to get shit-faced.

My alcohol-soaked brain focused on the shop. It looked like this was going to be the only game in town. I had thumbed through the phone book earlier. There were a couple other mom and pop repair shops at the end of town but they weren't looking any mechanics.

Down below the broken El Camino sat. Broken, wilting away under the Moriarty evening like my soul every time I looked at it. I could feel the weeds growing under the tires. Growing old by the second, time lapses on fast forward forever, and time is a constant enemy.

I drank another shot away and my mind drifted.

I had been pounding concrete for eighteen years as a diesel mechanic.

Some guys get to do incredible things in life like being a badass in the military with a list of ball sack curdling events stamped across their DD214s. Others go to college to make it big in business by slitting the throats of the competition on the way up the corporate ladder. Others become lawyers or doctors, but for the majority of Americans, we choose the lesser professions whether we like it or not. We enlist our services under the many banners of corporate or business armies, swelling their ranks to wage wars for customer's dollars across the battlefields of the American economy. We become fast order cooks, grocery clerks, dispatchers, truck drivers, parts runners, cashiers, cops, and or bad guys. I happened to choose the life of a diesel mechanic.

I would be lying if I said I didn't love every minute of it.

My first days as a diesel mechanic were nothing more than forgotten blurs and fragments of memories lost to the fogs of time. I had graduated high school in 1988 and took to the party life for a time. Every night was good times celebrating with friends our triumphs and our new found freedom into adulthood. We cruised the highways around Middletown, Connecticut with our cars or trucks and picked up and banged willing skirts. The popular beats of Def Leppard, INXS, and Guns n' Roses thumped from tinted windows and we drank as much alcohol as possible.

But eventually the season of freedom ended and the tainted tentacles of life began creeping in. Everybody was in a hurry to get on with life, jobs, and careers and eventually, I was the last man standing out of the group. I didn't know what the hell I was going to do with the rest of my life.

I had just broken up with Jenifer McDowell. We dated on and off throughout our senior year in high school and it carried over into the summer months. It was early September and one could feel the beginning shifts of the seasons. She had been offered a scholarship from a college in Texas. She didn't want the long-term relationship thing nor did she want me in the picture anymore. The sex and parties were good but life was knocking at the door and plans had to be made. She wanted a man who had an idea of a career path worked out. The idea of working on a career as a future alcoholic with a bad case of some weird unpronounceable STD didn't hold much promise. She wanted a man with a financially promising future and stability on the home front. Neither point I could provide at that time. She knew I was messing around with a few other broads on the side.

I was cruising the outskirts of Middletown headed home after a night of howling at the moon and bad feelings from the break up when I saw the sign. It was a sign from God that changed my life. Well, it was a help wanted sign, but it steered me down the road to a career as a diesel mechanic. I saw the wooden sign posted by the side of the road with thick hand-painted words scrawled in white.

Help wanted: Lube Mechanic.

I turned the El Camino onto the gravel lot leading to the trucking terminal. There was no thought, only action. That's why I say it was the hand of God guiding me down the road to destiny. I got the job as a lube tech, worked there a few years before making the jump to a dealership in Las Vegas, Nevada. Now, after eighteen years, here I was a full-fledged diesel mechanic.

Eighteen years....

The shop was packed two deep outside the tarmac. I resigned myself to the fact that tomorrow I would go in and see if they were hiring. I was sure they would be. Mechanics are a necessary evil. If I could stitch together enough money to fix the El Camino and pocket a few bucks for gas, Texas would not be out of the question in the future. The itch for the oil fields still played strong in my hopes to knit my tattered life back together.

To hell with it. Adapt or die.

I flicked the cigarette butt over the balcony and downed the last of the Crown before pulling the glass door closed. It had taken a fair amount of alcohol to convince myself that the job and new life in Texas were gone. I was going to have to shift gears.

THREE

The sights and sounds are the same. There was the blistering hammering of impacts spinning off lug nuts or rusty bolts, mechanics swearing and yelling and diesel motors knocking to life. A thick cloud of gauzy smoke from exhaust stacks floated lazily out the bay doors. The smells are the same. Hot coolant, burnt brakes, and used gear oils mixed with the lingering stench of diesel fuel hung thick in the air. The walls had once been white but were now black from years of exposure from exhaust fumes and dust. The floors had the same coated color of dull black dust ground into the concrete from years of exposure to chemical spills and brake dust and the elements.

Every shop I worked at was in the same sad state.

I wanted in on the action.

I loved the sound of heavy diesel motors roaring back to life, lifters clattering, pistons pumping, and gears whining. All motors have their own distinctive sounds. Detroit 60's, DD15's, Cummins ISX,

Volvo D12 and 13's, Cat 3406's, A-Cert engines, they were all different. There's nothing like getting a truck that doesn't run for whatever reason and making it live again. It could be a bad cam, a bad head, or something as simple as a thermostat. The feeling of getting a driver back on the road was one of exhilaration something akin to slaying the demons that so often plagued the mechanical machine.

I watched the shop techs moving about, performing various types of repairs, changing tires and oil. The man named Hendricks was nowhere to be seen. The other techs looked up from time to time, concern and questions etched across their faces. I know what they're thinking. Some care too much when a potential new guy shows up for an interview. They're worried about how much money the new guy is going to be making and how much was it going to cut into their paycheck. Management usually had a bad habit of offering sweet deals to get an experienced guy on board.

I filled out the application with a borrowed pen, cursing while filling in the required blank spaces. Even though I had a resume, the shop ram-rod insisted on listing everything on a paper application. Thirty-minutes later, I emerged from the break room and turned in the application to an older woman with auburn colored hair working the counter. Her cold blue eyes said she could've cared less. With a cigarette burning between yellowed fingers, she pointed toward the employee breakroom and told me to wait in there.

I found a chair free from grease, slid it out and sat down. After several minutes of nothing, I stood up, stretched and resisted the temptation to exit the back door to have a cigarette.

I saw the yellowed map hanging on the wall. It was a map of the US with nine red stars carefully placed over cities or towns where other Duggan's Truck Stops were located. I took a closer look. The stars were painted over Tulsa Oklahoma, Tucson Arizona, Moriarty New Mexico, Lubbock Texas, and a few other locations sprinkled across the south-west and east regions. A single blue star was stuck over Biloxi, Mississippi. The only rationale for that blue star would have to be it was the main headquarters. Looking over the old photographs on the nearby wall proved my thought correct.

A couple of Confederate flags waved in a soft breeze over what looked to be the main entrance way to a truck stop with a large group of employees posing beside the flag poles. Everyone was smiling with the exception of four men dressed in dark blue or black suits. One of them was different. He wore grey slacks with a pastel peach-colored shirt and he was smaller, older but held a sense of dignity and authority.

The others were tall, muscular and hard looking men. Maybe the man in the peach colored shirt was the main head honcho for Duggan's. They looked out of place when compared to the rest of the employees. I wondered why they weren't smiling. Maybe the stresses of having to manage a chain of truck stops had taken its toll. Perhaps they were bored with the whole photo op thing, and they saw this as a waste of time and money since they were paying these employees to pose for a group photo.

Looking over the other photos, I didn't see any Confederate flags waving in the air over the other locations. I wrote this off to the fact that people and politicians had started complaining about the use of the Stars and Bars.

There was another picture, this one in Lubbock. This looked like the same man from the earlier one. In this one though, he was wearing a white Polo shirt that looked several sizes too small or he had giant arms indicating he worked out on a regular basis. He wasn't smiling in this one either. I moved on to the other photographs of Duggan's and saw the dates ranged from the early sixties to the latest photograph being a little under ten years ago. No recent photographs could be seen.

"Logan Pierce?" The voice sounded deep and thick like it was mixed with gravel.

I turned and saw a man pointing a cigar at me. "Me?"

"Anyone else in here? Yeah, you, what're you applying for?"

"Technician."

He stabbed the cigar in between thick lips. "We got openings to spare since I fired a couple guys this morning. You got a resume?"

"I do." The part about firing a couple mechanics this morning had me concerned.

"Come on back and let's talk."

I moved away from the break room and down a short hallway where he met me with a hand resembling a slab of pork roast more than flesh. "Names Johnson, Ty Johnson."

I took hold of it and was surprised his grip was not hard but controlled. "Logan Pierce."

Johnson was short, around five-foot-four and just as wide. His arms were thick as tree stumps and he pushed his glasses up the bridge of his nose with one thick sausage of a finger. His hair was a thinning mop of shiny black. He used a dye of some sort to hide his aging features. His gait reminded me of a slow-moving gorilla, or maybe an orangutan. I was surprised his thin legs could support that much upper body mass.

His office looked more like an oversized utility closet. Papers were scattered about or in large stacks on a large desk stretching across the length of the room. A couple computers stood by and looked like old Apple systems from the eighties. He sat down in his chair and I thought it would break under the sudden shock of his weight but it only moaned in protest.

He shuffled a few papers on his desk, tucking them away in a manila folder. "You said you got a resume?"

I handed over a sheet from my file. He took hold and glanced at the letters with interest.

He furrowed his eyebrows. Thick cigar smoke drifted up over his glasses and combined with the glare of room's light fixture from above, reflected off the glass lenses to hide his eyes. "Looks like a lot of experience."

"Just about anything, sir."

"Oil changes? You got a problem doing those? I got guys here who won't touch the damned things."

I shook my head. "No, no problem."

"Tires…it says here you worked at Consolidated Express. They're union…were anyway, and I know they didn't do tires. They went under didn't they?"

"They did, sir. Tires are not a problem."

"I mean taking them down off the rim, maybe patching them and reinstalling them."

"Been awhile but I can do them."

"Air conditioning. You got a 609?"

A 609 is a license that says you can handle refrigerant for automotive. I opened my folder and took out a copy of my license and handed it to him. "Yes, I also have a 608."

"What the hell's a '608'?" he asked as he took hold of the paper.

"Commercial refrigeration."

"Like building HVAC systems and chillers like in a restaurant?"

"Yes."

"No need of it. ASE's? You got any?" He leaned over to the desk, clicked a pen and began scribbling heavily onto a notepad.

I took a deep breath. "I have one."

Johnson looked up. "A guy with your experience level and you only one ASE certification? What's it for?" he asked. Cigar smoke sputtered out from thin lips like a motor with a busted piston ring

I didn't have the heart to tell him that on a personal level I didn't believe in them. Not that I'm knocking the guys who have them and are Master Technicians, as a matter of fact, I envied them. ASE certifications are nice to have but the tests are a pain in the ass. I was lucky to have passed one let alone all eight parts. I was better at working out problems with my hands rather than taking a written test to prove I was a diesel mechanic. "Diesel Engines."

He thought for a moment. The resume quivered in his hand. "Maybe you'll work on that and get some extra money in your pocket. This company believes in ASE's. One is all right but work on getting more. A master tech here pays about forty-eight percent of the labor dollars. You'll get maybe forty percent." It was not a request but a demand. He stuffed his face back in the resume. "Wheel seals and brakes?"

"I can do them." I swallowed hard. "I can do in-frames, transmission rebuilds, clutches, differentials, injectors."

"We don't do that kind of stuff here, too much of a liability issue. Sometimes we do clutches and such but we let a couple other guys work those things."

"Sounds fair."

"Says you from Nevada?"

"Yes sir, Las Vegas. I broke down yesterday."

He leaned back. The chair made a heavy creaking noise. He blew out another plume of blue-hued smoke. "So why you need the job kid?"

"Money, sir."

"So, you planning on splitting once you get your money? I need guys in here for the long haul."

"I plan on sticking around for quite a while, sir. I really don't have anywhere else to go." I lied, knowing full well he knew that was not my intentions.

He let out a grunt, turned back to the computer and began hammering the keyboard. I didn't say anything and stayed quiet while he thought. The quiet between us grew. I could hear the seconds ticking away on the wall mounted clock and the clicking of the keyboard as his fingers danced across it. He finished pounding the keyboard and turned his attention back to me. He had the cigar still clamped between his teeth and it reminded me of some Cheshire cat, pondering on what to do with his latest acquisition. He removed the cigar, pointed a thick finger at me, blowing out more smoke.

"Kid…you're in luck. Even though you're not a resident of New Mexico, I'll give you a shot. Just get a New Mexico driver's license when you can. God knows we got plenty of work and we're short-handed. When can you start?"

"Right now would be good."

"Good answer, kid. You in for the long haul or to screw me over in a couple months? I'm warning you now you mess with me and your last checks going to be a long time in coming."

I acted surprised. "Long-haul."

His smile widened. "I like you, kid. Let's set you up for a drug test." He paused and pointed his cigar at my chest. "I forgot to ask, this always bites me in the ass. Can you piss clean? I got plenty of people who can't get in here because they're dirty. A lot of dopers here in Moriarty."

I nodded. At least I had that going for me. Being a Teamster at one point had told me not to touch dope. Consolidated Express always performed random testing. "It'll be clean."

"Alcohol?"

I paused for a second, trying to find the right combination of words. He held up a thick paw. "Before you answer, you smell like a damn brewery."

"I had a few last night."

"More than a few I'd say. As long as it ain't an issue, you understand?"

"It won't be, sir."

"We'll see, kid. You got a toolbox? That's another damned thing. You'd be surprised how many guys come in here with a 'toolbox' and it turns out to be nothing more than a god-damned fish and tackle box or a five-gallon bucket of rusted Chinese tools."

"I gotta triple bay."

"Well, I'm gonna gamble on you pissing clean so go get your box and here's the paperwork to go get the piss test done. I need it done today as in ASAP." He handed over the paperwork. "What about transportation?"

I held the paperwork and frowned.

"Tell me you got wheels, kid."

I shook my head then explained what had happened.

He nodded and frowned. "I got a deal for you, but remember what I said about screwing with me. You got it?" He stood up and motioned for me to follow. "I don't do this for anyone and any other time, I would've told you to pound sand, but you got the skills and work history that tells me you gonna make me money." We exited the back door into the bright sunlight. "So you help me, I help you but don't, don't ever try to pull one over on me."

"I swear, I won't, sir."

We walked behind the shop. There were piles of scrap metal with tall weeds growing all over. There within the weeds were several trucks, one was a newer model wrecked Dodge Ram, a flatbed Chevy with the doors, hood, and engine missing. The third truck, an old Ford, looked intact.

"That Ford there," he pointed.

It was a 1971 Ford F250. Its forest green paint job had faded to near grey and the fenders were pushed in. The windshield had a sprawling crack stretching the vast expanse of glass and a layer of dust had settled over the metal and interior. The poor thing looked like it hadn't been used in months.

"Don't look like much but this truck was a beast on road calls. Never broke down on us or gave us too much trouble." He patted the fender. "I like to call her *ol' reliable*. The mechanics in there hated using it but to hell with 'em. Since we got a couple new service trucks, this one was retired and no one wants to buy it. So fortune smiles on you."

Looking it up and down, I couldn't complain. It was a set of wheels to roll around on. "How much are you asking?"

He pointed the cigar at my chest. "Not *asking* anything, kid, it's *wanting* and you ain't got no negotiating on it from my standpoint. Five hundred and that's a hell of a deal."

"It seems a fair price since you put it that way."

He blew a plume of smoke in my face. "Beats walking now don't you think?"

Five hundred wasn't anything but it did hit the pocket. That would leave me with eighty bucks to my name, provided I could find a place for five hundred down. I slowly stabbed a hand in the pocket, pulled the bundle of currency and counted off five hundred in bills and handed them over to Johnson.

He took the bills and stuffed it away in his shirt pocket. "I'll turn this in to bookkeeping and they'll hand over the title." He turned and waddled away and stuffed his face back in the fistful of papers. "Tomorrow, show up around four in the afternoon and we'll get you started."

I looked back on the Ford and popped the hood open. It took a few slow cranks to fire the thing over but the 390 rumbled back to life. It ran like shit but it was better than having to hitch a ride or walk to work every day. On payday, it would need filters and a tune-up. Whenever I did leave New Mexico, I might be able to sell it for more but even if I only got my five hundred back, then so be it.

And that's how it starts. You get in a place, work for a while and gather up your money and live, survive. There was nothing formal about the interview. As a matter of fact, it was unconventional. I felt deep down, looking at Johnson as he walked away, that I had been forced into making a deal with the devil in staying here in Moriarty.

FOUR

I pissed clean. That surprised me considering how much booze I had soaked my liver in over the last twenty-four hours. I planned on destroying the precious organ later on. I took the Ford and hauled the cargo trailer over and off-loaded the toolbox. I handed Johnson the drug testing paperwork before hauling ass on a quest for a place to rent and to check out Moriarty in general.

The choices were limited. I either plunked down my remaining five hundred bucks on a hotel room for a week and end up living in the Ford truck until payday or find a place for the month. If I did manage to pull off this feat, I'd have around eighty bucks left to my name until the first check. I was sure the old Viet at the bar had swiped some extra dough. I grabbed a pack of Marlboros, a Thrifty-Nickle ad paper, and a couple pints of Crown from the Circle K and began scanning the rent ads.

Mobile homes. That's all I saw listed for rent around town. There was the close cluster of houses in residential areas in town but I wanted something a bit more out in the open for a change and a bit cheaper. I was hoping for a garage for the El Camino but I didn't want to pay an arm and leg either.

The further south I drove from town, the more single and double-wide trailers. The homes resembled derelict cardboard ships left adrift on a vast ocean of brown earth. A large portion of properties was nothing more than acres of collapsed buildings, smashed junk cars and rusting farming equipment piled up everywhere. Some of the nicer properties everyone wanted a good chunk of money to rent and I couldn't justify paying what they were asking. I was used to having solid textured walls, insulated windows, central air, and solid flooring back in Vegas. I wasn't used to particle board flooring that sagged under my feet.

I finished the last of one pint bottle, tossed it out the window before taking up the crumpled copy of the Thrifty Nickel. I crossed off a potential rent ad from the growing list of rejects. I was still parked outside the mobile home I had come to look at. Several mutts were keeping me pinned inside the Ford. They had erupted in a cloud of barking fury from under a large pile of heaped up broken boards and plywood when I pulled up. They let me know right away I was trespassing on their turf. Maybe they didn't want me here and I was fine with that. I sure as hell didn't feel like getting eaten alive just to see the place.

Fine, keep it.

While the dogs barked, I scanned further down the list and cracked open the second pint bottle of Crown. I was getting tired of looking at mobile homes and started looking for something resembling a real house. About halfway down the column, there was an ad for a two bedroom and fairly priced. I flipped the phone open and dialed the number. A tired old man answered and after a few minutes of talking, gave directions. I scribbled them down as we talked, hung up and headed back to Moriarty, leaving the trio of barking fleabags to maintain their grip over their domain.

I hit Martinez Road, hung a left and drove out to where the blacktop came to an end and a dirt road began. Five miles later I saw the large cluster of trees as described by the old man. There within, was the house. After meeting with the potential landlord, an inspection of the house, a few questions later, money changed hands, and papers were signed. I was now an official renter.

Driving back to the hotel, I finished off the second pint bottle and tossed it out the window and made a beeline for the lounge bar. I was thirsty and decided to celebrate, alone, my victory of at least finding a job and also finding an actual house to rent. The joint had a few patrons and Lee the bartender was wiping down the counter like last time.

The lounge lights were turned down low. An old Vietnamese woman sat perched at the end of the bar. She looked up and flashed a smile exposing teeth that were stained from years of eating betel nuts. We exchanged greetings before she turned her attention back to a Jerry Springer rerun. Soft jazz music drifted down from the overhead speakers, giving it a nice touch of quiet peace. I ordered several shots of Crown and a Heineken.

Lee poured a shot and produced a Heineken. We made small talk and I reminded him about the eighty bucks from last night. He smiled and said he would set me up this time. "Many lonely men go to club."

"What's that?"

"Strip club. Many women, there are none here. You should go."

"No thanks, I ain't got the money or the time for that."

"*Ahh*," he said. "So, you have no honey?"

I was a bit put off by the conversation and the direction he was headed. I was expecting to hear next that he knew a friend, who knew another friend who had access to cheap whores, but he stayed quiet. "No, no honey."

"Shame it is," he rubbed at an imaginary spot on the countertop between us.

Changing the subject, I waved a hand indicating another shot. "I got the job."

He smiled as he poured the shot of Crown. "*Ahh...*Duggan's. That is good. You will soon make much money there."

"I hope so," I said while looking around the bar. "Is Hendricks here?" I felt I owed him a drink.

"No, he not here today, he come sometimes but work all the time."

"Duggan's got to be good then."

"Many rumors come from the place, much about missing money."

I realized many businesses had the usual rumor mill, but hearing about missing money was a new one. "Missing money?"

He leaned forward and his voice dropped to a whisper. "Yes, thousands of dollars, much money, they say embezzled by mafia but no one knows."

"Mafia? Out here?" I chuckled. "I doubt it." I knew Las Vegas was prime territory run by the mob back in the day. They say they got busted out of Vegas, but rumors say they just went a little deeper out of sight and still had controlling interest over some of the gambling joints and unions. Out here in Moriarty, New Mexico though? I doubted any legit mob unit would be operating this far out. There just wasn't anything here.

"Rumor. It is a small town, many people talk."

I waved it off with a numb hand. The liquor was beginning to run thick through my veins. "Mob, as in Chicago or New York?"

"No, not Italians. I heard somewhere from the south, say

Mississippi." He produced a pipe and packed it with tobacco.

"Cornbread Mafia?" I laughed. This was a new one on me. I had never heard of another mafia other than the Italians, or the Jamaicans or the common street gangs such as the Bloods, the Crips. I snorted and downed the last shot of Crown. "This town is a long ways from Mississippi."

"True, but no hear of Cornbread Mafia. Hendricks say they Dixie Mafia. They run strip club up road also I hear." He lit a match and puffed on the pipe while lighting the bowl. Content, he waved his hand to extinguish the match.

I stopped mid-sip on my glass of Crown. "The strip club?"

"Yes, it true, we growing town, also growing bad things."

"And you wanted me to go there, you are one funny guy, Lee. Have you ever been there?"

He smiled and a chuff of smoke blew through his thin lips. "Me? Have no reason to." He pointed the stem of his pipe toward the old woman with stained teeth. She was still content on watching the television. "Why go there, when I have rose from garden here?"

"Wise words, my friend," I waved for another shot.

He poured a shot of amber gold. "You have no honey?"

"I was married…once."

"Ahh, it no work?"

"No, didn't work out."

"No man should be alone in life. Being alone brings bad things within the hearts of men. Women needed to calm the storm in the heart," he placed a hand over his heart to emphasize his point.

"Yeah, it didn't work out for me." I downed the shot and he poured another.

"Rumor of money missing could prove to be true if one listens," he said while seating himself on a stool behind the bar.

"It's just rumor, Lee. You can't put a whole lot of faith in a rumor unless you got a certain number of facts that make it the truth."

"Then it would no longer be a rumor," he smiled

I started wondering on his angle. "What you getting at?"

He shook his head, smiling. "Nothing. I always listen to people talking. Here at the bar, you hear many things from employees who come here."

I took out my cell phone, looked at the time. "I gotta get going. My day starts early tomorrow."

Lee leaned back, taking a long drag from his pipe. The tendrils of smoke rose upward between us. I stood up and grabbed my jacket from the chair back. I wasn't going to let in on the fact I was here in Moriarty for a short time, not a long time. My game plan was simple. Stay under the radar, make the money, fix the El Camino, and then haul ass out of here. Don't get me wrong. Moriarty and the people who lived here seemed nice enough, but it wasn't for me, but then again where else was?

I tossed a twenty on the table enough to cover the last few drinks and a tip. I turned to walk away but the soft whisper from the Viet made me stop mid-step. "Be careful."

I couldn't tell if he was warning me about the so-called mafia or if it was about stumbling into the nearby chairs. I looked back, and he was leaning back in his stool, still smoking his pipe.

There was a calm expression on his face and I wondered what he was thinking. It was hard to read emotions from Orientals. Sometimes they had this dry sense of humor that was hard to read.

I had my plans on a roll. Regardless of the Mafia rumor, I was here for the money and then off to Texas. I knew things were headed for the better and all I had to do was hang on. If I knuckled down and went to work, I'd be out of here in six months. Six months should be enough time to gather up a few coins for the spring and early summer jump off when companies hiring for the oil fields were at a peak.

That's all I had to do. *Stay out of the bullshit*, I told myself.

FIVE

Several months had passed since I first drifted into Moriarty. It felt like a lifetime in my career as a diesel mechanic. The month of February was locked in the firm grip of winter. The surrounding landscape held several inches of fresh snow and the parking lot was a sheet of ice. The weather forecast was predicting more incoming.

Life at Duggan's had settled into a steady routine of repairing the broken, shattered machines rolling off the nearby I-40 corridor. I was nowhere close to leaving New Mexico despite my best efforts. There wasn't much else to do in Moriarty except work and sleep and maybe throw down some Crown or a Heineken from time to time, but there was always plenty of work rolling into the truck stop. I kept pounding metal and concrete twelve to sixteen hours, sometimes longer, for six, sometimes seven days a week.

Working as a diesel mechanic for as long as I had, I recognized every problem and solution for the trucks or trailers rolling in. It didn't matter what model truck or engine or transmission. I knew each one intimately or the problems crossing over from one model truck or brand to another. There was plenty of variety to choose from and that made the job at least tolerable. Mechanics get bored easily with no variety.

One moment I would be working on switching out an air compressor, or dumping oil, changing a shattered differential to changing a set of injectors. But the bottom line was money. Working for forty percent of the chargeable labor billed hours, I was content on gathering as much of the green stuff as I could. I intended to make every company rolling through the shop pay me the money necessary to leave New Mexico even if it meant taking money off another mechanics dinner table. Not that I'm a dick, but I really wanted out of New Mexico.

I was banging away on a yellow Peterbilt with a Cummins ISX. The elegant stylized red lettering on the doors read *Sleepy Quinn*. The injectors weren't firing right. I popped off the valve cover and examined the rollers and found them to be pitted and scored. The cam was just as bad of shape. My pile of replacement parts had arrived and took up a whole workbench. The driver was elated we had managed to get all the parts before the storm settled in.

I had befriended the tech known as Hendricks. He was the obvious alpha dominant and the top earner in the shop. He had a sure-footed swagger that drew the other lesser mechanics to him like he was some sort of demi-god. Everyone asked him for advice whenever they ran into a problem with an engine or truck they couldn't figure out. He had the solutions all filed away in his head of long grey-black hair. The exception to this though was he had to like you for him to open up the Holy Book he held deep within the vaults of his brain. If not, the mechanic was pretty much screwed. I figured he had been busting wrenches for as long as I had.

Even though we were friends he could be a royal pain in the ass. He was quick to brag about how much money he was making like it was a competition to him. I usually fell short and just under the total dollar amount he had earned for the pay period. I had to smile and refrain from punching him in the throat. The one thing that was certain though he earned every penny. His uniforms showed it by the end of the shift. I had seen him do two clutch jobs on a couple of Volvo VNs back to back and he was covered in clutch dust and burnt grease by the end of the night along with a couple of cigarette butts tangled in his hair. No one told him anything about it either. Hendricks was known for his temper.

The shop was a bustling hive of activity. Mechanics were bundled up in oil-soaked overalls, coats, or anything that would trap in the body's heat. They moved from one truck or trailer to the next, repairing tires, broken air lines, water pumps, or anything else ailing the sick machines. Everyone was covered in a light sheen of oil and grease, mixed with a streaking pattern of dirt and brake dust, creating some sort of camouflage soaked deep within the fibers of the uniforms. My new dark blue uniforms had become soaked with the blood and dust from the trucks I worked on.

Hendricks was working on a Freightliner that was puking coolant on the snow-laden tarmac in front of bay two. A split hose on the EGR cooler mounted on a Detroit 60 Series was giving him fits. The cold winds and thick flakes of snow only added to the misery. He cursed the cold breeze that had kicked up and sent every man's balls crawling further up into their gut. Derek was busy changing out a tire. His stocky form shivered while his cold blue eyes focused on running the one-inch impact. Everyone said he was a former convict and he wasn't denying the quiet allegations. He stayed to himself and hardly talked to anyone. He had started a couple months before me and no one really knew anything about him.

Johnson waddled out of the side door, cigar smoke followed in his wake. He yelled something derogatory across the shop, something about fornicating with a sheep and shitting on a southbound flock of birds. No one could understand his analogies and no one tried.

A pair of techs poked their heads up out of the oil change pit, young guys, new to the profession and hating every minute of it especially when Johnson was around. Johnson yelled for the two idiots to quit screwing off and finish the oil change. There were several more waiting and the customers were bitching about them being slow.

Hal was finishing up replacing a turbo. He flashed a toothless grin and wiped his hands on his shirt tail. He had been a meth head at some point and spent time in the crossbar motel for dealing in crystal dreams. He kept a photo of his wife in assless chaps taped up in his toolbox. She had been a stripper up at the 203 and, to hear him tell the story, he asked her to marry him the first night he saw her stripping and hanging off a pole. She said yes and it had been a caustic dangerous marriage ever since.

Then there was the counter guy. I wasn't sure why they called him Big Mac. Maybe it had something to do with eating burgers all the time or perhaps it was his fixation on the Mac 10. He owned several. He was big as hell, half Samoan and half Spanish and not too many drivers lipped off to him.

His sidekick was an old high school buddy known as Mongoose. Don't ask. It's been said he was fast with the women and he had disappointed more than just a few. Big Mac always ribbed him about his short-comings. Mongoose didn't seem to mind though and laughed along.

Where Mongoose smiled and laughed easily, I didn't think Big Mac understood the natural laws associated with jokes, but when he did his laughter was deep and loud and rolled across the room like two colliding boulders.

I slid the old pitted camshaft out of its place, set it down, oiled the new one and began working it into place. Once it was positioned, I jammed in the cam wedges and began installing the new rollers, injectors, and jakes. I set the torque on the bolts and began the overhead process. I was shivering while trying to adjust out the valves. The night was coming on and the temps were dropping. I paused once for a shot of Crown from a pint bottle I kept stashed in my box. The liquor settled into a nice hot glow in the pit of my gut.

I wondered if this was how doctors in an ER room felt working a Friday night in downtown Chicago. I liked to think diesel mechanics and doctors serve in similar ways. Doctors patch and save people while diesel mechanics repair and save the economy. The key difference between us is money.

Doctors save lives and rake in a small fortune, mechanics save company assets, profit margins, and the American economy but are paid pennies. Mechanics spend thousands on tools and tool boxes. My own toolbox and the tools within equaled out to the price of a small three bedroom house. Doctors don't pay squat for their tools and live in mansions. They also get to have a fleet of busty blonde nurses at their beck and call. I zipped up my jacket and shivered as a cold wind picked up. Come to think of it, I should've been a doctor.

So far, the job at Duggan's had been a fair move despite the few things that were wrong with the people who worked here or the drivers floating in from the outside world.

Throughout all of this, rumors swirled. Johnson had stated Duggan's was a miniature city within a city and with it came distorted forms of truth. If you wanted to, you could find out the latest words on the wind just by listening to the people talk. You didn't really have to pry the info from them, most gave it freely in casual conversations. Dwayne, the complex manager, was screwing the blonde bookkeeper named Andrea. You hear all the company hype about 'ethics' and 'integrity', but its bullshit. Managers have always screwed the employees both physically and financially. Around lunchtime, you could see both of them running across the street to the same motel I had stayed at during my first days here in Moriarty. Then there were words about the groundskeeper slinging dope to truck drivers looking for a quick high or for the speedball to help them push on through the night.

There were whores to cater to the flavors of the highway drivers. Several women of the night traveled from Albuquerque to Duggan's and worked the lot. There were also a few local broads who were hooked on meth in on the gig too. You could get a blow or hand job for twenty-five bucks if you didn't mind a broad who was missing a few teeth and had sores all over her face. You could see them from time to time but as soon as they caught wind of the local PD roaming the lot, they vanished.

Even some of the female employees at Duggan's were in on the action. There was a broad who worked the C-store register, who lined up her customers for the night throughout her shift. Once she punched off the clock, she began hopping trucks across the lot spreading her pixie love dust for handfuls of cash.

Then there came the first whispers about the missing money. Before Andrea, there had been another blonde gal who worked up in bookkeeping. Everyone knew her as Lonnie Blonde who was really blonde, like true Scandinavian blonde. Her real name was Lona Sabir from some small town in Oklahoma. She was one hell of a looker. She began an ongoing affair with Dave Musgrave who had been the shop manager at the time. I'm not sure on details but they couldn't keep their hands off each other.

Word was around the campfire, Lonnie Blonde and Musgrave were making, growing and slinging dope, but as a side gig, she was responsible for skimming money from the Duggan's coffers. I guess it was to support her new-found drug habit.

When one first enters the Duggan's complex, there is a wall where people who made Employee of the Month have their pictures hung up on a turquoise colored bricking. Next to those photos were photographs of those employees no longer among the living. It was called the Wall of Remembrance. To be added to this wall you had to be employed at Duggan's at the time of your death. Photographs of Musgrave and Lonnie Blonde were the most recent additions. They had been dead a little over eight months now which was why people still talked about it. Looking at Musgrave's photo, I couldn't for the love of God, see what Lonnie Blonde saw in him. He was one ugly bastard. I was sure it was either the drugs or he was hung like a horse.

I had heard a wide range of rumors about the 'dynamic duo.' That's what the rumor mill called them. They had been shot to shreds and found lying out in the elements several days later over at Musgrave's sprawling ranch south of Willard. There was nothing out there for miles around, just a vast void of rolling prairies with large swathes of piñon, scrub oak and twisted Juniper trees. Out in the wilds, no one can hear you scream once the bullets start flying.

Some rumors speculated Musgrave and Lonnie Blonde had a falling out and were trying to kill each other their last night on this earth. The other part of the theory was they had crossed someone and paid the price for it. I was betting on the later.

Then there was the main part that raised my concern levels a notch. I remembered Lee the bartender claiming the 203 strip club and Duggan's Truck Stop was owned and operated by the Dixie Mafia. I hadn't seen anything close to the mob in suits and Thompson machine guns running around Moriarty but then again, maybe they were management. They ran the place like Nazi thugs.

It was known the FBI had raided Duggan's a year before. The reason was someone on the inside of the truck stop chain had said they had bilked the government out of millions of tax dollars. The US Government hates competition as it is and quickly opened an investigation into the claims. Nothing came of it but the investigation was apparently still ongoing. A couple months after the raid, Musgrave and Lonnie Blonde got murdered and the State and local cops were investigating their deaths.

The troubling aspect of having the local police asking around about anything was they put the fear of God into you. I was finding this out when Big Mac stopped me from finishing up the *Sleepy Quinn* truck and asked me to fix a flat tire on a Crown Victoria belonging to the State Police. Duggan's repaired them for free for law enforcement, medical and fire department vehicles. Two officers stood behind the cruiser, watching intently as I walked up and introduced myself.

They didn't offer up their names and remained quiet and stiff-lipped. I started working on removing the flat tire

It was the taller white cop who spoke first.

The name tag on his neatly pressed uniform said his name was Richardson. When he removed his duty hat, it unveiled a large bald slick patch. He seemed like a grandfatherly type of person and I could see him playing with his grandkids, but his sidekick was another story. He was also dressed in the standard black and grey uniform and was walking around, looking at the shop. His oriental features reminded me of Bruce Lee, just a heavier, meaner version. His hand rested on the Glock .40 hanging on his hip. He pretended not to be interested in my repairing the tire or of the conversation Richardson and I was having.

"New face," Richardson said.

I had found a nail buried in the rubber tread. I took the tire off the Crown Vic and nodded in agreement.

"Always a new face," he placed a toothpick between his lips. "You probably wouldn't know much."

"About?" I marked an *x* over the nail head with a grease pen before lifting the tire and rim up on the Coats 40-40 tire machine.

"Naw, you wouldn't know anything."

The machine hissed and I worked the bead-breaker bar under the lip of the tire. "Maybe you're right." I concentrated on the job at hand.

"You hear anything about missing money?"

I found the question surprising. "What money?"

He smiled. "You see? No one knows anything, Nguyen."

Nguyen shrugged. He tapped his fingers across his service pistol.

"Don't know what money you're talking about."

"The quarter million in missing money? Supposedly it was embezzled?"

"Haven't heard anything." I concentrated back on the tire. Taking a pair of pliers, I removed the nail, buffed the inner surface and applied a patch before working the tire back on the rim.

He grunted. The toothpick quivered. "Surely you've had to have heard something?"

I aired up the tire and doused the patched area with soapy water. Satisfied the patch wasn't leaking, I slapped it on the Crown Vic. "Something about money being embezzled that's all I've ever heard."

"That seems to be the word anyway. Did you know Dave Musgrave?"

"No."

He looked off into the rafters. "Poor bastard got his ass blown away down on his ranch outside Willard, both him and that cute little druggy girlfriend of his."

After finishing the tightening sequence, I lowered the jack and pulled it out from under the Crown Vic. He pulled out a business card and offered it over. "You'll call and tell me if you hear anything…right as a virgin's virtue now won't you?" There was a firm, tense tone. It sounded more like a veiled threat.

"Sir?" I took the card.

"If you hear anything, no matter how small the detail, you'll give me a call."

Nguyen gave a casual look, never smiling once in the exchange. Somehow, I felt there was a hidden motive in Richardson's request. I wasn't sure but the glint in his eye told me he was dead serious about the money.

"Yeah, sure."

Richardson placed his hat back over his bald patch. "I'm sure you will." He slid behind the wheel and started up the Crown Vic. Nguyen slid into the passenger seat and they pulled out into the dark winter morning and disappeared into the blizzard.

Big Mac waddled over, hands in his pockets. "So, what were you guys talking about?"

I looked at the business card, shrugged and stuffed it in my pocket. "Something about missing money."

Big Mac grinned. His breath reeked of onions and garlic. "Dave Musgrave's missing fortune? They've been looking for months for the missing money and they'll never find it because it doesn't exist."

"That's the thing. I've heard about it but never thought about it."

"It's bullshit. It doesn't exist."

"It is," I replied but I was starting to think about those rumors. I went back to the *Sleepy Quinn* truck while thinking about the missing money. If the cops believed it as truth than it had to exist. The possibilities were endless for anyone who found it. *Hell, I could get the hell out of here,* I thought. *But where would you even begin to look?*

I shook it off and focused on the yellow Pete. I didn't have time to daydream about the missing money. I had a stack of cash riding on this job. The radiator, charge air cooler and AC condenser were back in place and coolant was topped off. After a few cranks, the Pete fired back to life and purred like a kitten. The owner was elated. He'd hoped to get back on the road with his load of hay.

Hendricks felt different about the money. There were times he would talk about the money and Dave Musgrave like it was some sort of treasure waiting to be found and other times he wouldn't give the time of day. On the rare times he spoke about it, he felt the money was out there. I wondered why he was even talking to me about it. He would never talk to anyone else about it.

Richardson's words hung thick on my mind. I replayed the conversation while putting the finishing touches on *Sleepy Quinn*. The February winds were bitter cold and carried thick snow within its currents. Winter had blasted the area with several inches of snow and more of it was coming down. The snow fell at such a steady rate that hordes of big rigs and four-wheelers were pulling off and seeking refuge in Moriarty. A steady stream of traffic flowed into Duggan's looking for holes to park and wait out the worst of it. The snow relented only for a short time before dumping another couple inches.

The weather reports coming off the radio said the canyon going into Albuquerque was officially closed. It only got worse when I-40 shutdown going east toward Santa Rosa an hour later. Weary travelers and another wave of truck drivers flooded into Moriarty. The hotels had sold out hours forcing many to park along the streets. A solid wall of big rigs lined the main drag all through Moriarty. The town had become one giant truck stop.

The shop continued on despite the inability of the dealerships in Albuquerque to run any parts out to us. We were relegated to nothing more than oil changes at this point. The inventory was running thin and radiator and heater hoses and fan belts were all used up. In some cases, we managed to have a water pump in stock or an alternator, but there was a large chunk of trucks currently waiting on ordered parts. The snow continued falling for a few days. The pile of broken trucks continued to grow.

If I kept my nose to the grindstone, this storm could pay off big to my advantage. Hendricks was thinking the same thing. We had several trucks in need of clutch jobs, one with an injector out, another with broken motor mounts, heater blower motors, busted coolant hoses and they were sitting for lack of parts. We concentrated on the trucks and trailers we knew we had parts for and could repair. It wasn't like the drivers who were waiting on parts were going anywhere anytime soon.

The only time we left the shop was to head up to the C-store or restaurant for a quick bite to eat or a coffee refill. The main complex was packed with drivers who watched the weather channel for any signs of hope in hitting the road. They were losing money sitting here. We took little naps in between jobs. I took up an old tattered blanket and disappeared into the tire room just under the heaters, and crawled inside the tires in the racks to sleep. I was too tired to drive. Hendricks had an old sleeping bag in his locker and would fall off into la-la land tucked inside and laid out on one of the break room tables.

We waited, watching the skies and hoping and praying for the snows to stop just long enough to get our parts in from Albuquerque. On the third day, God answered our prayers and the grey skies cracked open to reveal the morning sun. The storm had passed and we breathed a sigh of relief when the first of the delivery vans loaded down with much-needed parts arrived. The delivery driver cursed the weather and the roads while he unloaded the parts. Now that we had the parts, the pain in the ass was playing catch up. We set about repairing everything we could. Money was the objective and we intended to mop the floor clean.

The shop was catching up on tickets that were waiting on parts. I heard the dealerships were hammered just trying to run parts out to us and other shops in the area. The past several days of snow had melted away from the highways and trucks slammed gears getting the hell out of Moriarty. Thin tendrils of vapor rose off the asphalt as the sun showered the lands with its rays of warmth. It reminded me of spring, which was strange. It was only the middle of February.

Hendricks was finishing up a water pump job on a Detroit 60. We had been running hard for over three days straight. He looked up at me with red-rimmed eyes. "Beer?"

I was wiped out. The Crown had run out the day before. I

wanted to go home. My energy levels were running on reserve. "Naw, sleep would be better."

He was too tired to protest. "Yep."

I expressed my concerns with the State cops from the other night.

He wrestled a clamp into place. "State cops? They're always coming around asking."

"All the time?"

"They like to ask the new guys. I think they get a kick out of the deer-in-the-headlights look they get."

"Yeah, but they think it's real."

He stopped and took a pull from his coffee mug. "They're still looking for the money. They'll never find it if it even exists."

"Do you think it exists?" I asked.

He scratched the stubble on his chin. "Hard telling, maybe, besides, what's it to you anyways?"

"Yeah, what the hell do I know," I was too damned tired to try and angle any information out of him.

We both went back to work but from time to time, I caught Hendricks looking up with concern etched in his red-rimmed eyes. I wasn't sure on what to make of it but shrugged it off and kept working. The day rolled into the night and early morning but the two of us stayed on, picking up the dollars as each driver cashed out and left. I-40 was currently open for business but another storm in the forecast and everyone wanted to haul ass before it came around.

The last ticket of any kind of pressing matter was an oil change and I told myself to hell with it. Hobart, a new mechanic who had started several days prior to the storm, was finishing an oil change. I figured he could get to it.

He was a strange character. Hobart Mills. Who named their kid 'Hobart' these days? Regardless, he kept up on oil changes throughout the graveyards and we had less to contend with in the mornings. He was in his fifties and had a southern or Texas accent and spoke little to anyone. He would do tires, oil changes and maybe change out a light or two but nothing too strenuous. He saved the heavier stuff for everyone else. Some guys complained about his lack of capability but I wondered if he was fooling everyone. There was this glint of intelligence in his eyes and he moved around on oil changes like he knew everything step by step and had tackled a few projects that baffled some of the other guys. He looked familiar but I couldn't place him and as hard as I thought about it, I drew a blank. I gave up trying. Johnson was just happy to have a mechanic on overnights.

My eyes felt like they were going to roll out of my head. My lungs were clogged from cigarette smoke and exhaust fumes. Hendricks had left hours before and it was my turn to haul ass to the home front for a shave, shit and shower session. After catching the wrinkled expressions of disgust from drivers and Big Mac, and smelling myself, God knew I needed it.

I locked up the toolbox and made a beeline for the locker room to grab my coat. I slammed the locker door and was putting on the jacket when I noticed something out of the ordinary. Looking closer at the wall of photographs, there were several bare spots with rectangular shaped rings of dirt and the lone nails that had once held them up in place.

There were several pictures missing off the wall. I found it strange. I walked over and studied the remaining pictures carefully. I remembered the pictures with the men who were out of place under the Dixie flag but I couldn't remember what they looked like. Those pictures were missing. Johnson had said he had planned on repainting the break room. The question remained. Why only take down a few pictures and not all of them?

I shrugged it off and slipped out the door, fired up the Ford and let it idle until the heat from the defroster started melting off the ice from the windshield. I flipped it in reverse and plowed through the snow drift that had built up around it and floored it on home.

Five miles of snow and ice packed roads later, I was glad to finally see the driveway and home. I pulled in and left the keys hanging in the ignition. My body sagged under the weight from days of lack of sleep and the joints in the hands and knees were aching. After stumbling into the cold house, I kicked on the heater and stumbled for the kitchen where I found a bottle of Tylenol and my last Heineken brew. Downing several pills chased with the beer, I went for the shower and kicked it on for a minute before realizing I was just too damned tired.

Filthy, greasy and damned the stench. I crashed on the couch just as the morning sun's tentacles of light had begun pouring in through the living room window. As a habit, I empty out my pockets of everything. I could feel the grime and dirt in my pockets as the State cop's and the owner from the Sleepy Quinn's business cards materialized in my fingers.

I starred at Richardson's card for a long time.

You'll call and tell me then…right as a virgin's virtue, now won't you?

The State cop's words hung thick in my mind. I held the business card for a minute before dismissing the veiled threat in his tone and tossed the card on the table. It seemed everyone was looking for the so-called 'missing money.' I already resolved in my mind it was nothing more than a rumor at least for now.

The owner of the *Sleepy Quinn* truck had left Moriarty long ago. He was just happy to get back on the road. So much so that he handed me a fifty dollar tip along with his business card offering me a job if I was ever looking in the future. I tucked it away. You never knew if you were going to need them.

I fell back on the sofa. What I really needed right now was sleep, deep healing sleep.

SIX

The first time I'd spoken to her was up at the C-store.

I had seen her floating around from time to time. When I had gone up for a coffee refill, she was refilling her coffee mug and pouring in shots of Irish Crème creamer singles. We greeted each other with the simple 'hello' and that's the start of some things.

She was sculpted perfection, the green eyes, the small up-turned celestial nose, the long honey-blonde hair that cascaded down to the middle of her back. She wore form-fitted jeans that accentuated an athletic frame. Her nails were long, uniquely long and I wondered how she opened a jar or popped the cap off a Heineken. In my eyes, there was nothing imperfect in God's creation of this woman

The only noticeable defect was a scar that ran under her left eye. A small two-inch gash no makeup could cover up but it didn't take away from her natural beauty. I suppose even fine china has the occasional blemish. She was still hot as all hell and I was sure she knew it.

I reached over, took up a coffee pot and began pouring a cupful.

She stirred her coffee with a single plastic stir stick, looking me over. "Shop?" She had a southern accent but there was no way to gauge if she was a true dyed in the wool southern. But her tone sounded pleasant and sparkled of intelligence.

I finished topping off my cup, looked at my grease-stained hands. "Yes."

"How is it?" she asked as she stirred her coffee.

"Not bad seems pretty good."

"It looks pretty busy back there," she smiled.

"More than we can handle."

"Money is good then?" she placed the cap back on her own coffee mug, smiled again. "I'll see you around." She walked away with soft lofty steps.

"See you," I said softly but I wasn't sure if she had heard me.

We parted ways. I didn't know her name but her residual beauty remained in the forever files of memory. Over the next few days, to my surprise, she would drop in and talk with Johnson. She would go in the office and watch those mandatory company videos on customer service and other nonsense. I took it as a sign she was going to be working the counter.

The other guys in the shop also took notice of her. Some making crude comments about what they really wanted to do to her. The only one, who hadn't said anything on the matter, was Hendricks. He had noticed her but held silent judgment with a glint of concern in his eyes. He had been here at Duggan's for the better part of five years and maybe had seen the drama some attractive women working in a shop environment create and the damage left in their wake.

No one working at Duggan's knew who she was or where she

had come from. No one knew anything about her but I was starting to like the idea of seeing her around. It beat looking at Hendricks' ugly mug all day.

I came into work early, dressed out in a set of uniforms that the cleaning company had just bought back. They were heavily stained and I wondered if they had washed them at all. I looked the rest of the uniforms over and found them in the same sad state. I went to complain to Johnson and knocked on the closed office door. Johnson bellowed to enter.

I forgot about complaining when I saw her in the office with Johnson.

Johnson stabbed a thick finger toward me. For once, he didn't have a stinky cigar clasped between his sausage fingers. "What the hell you want, Logan?"

I tried focusing back on the topic at hand. "Uniforms."

He rolled his eyes. "Hendricks and everybody have told me already."

"I thought you should know."

Johnson nodded. "I'll be calling the uniform company and get it handled." He saw Amy and me looking at each other. "Logan, this is Amy. She'll be working the counter, swing shift."

"Swing?" My interest level shot up a notch.

"Big Mac's moving to days. Need an experienced guy running the counter since Lucey quit this morning. Swing is a bit slower so she'll learn quickly."

She smiled and I returned it. "She'll be in good hands."

He grunted. "Just watch those drivers. Damn bastards'll try and take advantage," he thumbed through his papers and stood up. "I'll be right back. Have to go up front and make some copies." He left the office leaving me and Amy looking at one another.

I extended a hand. "Logan Pierce."

She took it and smiled. Her southern accent sounded sweet on the ears. "Amy Hauser."

"I think you'll like it here."

"I hope so," she smiled.

We were still holding hands when Hendricks came up from behind. "Logan, we got work to do. There's a fan clutch with your name all over it."

"Okay," I grunted. I was annoyed with him.

"Well, c'mon, let's go. She's got things to do and we got things to do," he placed a hand on my shoulders to direct me out of the office. He greeted Amy and shut the office door.

Hendricks pushed me along before I decided it was best to get to work. Dayshift had left a pile of broken trucks and trailers stacked up in the bays and customers were lining up and complaining. Hal was finishing up with a tire and running the impact hard. Hendricks slid under a Century Class Freightliner to replace a worn u-joint. I focused in on the W900 KW and began removing the components necessary for the fan clutch replacement.

Hal had control of playing radio DJ for the evening. The radio was banging out some heavy speed metal music that sounded like a sack full of angry cats going through a wood chipper. There was an agreement between the mechanics. We alternated radio control daily for the shift and it saved a lot of arguing and heartburn. Hendricks played country or punk rock when it was his turn. I played old time rock with a mix of the Rolling Stones. Hendricks and I lamented it was Hal's turn playing his speed metal music for the day.

The fan clutch didn't take too long and I found myself lost in a whirlwind of broken machines, tires and electrical work. Before long, I had been working for five hours into the shift and cleared up most of dayshifts mess. My stomach grumbled in protest and decided to head up front to stuff the feed bag.

The truck stop was loading up with rolling off I-40 for the overnight siesta fest. The lot could hold up to two hundred trucks and as the day faded away, the watermelon sunset cast a bright orange glow over the parked rigs. Truckers wandered to and from the main complex, worn out from the road or getting ready for the graveyard run.

I moved across the back lot along with a few straggling drivers and entered the C-store. I maneuvered through a large group of kids and parents buying junk food, DVDs and energy drinks for the road. Their wave of enthusiasm and clean-cut clothing contrasted sharply with the sleep-deprived gaits of the truckers waiting in line to buy fuel. The restaurant was filled with drivers talking on cell phones, tapping away on laptop computers, or groups of drivers talked with each other. I spotted an empty booth in the far corner, walked over and slid in feeling the weight fade from aching feet. I looked around and the first person I saw was her.

Amy.

She smiled and put the magazine she was reading down on the table. "Hello, stranger."

"Hello," I replied.

She took a sip of her tea and removed her glasses, folding the arms away and placing them in a nearby handbag. Her soft southern tones sounded like heaven. "So, you managed to break away from the shop?"

A waitress came up and I ordered a coffee black to start. After she left I returned my attention back to Amy. "Yes, looking like a busy shift."

She smiled. "How you like it? I mean working here?"

"It's okay for now."

She pointed a long, delicate finger to the other seat across from me. "I hate talking like this, being far apart. Mind if I sit with you?"

I gave a nod and indicated with a hand to take the seat across from me.

She slid her chair back and stepped over. Her frame was small, delicate even but there was toned muscle under her loose print blouse and black slacks. Her perfume floated under my nostrils. I found the fragrance rather appealing. Not like my ex who used to douse herself in the stuff. She slid into the booth and plunked her handbag and coat down beside her.

"Where were we since we were so rudely interrupted last?"

"I think we had just introduced ourselves," I smiled.

"Who's the other guy?"

"Hendricks, he means well...I think."

She sipped on her glass. "I am going to assume he does."

"When do you start?"

"Tomorrow. I finished watching those new hire videos. Didn't they suck?"

"I didn't watch any."

"No?"

Before I could answer, a shadow fell across the table. Dwayne stood there wearing a shocked look on his face. He was the complex manager here at Duggan's Truck Stop and not a very good one from my understanding. He was too busy banging the bookkeeper rather than attending to the day to day managerial duties here at Duggan's. He swept a hand across his sandy brown hair. His brown eyes were etched with concern, surprise even, like he was the protective brother over a wayward sister he hadn't seen in years. He looked at Amy then me and back to Amy. He looked nervous. I couldn't explain the expression on his face but his voice held a high measure of concern. "Amy?" he looked to me and flashed a weak smile. "What a surprise."

Amy sipped her tea. "Just like you, Dwayne, late as usual."

"What're you doing...here?"

"Working," she looked up. "Something you should be doing."

He grunted. "*Ahh, sooo* what will you be doing? This is news to me." I wasn't sure how he didn't know about Amy working in the shop but then again Andrea was probably keeping him busy.

She looked back to me and we held each other's gaze for a moment before she looked back up to Dwayne. "I'll be working in the shop as counter help."

"I don't think that's necessary, is it? I mean..." he looked at the name patch on my jacket. "Logan, right?"

I guess he couldn't see the obvious. I nodded.

"Can you give me and Amy a moment?"

I rose out of the booth and moved out of earshot. Dwayne slid in my place and I could tell the whispered discussion was heated with Dwayne being animated with his hands. Amy remained calm but there was a look of annoyance on her face. She said something and Dwayne shut up. He froze and Amy continued talking. She leaned in as to emphasize her point and Dwayne's neck turned red. After several minutes, he rose up slowly and walked over to where I stood.

"Make sure you wipe down the seat. You got grease all over my suit," he pulled the suit sleeve down, straightening the wrinkles. "This suit cost more than you make in a month." He strode off and the cloud of anger followed him.

"Yes sir," I replied but I wasn't sure if he heard.

Amy was looking outside the window sipping on her tea. I slid back into the booth seat and looked at my coffee. "Well, that looked..."

"Looked bad didn't it?" she answered.

I looked in her eyes, surprised she still held a glint of happiness. "I've just never seen him pissed."

"He can be more of an annoyance," she chuckled.

"You two know each other then?"

"We do," she didn't offer up any more information.

We were quiet for a few minutes, but one of those not too uncomfortable moments.

She eyed me with those green eyes. "You're nervous."

"You see the obvious."

She smiled. "Dwayne is just raising concerns about me working but nothing to be worried about. It's been years since I've had to work, in this case though, I want to work."

"I wasn't worried in the slightest, just concerned."

She rolled her eyes. "He wouldn't hurt me if that's what you're implying."

"No, he just looked concerned, I guess."

"He's concerned about my possible failure and also what my husband might say."

I didn't see any ring on her hand. "Husband?"

"My husband works for Duggan's in various capacities," she sighed. "It's how we know each other."

"I see." Hearing about a husband in the picture dashed my spirits. She saw the expression on my face.

"I left my husband months ago in case you're wondering."

"Thought never crossed my mind."

She leaned in, smiling. "Don't lie, you're really horrible at it."

"My ex-wife said the same thing." I wasn't sure how people could look me in the face and tell I was lying. I had people tell me my eyes would look away for a second or, there was a nervous tick at the corner of one eye.

She leaned back and picked up her tea. "Well...I'm looking at enjoying entering the working world again even if it's just being a counter person. I'm nervous since it's been so long since I've worked at all."

"I think you'll do fine."

"You think I will?" she smiled.

"I have faith you will."

She smiled, leaned forward. "That sounds heartfelt. Thanks for the confidence boost." Her voice dropped to a whisper and her face was filled with examining wonder. It was hard to tell if it was an act or not. Women have this capability to play a man along and then drop him like a hot rock. One has to be careful regardless. "You have really great eyes, you know that?"

I didn't know what to say at this point. The silence fell into long thoughts of what could be, but I knew there had to be a catch of some kind. Maybe she was toying with the emotional string most men have, that one string that makes men think they're going to bed down some great looking broad and then...all hope smashes on the rocks of despair. Regardless, I was going to walk a straight line here. Women also played with men's hearts for ulterior motives to file a claim with the human resources department for sexual harassment.

Before I could answer, she smiled, rose up from her seat and donned her jacket. "I have to go but it's nice to meet you, Logan. I'm sure we'll be seeing more of each other."

"I'm sure we will."

"That does sound nice, Logan."

She wandered through the maze of truck drivers crowded in the diner and as I watched her leave, I wondered what she meant but shrugged it off. *Keep your eye on Texas,* I told myself.

But it was difficult watching her swinging hips moving through the diner.

SEVEN

I swung the motor out of the El Camino. The early signs of dawn stretched across the distant cold skies. The 396 popped free from the engine compartment and dangled from the cherry picker like a rotten tooth. I had spent the better part of yesterday working at Duggan's and decided it was high time to get things moving and inspect the engine to see if it was salvageable.

With a cigarette smoldering between thin lips, I pulled the oil pan and valve covers only to confirm my worst fears had come true. Number four rod was bent and the crank main bearing had spun. The piston was sitting at a weird angle and the gouges in the cylinder bore told the story that it was beyond saving. Further inspection revealed cracks at the main cap joint along with the side walls.

Finding another 396 was going to prove to be a royal pain in the ass. Even if one could be found everyone wanted a left nut money-wise for it. I mulled over my options and remembered the number Hendricks had given me. We were talking about engines one night. I told him I might need one for the El Camino. He had jotted down a number on a scrap piece of paper and told me to call a guy named Peterson. Peterson might not have been rich money wise but was rich with junk cars and farm equipment.

Digging around the uniform trousers, produced the number and I thumbed Peterson's number in the cell phone. After a few rings a tired, old voice answered. We talked for some time explaining I was looking for a motor and was told, by Hendricks, he might have an old 396 lying around. He wasn't too sure if he had one but to come out and see what motors he did have. I jotted down directions to his place.

I took off north on 41 towards Stanley, making a right on a dirt road called Jaymar. The road was fair in some spots and rough as hell in others. A giant plume of gold dust followed in the wake of the old Ford. I steered to the right on a side trail called 16A before circling back around to the north. Herds of cattle were sprinkled throughout the countryside, chewing on the sparse vegetation.

A mobile home along with a few large outbuildings, various farm tractors, cars and trucks, and equipment lay rotting under the sun and a series of wooden corrals loomed in the distance. I hoped the directions were correct. I had heard of ranchers running off people at gunpoint but when the old rancher appeared from the weathered and worn mobile home dressed in greasy coveralls and a can of Pabst Blue Ribbon, I felt I had the right address.

"It came out of my old Nova, a '68. I think, rolled that car back about..." he mulled over the years, the can of Pabst Blue Ribbon twitching in his hand. "About twenty-six years or so back, maybe longer." He pushed open one of the nearby outbuildings doors. Dust floated lazily in the air. "I'm sure originally it came out of a Camaro my brother had but he wrecked that too. My Nova needed a motor at the time."

I doubted the building had seen any use for some time. The building had served life as a shop. Within were several Ford tractors in various states of repair. Workbenches and shelves were piled high with old, used oil and dust covered parts. Off in the corner were several engines.

"Rolled?"

The old farmer smiled. "Back then it was an acceptable fashion to have a few brews for the ride home," he scratched his chin. "Yep, had a few too many I reckon."

"Been in here ever since?"

"Well, used it in a two-ton flatbed for a while. It was tired, rings wore. It was blowing smoke and such, but still ran," he waddled over to the stack of engines and pulled back on one tarp. "There it is."

It wasn't a 396. It was an old 427 or I was hoping it was. I took hold of the harmonic balancer and found it still turned. If it turned, it could be saved provided nothing was broke on the inside. We got down to business: price. After a few minutes of haggling, the 427 was loaded up in the Ford. I took it back home for five hundred bucks. I doubted the old man knew exactly what he had or perhaps even cared. He was happy to have beer money for the next week.

Over the next few days, I took it apart and examined everything and found, despite having been wore out from years of use and abuse, the motor was still in pretty fair shape. A lookup of the block and head casting numbers in my manuals revealed it was a genuine 427. A good solid rebuild would give me the legs I needed to get out of New Mexico.

The following morning, I ran to Albuquerque and dropped off the block, crank, and heads at a machine shop. Everything would be blasted clean, machined, and ported. I thought over my options on what to do with the old motor before finally coming to the conclusion I might as well make it into something worthwhile. A few calls to the machine shop and work began with my specifications in mind. I could've done the work myself, or most of it, but with work at Duggan's, I had my hands full. The finished product would take a couple weeks to complete but I had other things to keep me occupied in the meantime.

The winter air had returned again from the teasing taste of Spring-time reprieve, but the temperatures had not gone down below freezing. I had been watching Amy for some time but kept focused on the jobs rolling through. We had talked here and there, but really nothing more than small talk. She was focused on learning the counter job and had her hands' full writing up work orders, cashing out tickets and dealing with the drivers.

I had finished up a wheel seal, an oily mess that had coated the brakes and drum in a thick layer of black sludge. After a thorough cleaning and replacing the brake shoes, I went out back for a smoke break. It was slow for a change. Hendricks was working on a radiator swap in an old Pete 379. We were the only two techs working the shift and Hobart would be coming in soon.

The door to the counter office opened, Amy popped her head out looking both ways and saw me standing there getting ready to light one up. She came out bundled in a large overcoat to hold in what body heat she could. She smiled. "Mind if I join you?"

I looked over surprised. Not many women would want to go hang out outside, especially when it was cold. "Sure."

"Mind if I share a smoke with you? Hate to even start, but it seems to help keep me warm."

I lit up a cigarette, took a puff. "No worries."

We watched the distant night. The skies were clear and you could see the distant stars pulsating those millions of miles away. "Where are you from, Logan?"

"That's a deep question. My parents were in the military. I guess overseas." Being a military BRAT, no one cared where you came from. In reality, you didn't have a home.

"Really? Where were you born?"

I took a puff from the cigarette. "Ramstein, Germany."

"*Ohh*, a world traveler." She opened her hand for the cigarette.

"A few other places but don't remember them much," I handed her the cigarette. "What about you?"

"Mississippi native. Moved around to a few places but nothing big."

"Nothing?"

"Poppa worked for a large computer firm so we moved around to some places. Parents decided Mississippi was home no matter where we went, so we moved back." She took another drag and handed the smoke back. "Kids?"

I took the smoke and took a drag. "No."

"Why's that, Logan? You seem the fatherly type."

I blew out the acrid smoke. At one point, the ex-wife and I had discussed having kids. The idea had some appeal to it then but now looking back on it, I was glad we hadn't. Child support kills a man financially these days and the trauma of a divorce on a child would've been too much to bear. "No time for it I guess. We were both too busy for a kid to be in the picture. You?"

She seemed a bit fidgety and took a quick drag. "No, no kids, thank God."

I felt there was a twinge of animosity in her tone but dismissed it. "We're both fortunate then," I offered the last drag off the cigarette but she declined. I flicked the butt out in the parking lot and proceeded to light up another. "At least for any kid's sake."

"I'll just be glad when it's done," she pointed at my hand. "Are you glad?"

I held the hand out and looked down. She was referring to the pale ring around the finger. The ring had come off once the divorce was finalized. Just before blowing Vegas, I had given it to a homeless guy panhandling at an intersection while waiting for the light to turn green. "Finalized last October, and I don't miss it."

"Were you glad it was over though?"

I looked away to the night skies. I had come home late one night from the dealership and found the ex-wife getting pounded into the sofa by the next door neighbor, Ted. Things went dark. The only thing I remembered was I grabbed the baseball bat behind the front door. I chased Ted around the house with his throbbing member bouncing all over the place. A few smashed walls, a dented refrigerator, and a busted flat screen television later, Ted had run off through the back door in all his naked glory. I didn't have the heart to say I cried once the wife told me it had been going on for over a year. "Yes…yes, I'm glad."

"I know I'll be glad when this chapter of my life is over."

"I figured your husband would've been spoiling the hell out of you."

The scar under her eye twitched. "No," she smiled but I could see something in what I had said made her uncomfortable. "What happened in your case?"

I took a drag, staring out into the night. "She ran off with the neighbor. I guess I should've seen it coming."

"Why?"

"Married seven years, you'd think you'd know people by then but I find, now anyway, I didn't understand that she was just a lonely woman I had neglected."

"I wouldn't do that."

"You wouldn't? What would you do in this case?"

She gave a look of surprise, brushed those long bangs from her eyes with delicate fingers and smiled. "You mean if it was you and me?"

"Sure, why not?"

Her soft laughter reminded me of wind chimes moving around in a gentle breeze. At that moment, time slowed down enough to burn her smiling image into my brain as a forever portrait. "Ambitious, I like it. First, we'd get out of here. New Mexico is a great state but there are too many problems here, somewhere north, maybe Washington or maybe Alaska. Find a job where the company is second to marriage and family. I'd much rather have you around for the kids' sake."

"Kids? Already?"

She smiled and placed a delicate hand on my forearm. "Maybe two, but this is just a theoretical relationship, so don't get your hopes up," she looked away toward the winter moon again. "I'd settle for a small house built around the turn of the twentieth century. I always liked the feel of old homes."

I got the impression she wanted more out of life but her marriage wasn't into those things. I wondered if her husband really paid her any attention on what she wanted out of life. "Why the northwest?"

She took the remaining cigarette from my fingers and dropped it to the ground. "Smoking would be another thing you would need to work on," she looked away, lost in thought for a moment before continuing. "My grandparents lived in Idaho. My sister and I always stayed there during the summer months and the land seemed so green, so full of life. There was plenty of water. You never heard of peoples' wells going dry like around here. I kinda miss it. It would be a good place to raise kids."

"Sounds like a plan. When do we start?"

She mockingly slapped my arm and laughed. "Don't go getting happy. It's just theoretical."

I smiled and shook my head. "No, just messing with you."

She laid a hand on my crossed arm. There was a long silence between us while we looked into each other's eyes. A man could get lost in those eyes of hers. It was as if our souls were open to interpretation of our true feelings for one another. "You know, Logan,

I like you. You seem down to earth."

The door to the counter swung open, Derek poked his mug out and signaled to Amy. He carried an olive green backpack. He was ready to go home since it was end-of-shift. "We got a customer at the counter and time for me to punch out."

"Oh," she turned to walk away but then turned back and faced me. "We'll talk in a bit, maybe have coffee after we're done working if you're interested."

I looked at the clock. "Probably not tonight, I got a few things to do at home." I hated to do it but I wanted to get started on the El Camino.

"Some other time then."

I watched her as she walked away and I had to admit that she did look good. I was surprised at how small her feet were but she looked…real good even with that oversized coat on. *We'll talk in a bit, maybe have coffee after we're done working if you're interested.* The line alone seemed to have given me a key…a key to her heart.

EIGHT

You run into all kinds of TWN's, or Third World Nationals, working the circuit within the American trucking industry. I have to admit they are some of the hardest working guys in the business. I'm not knocking the true red-blooded American truck driver either. Anyone willing to haul freight to all points scattered across America deserves a hats off. Not many people have the testicular fortitude to climb up behind the wheel of a big rig and deal with the host of problems that come with it. They miss out on family events and miss out on their kids growing up, divorce rates are astronomical and they deal with crappy traffic and weather conditions. To make matters worse, they have to deal with bad management teams and get paid crap.

The TWNs are a special breed though. They are literally strangers in a strange land. In the short time working at Duggan's, I met a whole slew of nationalities that would boggle the mind of most

Americans. Some of them are more memorable than others.

I ran into a Russian, a former soldier who was in the spearhead invasion force into Afghanistan back in the eighties, an East German guard who patrolled the Berlin Wall for most of his career, an old guy from India who held incredible strength in his thin arms enough to crank up the landing gear on a loaded trailer that winded me trying to do it, then the Chinese, the Japanese, the Romanians, French, Cubans, Brazilians, and a slew of many other countries. The number of foreigners running the highways looked to outweigh the number of Americans.

Then there are the guys from Africa. I found out they just don't care about your life or theirs especially when you go out on test rides with them. They have a different outlook on life I suppose. Like most other nationals, they come to America to get their slice of the American pie and have a stable and fulfilling, long-lived life. Long-lived life is the key word here. It has something to do with the fact Africans have been hunted, tortured, murdered, and persecuted in their homelands by bands of terrorist, bandits, or their own government forces. Tragically, they are forgotten to the rest of the world's top nations. Like many other nationals the world over, they come to America and slam gears on our highways hauling freight all across the nation.

The Nigerian smiled. "See? See? You hear this?" he throttled the pedal and grabbed the next gears with lightning precision.

"Go easy, Killer," I hissed through clenched teeth.

"I go easy but watch!" he flashed a toothy smile and grabbed the upper deck of gears.

We called him Killer. I wasn't sure why. It was better than his Christian given name. Most Americans and even his own countrymen couldn't pronounce it properly. He was a regular customer who rolled through every other week or so. He paid cash for everything and never complained about our work. We always did our best work on his rig.

As a matter of fact, he always called in a compliment about our service location.

Hendricks was finishing up a turbo swap and talked me into taking a ride with Killer to diagnose a mysterious sputter and power loss at highway speeds. *'Highway speeds'* to Killer meant dropping the hammer, scrambling through the gears and getting to a hundred as fast as he could.

At this point, I was going to agree with anything he said. I wasn't hearing anything but the illusionary sound of smashing glass and twisting metal. I gave a quick glance at the speedo. My gut tightened up. The needle was inching over ninety. *Ninety miles per hour in a forty mile an hour zone and we're not on the freeway.* Where were the cops? There's never one around when you *really* needed one. I clutched the clasp of the seat belt a bit harder, feeling the plastic starting to give under the death grip. The slipstream of wind was seeping through the rotted door seals making it hard to hear yourself yelling.

We hit the freeway and the needle glided over a hundred. Anything at this point could happen. A steer tire blow, the differential could lock up, a weak u-joint could shatter and throw a driveline. We could roll over with my guts being squeezed out to resemble Betty Crocker's cheesecake that had splattered on the floor. I envisioned the accident photo with me surrounded by the squashed goo of jellied pulp that had once been my brains. It would be God's righteous judgment.

God was telling me something, like knock it off with Amy. It would serve me right too for thinking about messing around with her. Forget about it, no matter how good she might be in the sack, no matter if she took an interest in you first at the restaurant. Forget it now. Fix your car and blow this joint.

When the needle hit a hundred and five, the cab of the old Freightliner began creaking and popping. I was willing to give up everything and hitchhike out of this god-forsaken land. The Nigerian would be left scratching his head wondering why I told him to pull over and hopped out to hitch hike back to Moriarty.

Killer let off the pedal, the engine sputtered a little but you could feel a power loss. The injector was giving out. I was sure of it but equally sure I wanted the ride to stop. "Injector!" I yelled.

"What?" he hollered through his grin.

I signaled to turn back and repeated what I said.

He nodded, hit the next exit ramp and turned back and ran hard back to the shop. Hendricks had finished the turbo job and was outside the bay smoking a cigarette and sipping on his coffee mug.

I hopped out of the truck. "Injectors."

"We'll sell him a six pack and be done with it," he flicked the butt away.

"I'll order and get started on it."

He shook his head. "Not even, Paleface. That's my job."

"I diagnosed it I should get to fix it."

"You got storage room duties," he stabbed a thumb behind him. "Johnson said for you to do it along with Amy."

I didn't want to clean the room out. "Hell no! You got to be kidding? Look, I'll swap a few jobs for it. I work out on the floor and you get the money."

"Nope."

"*Aww* come on!"

"Look at it this way, it'll be a character building experience." He lit up another smoke. "Get going, Paleface."

For some reason, Hendricks had resorted to calling me Paleface. He had a nickname for everyone working on the floor. "Fine."

I walked off to the storage room in the adjacent bays being used for tires and old core parts. There was a second-floor landing that hadn't been used for anything but a catch-all for broken furniture, cabinets and a mountain of files dating back to the sixties. It was a sure bet most of the busted furniture dated back to the same time frame including the thick layers of dust.

Johnson had ordered a dumpster and wanted all the furniture and busted office equipment tossed out the side doors above into it. When I opened the door, I swore. There was plenty of work ahead. I heard a rustling and Amy poked her head up from behind a stack of cardboard boxes of old files.

"So I guess you got stuck helping."

I slowly walked over to her, looking over the work ahead. Since she was here, things might not be so bad after all. "Yeah, you're stuck with me."

She smiled. "It won't be so bad I don't bite."

I looked down at the files. She was going through them and had a stack set off to the side. Most of them dated back several years. I thumbed through a stack of open files and saw they were old as hell. Any trucking historian would go nuts to see some of these files. Trans Con, Sam Tanksley, Merit Distribution, and a whole slew of other trucking outfits who were no longer around. The files were going to be destroyed. An outside document shredding company was slated to come within the next couple weeks.

"Johnson says these files are going to the shredder," I lowered the paper and looked at the mountain of filing boxes. Some of them were dated back ten years. "I thought they had to keep these for like twenty years."

She flipped a lid off another box. "Depends, payroll and register deposits and things related are usually around two to three years," she lifted a folder out and opened it and began looking. "Accounts payable, financial statements and general statements are permanent. It's an IRS thing."

"How you know this stuff?"

She looked up. "I went to school for accounting."

"No shit? School?"

"Mississippi State. You?"

I frowned. "School of hard knocks."

"No college?"

My father had offered a golden ticket for college but I turned it down. I was more into partying and other 'educational' methods. I made one attempt at furthering my education but was bored with it. "Community college stuff but dropped it after a year," I started grabbing the computer equipment and tossing them over the edge into the dumpster below.

She pulled more folders and was looking through those. "That's not bad, Logan."

"What's that?"

"School of Hard Knocks, everyone has taken a course or two in that school."

I sat down on a nearby desk. "No, I don't think it is."

She knelt down, pulled the lid off another box and began looking through the old manila folders. I started to reach for the nearby filing cabinet and saw the green silk thong riding above her jeans. I inhaled softly and marveled at her skin and how good she looked in green for contrast.

She looked back and our eyes met.

I turned away.

"What are you looking at?"

I slid off the desk, grabbed the empty filing cabinet off of it. "Looking at finishing clearing this room."

"What were you staring at?" she smiled with narrowed eyes.

I stopped, winced and looked at her. "I ...*ummm*..."

She stood up and walked over a few inches from my face. My cheeks felt flushed. She looked me in the eyes. I couldn't tell if there was anger in them or interest floating around in those green eyes. "Well?"

I was glad I was holding the filing cabinet. It made a good shield. "I...it is a..."

"Yes?"

My teeth clenched, the muscles working in my jaw. I was sure a slap in the face was coming. "I just got…distracted. It's rather…petite, heart-shaped, and all."

She nodded slowly and the seconds ticked by. Nothing was said but she slowly placed her fingertips on my forearm. "I didn't detect a lie. Thanks for the compliment but I think you really need to stay focused on helping me clear out this room, despite the distractions that could come along."

I put a lot of passion into a nod. "I agree, Amy, whole-heartedly."

She gave a smile, wicked maybe, but thin. "Stay focused."

"I will."

She went back to the boxes of files and began going through them again. After several minutes she pulled out a few folders and set them aside. She shifted through several more boxes and removed a few more files. I wasn't sure why she was going through those old boxes. Johnson had probably instructed her to grab certain files.

I shoved one desk out into the dumpster and tossed another empty filing cabinet in after it. There were several shelving units about to fall over. I smashed those flat before tossing them down into the dumpster.

I paused to take a break. The storage room was hot. Even with the loft doors open, the air remained stagnant. I lit up a cigarette watching Amy. Particles of dust drifted in the air.

She didn't look back but could feel I was watching. "Are you gawking again, Logan?"

"Naw, just taking a smoke break." It was a genuine statement.

She looked back holding a folder. "You sure?"

"You want me too?" A plume of smoke drifted between us.

"You should quit smoking, Logan or at least cut back a little."

"I should, really should but it's a hard habit to kick."

She stood up. "Is it your only bad habit?"

I exhaled. "Maybe drink a bit too much from time to time."

She stepped over, clutching the stack of folders. "Have you thought about quitting?"

I nodded.

"So, quit."

I didn't say anything just looked into her eyes.

"I've had my share of issues with vices, maybe try and quit."

"You're concerned?"

"It would be nice to see you around for a while, so yeah."

There was a genuine concern in her tone. The ex could've cared less and the habits had followed from the divorce. I had never run into anyone who had any concern about my drinking. My mind was flashing back over the years and realized I drank something about every night. Maybe a beer or two but Crown Royal was a weakness. "Is it that obvious?"

"There are times you reek, and drinking on the job *is* a problem."

"I didn't realize it was that obvious."

She started to say something but Hendricks's voice boomed from below. "Amy!"

She turned and leaned over the railing.

"Derek needs your help at the counter." He eyed me with a straight face. "Get to work, Paleface."

I flipped him off and he laughed.

She went to her olive green backpack, stuffed the folders away inside before looking back, "We'll talk in a bit."

She walked down the stairs and disappeared through the shop. Looking around the storage room, there was still a mountain of old desks to toss. I was losing money the longer I was up here. I grabbed the next desk and found it heavy as hell to move and difficult to find a decent handhold. I bent down, grabbed a leg and started to tip it on its back.

I felt something rake across my fingertips, tape but it was holding something. I dumped the desk over on its back with a loud thud and looked down at the dusty desk bottom. I took out my flashlight and stuck it between my teeth. I felt along the raised lump and wondered just what the hell it was. It must've been important to someone or they wouldn't have taped it here.

Carefully, I pulled away at the aged edges, peeling slivers instead of whole pieces. Sighing, I reached into my trouser pocket and fished out my pocket knife and opened the blade. Cutting along the edges of duct tape, the metal object came to light. Still covered in duct tape, I peeled back the layers to reveal an antique skeleton key.

Odd. *Damned odd.*

Ripping it away from the desk, I peeled away the stringy material. There were some stamped letters on the round edge and taking the flashlight, managed to read the only letters on it.

NNRR

I pondered its meaning for several minutes but gave up. My mother had an odd fascination for old keys. She had several small shadow boxes she had made, loaded with antique keys. When she passed away, I had taken those keys and put them in an old jar. It would make a fair addition to my mother's collection of keys and quickly stuffed it into my pocket. Without further thought, I pushed the desk through the opening where it crashed in the dumpster with a clap of metal thunder.

I cleared the room out after a couple hours, sweating my ass off but always thinking of Amy. I could feel the devils hand on one shoulder and the grip of God on the other, but for the moment, I felt good.

Damn good.

The broken office equipment was tossed out with the exception of the filing boxes. The scrap metal company would arrive in the morning and the document shredding outfit would arrive in another week or so. Amy told me she still had to go through some of those boxes. She made several more trips to the storage room and came out with handfuls of folders stuffed into her olive green backpack. I didn't think too much on it and really didn't care but I did enjoy seeing her walk. She saw I was watching her and would give that smile and wink, that same smile and wink she didn't realize she was doing. It was truly sexy.

I found myself thinking about her quite often. At work, I looked forward to seeing her. While I was at home, or the rare single day off, I pondered what she was doing at that exact moment in time as I looked up into the moon overhead. Just what was it we had in terms of a relationship? That was if one even existed between us. I started to think I wanted more from it, but I wasn't sure how she felt or how to go about it. It was if she had the main key to my heart and was toying with it. I often wondered how her body would feel against mine.

But then again, we have to be careful what we wish for don't we?

NINE

Days went by and weeks faded into lost memories. The trucks rolled off I-40 with busted tires, blown clutches, shredded differentials and a slew of overheat issues. Spring and the early signs of summer were in full swing and every truck or trailer had a blown tire. Thick, rubber carcasses lay scattered across I-40 like shattered souls on their way to the darker regions of Hell.

Usually, heavy line trucks would overheat coming up Sedillo Hill, the same hill where I toasted the 396. Sometimes just blowing all the dirt, dust and bugs out of the radiator, charge-air-cooler and air conditioning condenser would be enough to fix the problem, other times it was more involved. This sometimes meant a water pump, thermostats or even a radiator as the interior fins would be clogged to the point where coolant flow was restricted. The worst-case scenario would be a cracked head, a cracked piston liner or anything else that could cause an issue but these were referred to the dealerships in Albuquerque. There was a few of us who could do those kinds of jobs but Johnson nixed it. He considered those things a liability issue. That was his explanation anyways. Everyone knew he didn't want to tie up the bays doing rebuilds or engine swings. A tied-up bay meant lost revenue.

The other hot ticket items were air conditioning, transmission repairs, fuel injectors, fan clutches and such, so either way, there was still plenty of dough to go around. It didn't bother me one way or the other. It all meant hard currency in the bank.

There's a certain rhythm you get into, an orchestrated and organized pattern of order amongst the chaos of shattered machines swirling around you. You clock into one work order, mentally calculating the next three or four jobs, lining up all of those, hook up the ac machine, recover the freon and while the machine sucks up the precious fluid, you bust out a tire or troubleshoot a light circuit, fix it, move on to the next and troubleshoot an overheat issue and blow out the coolers. By the time you jump on three or four trucks, the AC machine has just finished recovering, next step, replace the ac compressor and drier, set the machine on vacuum for thirty minutes, dash off to the next truck needing a fan belt but in turn, also needs an idler pulley because the bearings packs seized and shredded the belt in the first place.

During oil changes, I managed to convince drivers there was additional work needing to be done. There's an art to talking a driver into giving you more of his hard-earned cash. It takes a level of self-confidence and a measure of assurance you are the mechanic for the job. Not many drivers are so willing to trust repairs to just any mechanic. Up-sale a wheel seal, maybe you find coolant leaks leading to the conclusion the radiator or water pump needed replacing. The list was endless and the money fell into the bank like mana from Heaven.

This goes on well into the late evening and you realize before too long, its midnight and you've pounded out close to the twelve-hour mark. Never mind, go up front, and grab a coffee, coke and a smile. You got a radiator job or a shattered differential waiting for you. You just chucked about a grand into your next check. Good times.

Amy and I kept our distance, but there was this tension between us. All it would take is a single moment alone I was sure. Some of the guys tried hard to be close to her, making small talk or hovering around her. I had to remind myself not to be a jealous prick. After all, she was the only gal working the counter.

The worst part in this business is having a gal like Amy working the counter. Truck drivers, by nature, are on the road for days, weeks and sometimes, even months at a time. They haven't been with a broad in all that time. A bunch of them use the 'left-hand-Lucy' or 'right-hand-Rachel method to keep the pressure at bay, but they'll talk to a woman for hours if you let them. It is also one reason why I hated working on the inside of a driver's truck. God knew what the hell they were doing in the sleeper with their right or left hand. Word of advice: don't go into a sleeper without a black light, nitrile gloves, or even a bio-hazard suit with an external respirator system.

The rumor mill at Duggan's was still cranking. There wasn't a day that would pass when someone wasn't puking a rumor. The latest fashion statements had something to do with the Dixie Mafia having controlling interest in Duggan's. I had heard the spew before but hadn't seen anything close to Dixie mobsters roaming around. I guess I was half expecting to see big Cadillacs running around Moriarty with Confederate flags hanging off the antennas or something, but I saw nothing. Rumors continued on about the missing money. I would pretend to act interested but in reality, I wasn't.

I had other focal points going on.

The 427 was finished and picked up from the machine shop weeks ago but sat neglected under a tarp by the El Camino. The block was bored thirty over, forged pistons, aluminum heads and crank installed. Most of everything I was doing would make the motor into a 427 cubic inch asphalt eater. I'd have a nice motor but the downside was it would pass everything but a damned gas station. I wasn't complaining though. Gas prices hovered around a buck ninety and I had money rolling in. The time was sucked away by Duggan's though.

Amy.

There were the occasional light touches of her fingertips on my forearm or that cute smile and wink she did without realizing she was doing it. We were also mindful of the fact we were at work and anyone might see what was happening between us. We just didn't want the drama.

The shop rush hour had died down. Amy was messing with the computer and I was sitting on the nearby steps leading up to the parts room. Hendricks and I were the only ones slated for swing shift and we had cleaned house and made our money for the night. He was still working on an air system problem on a KW.

Idle hands are the Devil's workshop. These were the words I was hearing from my late Grandmother as Amy's fingers danced gracefully over the keyboard. I pushed those words aside from my mind.

"I'm short," Amy said.

"I know, around five-foot-two."

Her focus stayed on the computer. "I'm short a filter and I'm five-four."

"Damn."

She looked back. "I'm not too sure on filters and Johnson wanted the filter inventory done tonight. Can you share your knowledge?"

"Sure." I found it odd. I knew she could access the inventory on the counter computer but I didn't care. Every moment with her was worth the time.

"I have to log into Johnson's computer, bring up the master

list, and when I do, I need to know how many LF2001 filters we have."

"I don't think I've heard of that filter."

"It's an old number, so I'm figuring it's an old filter. That's what I'm trying to figure out for upcoming inventory."

"Okay," I went back to the filter room and began searching through the rows of filters stacked on dusty shelves. Amy opened the door to Johnson's office and slipped inside.

I started looking across the shelves. "What was the number again?"

"LF2001!" she shouted.

I kept looking but didn't see anything close to the filter number in question. I went to the cross-reference chart hanging on the wall by the office. I ran my finger across the lines of filter numbers and saw nothing close. "Still nothing."

"It says we have one."

I shook my head. "Amy, I don't think that filter even exists." I opened the office door and saw her fingers working the keyboard and the orange glow of the thumb drive in the USB port. She stood up, smiled and took hold of my arm. "Let's go find it together shall we?"

She was smiling and I was watching her and admiring everything about her. She looked around through the filters stacked on the shelves. "It says we have it."

"I don't think we do."

She looked back. "How can you be so sure?"

I stepped up behind her closer. "Because I've never heard of it and I've done enough oil changes to know what filters we have in stock."

"Is this it I wonder?" she pulled out a filter.

"No, that's an FF1000 and we got dozens of those."

"For oil?"

"No fuel."

There's this moment that comes around. It's almost childish to think two grown adults could see into each other's souls in an intimate way. She paused and we stood looking into each other's eyes. I could get lost in those green eyes of hers. There was nothing but the sound of our breathing between us.

I leaned in and slowly we kissed. She wasn't complaining and slowly laid her hand on the side of my face. She unzipped my jacket and slid her cold hands in as we embraced and kissed deeply with a passion I had never experienced before. Right as I was undoing her jacket to slip my hands in, a voice grunted from behind.

Hendricks looked away quickly, pretending he was looking for an oil filter and hadn't seen anything. "Amy, Johnson is looking for you, something about past your break time."

"Oh…" she zipped up her coat, ran a hand through her long hair and left with a look of concern etched across her face. She ditched into the office for a second, then reappeared and smiled before disappearing to the counter.

I scratched at my stubble of a beard and watched as she left. Hendricks looked over at me with hard eyes. He chewed on his gum, nicotine gum no doubt. I was sure he was going to have a heart attack one day from chewing the gum, wearing a patch and still smoking. "Hope I wasn't disturbing something."

Johnson waddled into his office and his voice called out for Hendricks and me to come to the office. We ignored him for a moment.

"No, no you weren't disturbing anything." I looked over to the nearby shelf, studying the filter numbers. "I was helping Amy find a filter…for end-of-month inventory."

He frowned, his eyes bored into me. He always looked deep into a man's soul with a mixture of anger and forced will. The kind of look a parent gives a child who is misbehaving at the store.

"Please, don't give me that look," I said.

"That must've been one helluva filter. You should know

79

better, but anyway, Johnson's got a special gig for us."

"Gig?"

"It has something to do with that road call this morning, for the trailer that lost its duals."

We walked into the office and I expected to see the orange glow from the thumb drive still jammed in the computer station but saw it was gone. Amy had taken her break and had gone up front for coffee. Johnson banged away on the computer before turning his attention to Hendricks and me. "Alright, you two need to quit screwing around on my computer. This thing is for business use only, not for some God-damned game of Solitaire. You got it?"

I started to say something but held my tongue.

Hendricks frowned. His fingers produced a cigarette. "We get it, boss," he looked over to me. "Quit playing Solitaire on the boss' computer."

"Me?" I asked.

"Yeah you, quit it."

Johnson scowled. "Alright, knock it off. Since it's slow, I'm sending you two out on a special mission. We got the trailer that lost a set of duals outside Encino. We chained up the axle earlier this morning on a road call and it's in the lot waiting for parts." He stabbed a thick finger at the two of us. "I need you two baboons to head out there and look for those duals."

"So, you want us to go out there and search about several thousand acres of BLM and ranch land for a set of duals?"

I had made dozens of road-calls on that lonely stretch of highway 285 between Clines Corners and Encino. There was nothing out there save for the hundreds of cows and bulls eating, fornicating, and shitting across hundreds of miles of rolling prairie, cacti, scrub brush, clusters of juniper and salt cedar trees.

"The owner back in Detroit said for us to go out and see if maybe we can find them. It'll save him a few hundred bucks if we can find 'em."

"This is a goat-rope session, sir," I injected.

Johnson frowned. "You declining?"

I thought this was stupid and I wanted to clean up and head home or talk with Amy some more, but Hendricks had other plans. "You in?"

I smiled. "No, not really, I've been here for fourteen hours already."

"I insist."

I looked up. He stood there with his cigarette. His eyes narrowed to slits as he took another drag and blew out a thick plume of smoke. I could see he wasn't having 'no' for an answer when he wanted something done. I shook my head. "Fine, I'm with you, just quit looking at me like that."

"Good, I'll get the Dodge."

"The Dodge? Why not the Ford?" The Ford service truck was several months old and rode like a dream. The Dodge service truck was five years old and looked like it had been recovered from a chop shop in the bad part of Chicago.

He stopped and furrowed his eyebrows in thought. "Because it's a good truck, it just needs a little TLC." For some reason, he had an emotional attachment to the Dodge. No one could figure it out and he didn't give a reason why, but he was the only one who used it on road calls.

Johnson shook his head. "You two get the hell out of here."

"We'll take care of it. Where did he lose the duals?"

Johnson's jowls shook. "Somewhere about five miles north of Encino on 285."

Hendricks smiled. "Easy money."

We stepped out of the office, closing the door. Amy still wasn't back yet from her break. "We ain't going to find those duals in the dark."

"We know that, and Johnson knows that, but we can earn some money off this without having to sweat our asses off."

I went and grabbed the keys to the Dodge. Hendricks grabbed another pack of smokes out of his toolbox. After checking the fuel gauge, we were going to have to grab fuel before heading out. Hendricks needed to refill his coffee mug anyway.

After grabbing the gas and coffee, we blew through town and slid onto I-40 at seventy-five miles per hour before I kicked on the cruise control. Hendricks cracked open his window, flicked the burning cigarette out before pulling out another cigarette.

The drive was quiet but I could see Hendricks had something on his mind. He was making small talk, talking about how much money he made this week or talking crap about some of the customers. We were coming up on Clines Corners when he got to the point.

"We got to talk."

"About?"

"Something serious."

I figured he was going to talk about Amy. He lit up another smoke, took a deep drag and looked out of the windshield, staring off into the surrounding dark landscape. "You familiar with proverbs?"

I found his question surprising. "You mean biblical proverbs?"

"Yeah, kinda. Jesus used them stories to prove a moral point."

"Like, something to do with an apocryphal story or a parable."

"What the hells that?"

"A way of proving a point without providing hard data, kinda like ...a proverb."

"Yeah, whatever, I got one for you," he took a swallow of coffee and took another drag. "I knew this guy a long time ago. He was a truck driver, hyper all the time and popped or snorted more dope than most people so he could keep going. Back then, you only made money when the wheels were rolling. Anyways, he's after this gal who worked at one of his delivery stops. I never could see what he saw in her. She was just butt-assed ugly."

He paused, his eyes were distant lost in the memory and took another slow drag before continuing.

"She won't put out for him. She's put out for a few other guys, why not him? He wants into her pants in a bad way. She's making him work hard for her shit. Every night, he's trying. This goes on for a month or so before the big night finally happens. He finally hits the jackpot, says the right combination of words or something and she finally gives in."

I was sure he was going to bring up Amy at some point in his story but continued listening in silence. The lights from the travel center at Clines Corner stood out like a beacon of hope in a valley of darkness. We made the exit ramp at Clines and headed south on 285. The vast landscape of darkness flooded back into the cab.

"Well, they go back to his truck, crawl in the sleeper and bang dirties, they finish, she falls asleep and he's lying there all wide-eyed and shit, thinking 'Hey what if this broad has some type of STD?' He knows she's been with a fleet of delivery drivers for the last few months."

"A helluva question to be thinking," I snorted.

He nodded. "The question keeps nagging on him. He gets up, goes out and washes his dick in the fuel tank."

I lit up a cigarette and cracked a smile. "Get the fuck out."

He held up a hand. "Swear to God, but wait, it gets better. So anyway, he finds washing your dick in diesel fuel is a bad idea. The shits burning down below so he goes inside the Walmart, buys some Orajel, goes into the restroom and cleans off most of the diesel and rubs on some of the Orajel to get it to quit burning. He then goes back out to his truck and the gal's awake and wants another go around. She goes down on him to help him get it up and after a minute comes up asking 'Hey, why my lips numb?'"

I laughed, choking on cigarette smoke.

"Swear to God it's true, the shit happened but there's a moral to the story."

"That was immoral as all hell I'd say."

"But he got the broad in the end. Why? Because he was persistent, you see? Persistence paid off in his case."

I laughed again. "How'd you know this?"

"He told me in confidence, made me swear never to say anything about it to anyone. I never did until now but there's a point to the story."

He took the last drag off his cigarette, rolled down the window again and flicked the butt out. In the rear-view mirror, the butt exploded in a plume of soft orange-reddish ash before fading into the dark mass of night and shadows. Whatever was on his mind, it was eating on his soul and he was smoking more cigarettes than usual.

"So, what's the point of this?"

He leaned forward in the seat, ignoring my question. We were close to Encino, some seven miles out. "Looks like this is the area, let's pull over here."

I slid the truck over to the shoulder, rolled to a stop and killed the ignition. The air conditioning motor whined to a halt. He stepped out and moved off to the rear of the truck to take a piss. The summer night was full dark with only the clusters of distant stars providing any kind of light.

I got out, dropped the cigarette and mashed it with my boot tip and turned on the flashlight. I could see where there were a couple of black streaks gouged into the asphalt surface. When a set of duals come off a truck or trailer, they pick up speed and velocity. I heard plenty of accounts where a driver was clipping along at seventy miles an hour only to see a set of duals come off his rig and pass him. Those duals were probably well over a mile inland through the large open lands, maybe even wedged against a tree. I looked back and saw Hendricks leaning over the truck bed sucking on another cigarette.

"You coming?"

He zipped up his jacket. "Yeah, hold a sec," he reached in and grabbed his coffee mug and flashlight.

We moved off across the road and up the incline. We came up to a small wire fence at the top and climbed over it before going into the nearby surrounding tree line. We pointed our beams of light through the thick growth, looking for a path where the duals might've gone. But I knew Hendricks had other things on his mind. The topic of Amy being one of them.

"What did you want to talk about?"

Hendricks flashed the light over to his left. "And you're right, been hearing things. It's why I drug your ass out here."

"Oh?"

"Just grumblings."

"What've you heard?"

He stopped and looked at me. "You and Amy. Why are you attracted to her?"

I paused then kept searching. The trees ended and all that could be seen were the dark rolling hills of prairie grass and tall patches of cactus. I didn't really want to hear this conversation now. "She's a Rolling Stones fan, can't go wrong with that. You've heard what about her?"

"Don't play me stupid, Logan. You and Amy have got a thing going. Hell, I saw it in the filter room, both of you tangled up like a pair of rabid dogs. Ever since you two showed up at the shop, sparks fly and everyone notices."

I shouldn't have been surprised. Everyone was going to figure it out in time. A few guys were starting to question and this concerned Hendricks for some reason. "Is this why you drug me out here at two o clock in the morning? To have this talk?"

"I'm just tossing out a warning. I don't think you realize who she is."

"Oh? And just who is she?"

He took a look around with the flashlight. "I'm going to tell you something and you better listen. Amy is married."

"Nothing new, I already knew that."

"To a high-ranking member of a group called the Dixie Mafia."

I didn't know that and stood there silent.

"Oh? That got your attention did it?"

"Bullshit."

"Go ask her," he dropped his cigarette and mashed it under his boot heel.

Silence fell between us. A breeze kicked up and rustled the nearby trees behind us. "How do you know this? Some damned rumor scribbled on a bathroom stall?"

"I was at another Duggan's location in Beaumont, Texas for electrical training class a couple years back. I remember seeing her there with a guy named Thomas Hauser. He's a big guy. I didn't think anything big until this kid in our class, a local yahoo, who said he worked as an errand boy for the Dixie Mafia. We had a few brews after class and he bragged about his connections. Word was then, and still holds true today, Thomas is high up the Dixie Mafia ranks. I've heard he is an enforcer of some kind."

"And she's married to this Thomas character?"

"Yes, she is, but the kicker is he is also a roving manager for the other complexes. He comes to each facility and fills in when there is or even when there isn't a position open. What I can't figure out is why she is out here at this location without him. I've never heard of her being anywhere without Thomas being around, let alone working at our location. You understand?"

"I...don't know really what to say to this."

"Look, I'm just giving you heads up. What you two do is none of my business, but for some damn reason I like you and don't want to see you get hurt."

"Emotions don't mean jack-squat. My ex-wife took all of those in the divorce and I can take care of myself."

He nodded. "Screw your emotions. I'm talking about physical pain. Maybe you can take care of yourself but Thomas has relatives who consider protecting the family honor more important."

"Relatives?"

He nodded. "Big bastards, like in bench-press-a- Buick big. A couple of his cousins are enforcer types from the Dixie Mafia out of Mississippi. That's a no shit thing. They are part of a clan called the Devil's Dog Pound. Their uncle was a big-time enforcer for the Mafia. He was known as the Devil, an evil bastard from the info I got. He taught these nephews of his, the tricks of the trade. Let that sink in for a minute."

"Devil's Dog Pound? What kind of name is that?" I started hearing old Lee laughing at the hotel bar and the soft warning to be careful.

"As good a name as any. Thomas and his connections with the Dixie folk is a no shit, so be careful."

Mafia! Jesus Christ! I suddenly felt my chest squeeze in and adrenaline began coursing through my veins. "Why you concerned then?"

He stopped and shined the light right into my eyes. "Because it could get you an ass beating or worse. If everything about the Mafia connection is true, those bastards just might pay a visit anyway and then you two get busted, and bad things will happen. Regardless, I got something else to talk about."

I held my hand over my eyes to shield out most of the blinding light. "Get that damned light off me. Like what else?"

He moved the light away. "Don't laugh but it's about the missing money."

I moved away. "It's a damned rumor."

"Not too fast cowboy. I got a pretty good idea the rumors are blooming into truth."

"It's a rumor, nothing more, Hendricks."

"It takes a set number of facts to make it a truth."

"And let me guess, you found the truth?" I asked sarcastically.

"Let me ask you this then. How bad you want out?"

"What? Out of New Mexico? If I could, I'd leave tomorrow."

He nodded. "It's not just about Amy, the Dixie Mafia or the other nonsense. There's something new this is why we're having this talk out here." He paused for effect.

I raised my shoulders.

"Quarter mill, maybe more I'm thinking. The story I told you about being persistent earlier? That's the moral of this discussion."

"Okay, I'll amuse you for a few minutes, and then we're leaving and never speaking of this money again." I was tired of hearing the rumors even though I had daydreamed enough times about finding that missing money. I had even thought about looking around out here before but then Amy entered the picture and those thoughts were swept away. I resorted to facts. It was going to take some ample amount of evidence to prove that there was a shit-pot full of money at the end of the rainbow. Everyone I talked with apparently was looking for the missing money, which I believed didn't exist.

He nodded. "I might have a lead."

"Convince me it's not a rumor."

"Rumors that have a hint of truth to them and I have a piece of the puzzle. That night when Richardson, that State cop came asking you questions got me thinking. I told you the story about my buddy being persistent for a reason. We need to be persistent with this. If the cops are still looking for that money then it has to exist."

"You think you know where the money is? Look, Hendricks, this idea of a treasure hunt. I think we're a bit too old to start believing in tall tales or trekking across land and sea looking for the proverbial pirate's chest." I was sure he was joking.

"Maybe but…" He unzipped his jacket, crammed a hand inside his shirt and pulled out something dangling from the end of his necklace. He removed it from the links and handed it over to me.

I took it unsure what he was getting at. There within my fingertips appeared to be a coin of some kind with a square hole in the center. I had to admit, it perked my curiosity. "What is it?"

He shrugged. "Chinese coin. It's old as hell. I'm not sure what to make of it. I do know Dave kept this coin on him at all times. He said it was one of his most cherished possessions. He said he found it and another coin just like it, on the family ranch down around Willard, when he was a kid. It might be something or it may be nothing, but he said something about his retirement being under an old pole, which I found peculiar. Of course, he was stoned off his ass at the time."

"How did you end up with it?"

"He left it behind. I knew something was wrong when I found it hanging up in his locker the day after he was murdered. Dave would never leave this coin out for anyone to mess with. He said at one point, he wanted his daughter to have it."

"You think the mob had something to do with that?

He nodded. "His murder? I think so but I can't quite put the pieces together. Dave was Dixie mob-connected and murdered by his own people? Why? Your guess is as good as mine, but I don't think the money was the main bone of contention," he lit up another cigarette and inhaled deeply, allowing the smoke to bite deep into his lungs. "You want in? Just you and me? We go looking for the fortune, which, I believe, is buried on Musgrave's ranch."

I handed back the coin. "Why me?"

He fell silent as he looked over the coin and hooked it back onto his necklace chain. "Because you are just like me, broke, with no future prospect on retirement, stuck busting wrenches for life, while the big dogs on top? The ones who ramrod this operation or any company we work for? They'll be sitting on some beach down in the Bahamas, sipping martinis and getting blowjobs from high-dollar whores. They won't be thinking about us. They'll only be thinking about the money they made off our sweat and how many more whores, cars, and airplanes they can buy. Meanwhile, we end up walking away with nothing but a bad case of rheumatoid arthritis, hemorrhoids, and maybe a hernia or two. You dig on that?"

I shook my head.

"We got this one shot," he held up a single finger. "One shot, to be that guy sitting down in the Bahamas and damn it, the money is out there, waiting for us to find it."

I was quiet for a long time, lost in my thoughts. I knew a few guys who had hit their early to mid-forties and besides the slow suffering physical effects the profession had on their bodies companies treated them like garbage. They were some of the best in the field. Some of these guys saw the handwriting on the wall and made the change to being shop supervisors or parts counters help just so they could keep their fingers on the pulse of the industry. It ran thick in their veins.

Then there were the ones who had been busted out. Being busted out meant there was no way any other company in their city or town would hire them due to the fact that managers at most trucking companies or dealerships knew each other on a first name basis and even played golf together on the weekends. All it took to destroy a mechanics application and career was a simple phone call to the manager buddy at another company listed on the application. Soon, with no one looking to hire them, these mechanics would drift to lower paying jobs, others left the field altogether for totally different career paths. The worst part? They had no money and no retirement.

They say there's no age discrimination in this country. I got news for you all - there is, and even though there are laws on the books that say otherwise, companies don't like to hire guys over forty and do anything to get rid of them post haste, or make life a living hell until they do quit.

I was a couple years away from the magic number forty.

"Still doesn't answer why me?"

He slowly nodded. "I need a brain, a second look at things. I'm pretty smart but sometimes I overlook things. You seem a decent guy, not out trying to grab everything or screw over anyone," he paused and lit up another cigarette. The red glow flared to life with each puff. "This is the real deal. We go in fifty-fifty."

I stood silent, thinking about what he had said. A breeze kicked up and the junipers shivered under the summer moon. Really, what else did I have to lose? If the rumors proved wrong, then it was nothing more than shooting for a Lottery ticket and losing a couple bucks and time.

Hendricks pressed his point. "I'm going to look with or without you, Logan, but two sets of eyes are better than one. If one day I ain't at the shop anymore, it's because I found the money and ran off to the Bahamas with my girlfriend for an overdue vacation. I promised her one someday and life is too damned short."

I looked into Hendricks' face. His expression was firm and resolute. What else did I have to lose really? Time? Maybe a few bucks in gas driving out to the ranch? "Alright, Hendricks cut me in. I'll help take a look." I decided to tell him about the key taped under the desk. I wasn't sure if it was relevant, but maybe there was a connection with the coin Hendricks had. It also might explain why it was taped up under the desk.

"A key? What color was the desk?"

"A beat to shit almond color."

"Sounds like Dave's old desk, you still got it then?"

I nodded.

"Bring it with you in the morning. We'll talk more on it and maybe go out to Dave's place."

"Sounds like a plan."

He nodded and grinned wide. "This is going to be wild if we find it. Imagine no more debts huh? Damn, that would be sweet," he turned to leave, then paused and pointed a finger at me. His tone turned serious. "You got beer?"

"Heineken."

"Rocking, bring 'em along."

I stabbed my flashlight around into the darkness. He whistled softly, grabbing my attention. "You coming?

"The duals? Johnson wanted us to try and find them?"

He looked around and grunted. "Those bastards went a long ways and ain't no way we're gonna find 'em. So, let's roll.

TEN

I gave up trying to sleep. I sniffed through the pile of dirty t-shirts for the cleanest one and pulled it on before stuffing the key in my pocket. Things had been too busy lately to be concerned with washing clothes. I made a mental note to do a load before work. I crammed the Ford into gear and took off, drove past Duggan's before turning down the main drag through Moriarty. I stopped once at the Circle K to grab a pack of smokes before realizing I had forgotten the Heineken. I back-tracked to Blackie's Bar and Package store and grabbed a couple six packs before heading down Highway 41.

The noontime sun hung high in the summer skies and not a cloud could be seen. It was just a vast ocean of blue stretching from one side of the horizon to the other. Following the directions on the worn and crumpled paper, I made a left turn on Ice Plant Road. The dirt road was hard earth and the washboard ripples rattled the old

Ford. The homes closest to 41 started out looking nice but as I drove further down, the homes began to look more rundown, battered or were boarded up resembling a beat-to-shit boxer with bandaged eyes. Near the end of Ice Plant, the road came to a T crossing and I hung a right on CR121. The road was nothing more than a trail of silt sand cut through the surrounding landscape of scrub brush and prairie grass.

Driving down several miles, the depressing array of homes faded away to vast open fields. I guess no one wanted to live this far off the main road. CR121 curved to the left over a small rise revealing Hendricks's RV trailer, his Chevy truck parked just in front of it. His place was the only habitation out in the vast expanse of cattle land. I pulled up, killed the engine, and grabbed the two six packs. The radio inside blared out some old-time music reminding me of my high school years. It took me a moment to recognize the punk rhythms belonging to the band *Gun Club*. I rattled the screen door a few times and the music died mid-tune. Hendricks popped open the flimsy screen door and I handed over one of the six packs before stepping in.

"About damn time," he plunked the six pack down on the counter, pulled one of the green bottles and twisted the top off. After sucking down the froth, he lit up a cigarette and tossed the lighter on the counter.

"Had to grab some smokes," I answered as I lit up my own.

The camper was surprisingly clean for as old as it was. There were a few dishes in the tiny sink but nothing more in ways of garbage or dirty clothes. I figured since Hendricks was living alone, he would've been a slob but just like his toolbox, everything was neat, cleaned, and organized. Everything was a contradiction considering he probably hadn't shaved in months, or cut his hair which hung down to his shoulders. I had a feeling he drank too much though. He finished off the first bottle and took up a second. "Glad the beer's cold."

I dug the key out of my pocket and handed it to him. He took hold of it and rolled it around in his fingers. "NNRR?"

I took a pull from my bottle. "That's it."

"What the hell does it mean?"

"Haven't the foggiest but it must've meant something."

He grunted while studying the key.

I took another drag. "So are we going or what?"

"Yeah, let me grab my boots and we're off." He disappeared in the back room and several minutes later reappeared. He grabbed the beer and we took off back to 41 through Estancia until we hit highway 60 through a town called Willard. We hit Highway 42 south and Hendricks had stayed quiet except when he was giving directions on where to go. I was sure he had already made a few solo explorations out here looking for the money.

We had driven twenty or so miles before he indicated to make a left turn. I slowed and quietly steered the old Ford onto a dirt road with rough patches of washboard. I had to slow down and dropped a gear to pull a small hill before upshifting again. "We're going down a few miles. You can see Dave's place from here." Hendricks finished off another Heineken and tossed the bottle out the window.

Dave's ranch was a collection of run-down series of buildings hidden within a thick cluster of trees. Some were modern looking with pro-paneled roofs poking through the green clusters. Other buildings were made of wood that had faded to a bleached weathered look due to New Mexico's change of seasons. I counted eight buildings and lean-tos not including the large barn that had half-fallen in on itself.

I started to turn into the main drive but Hendricks nixed it. "We'll head down a bit and take the back roads in. We don't want people thinking anyone's here," he pointed ahead, "go down a few miles. There's a road that runs alongside the property."

Once on the road, I felt the excitement creeping in. Somewhere, out here, was supposedly a quarter million plus in cold hard cash. People were looking for it and had for the better part of a year and no one had found it. What if we did today? A long shot but the possibility was there.

Hendricks pointed to a large group of trees. "We'll park here and walk in. The trees will hide the truck."

I parked the Ford within the trees and killed the ignition. "You think anyone's in there?"

Hendricks leaned back, raised his shirt front up revealing a revolver with Pachmeyer grips. The sunlight reflected off the blued finish. It was a .357 from the looks of it. "If there is, we got security."

"Jesus," I whispered. "Should I have bought a gun too?"

"Too late now," he laughed, opened the door. Stepping out, he grabbed another Heineken and popped the top. "I've been out here a few times already, looking around but the place is pretty torn up. People have been running around through here taking all kinds of stuff," he pointed across the gate, "there was an old John Deere tractor over there but someone grabbed it a while back. All the antiques are pretty much gone. Dave was a hoarder of antiques."

I was feeling nervous about not having a gun. A lot of problems are buried out in deserts and prairies across America. I didn't want to be that kind of a problem. I tossed the cigarette butt then mashed it into the ground with my boot tip. "Let's go."

We moved across the trail and were greeted with a sign bleached out of all its colors. I could only make out '...*violators will be shot.*' I clambered over the fence, followed by Hendricks who insisted on holding his beer while he did the same. We moved down the overgrown trail.

We slowly moved across the overgrown fields onto a deeply rutted dirt path circling back to a series of buildings. One of the buildings was a newer style double-wide with an attached two car garage. Directly across from it was an old adobe bricked building that resembled an old barn of some sorts. We moved in closer listening for approaching traffic from the nearby road. Only the sounds of chirping birds or the occasional cawing from a distant black crow could be heard.

I stepped up the front steps on the porch to the double-wide. The front door was open and swinging in the breeze. I poked my head in and found the obvious signs people had rummaged through the house and destroyed most of everything. The elements had soaked their way through and had turned the once white carpets into a pile of brown mush. The musty stench of rot hung thick in the air. I stepped in and felt the floor sag under my weight. The walls had been busted out, plaster piles of torn sheetrock lay scattered all over and the furniture, what little there was, were torn apart.

Someone had wrecked the place…searching for something and it could only be assumed it was the missing money.

"Dave died around here?" I asked.

Hendricks leaned against the porch railing. "They found him out front by those cars," he raised the Heineken and pointed out the weather-beaten Lincoln Continental and a late eighties Mercury Cougar across from where we stood, "they found him shot to shreds along with Lonnie Blonde. From what I understand he didn't have a head left…closed casket."

"No known relatives?"

"None to speak of. He had a daughter somewhere back in Texas who wanted nothing to do with any of this. Come to think of it, she didn't even show up at the funeral either."

I stepped off the porch. The sun's rays danced around through the nearby tree limbs swaying in the gentle breeze. "How many acres are we talking?"

Hendricks finished off the beer and tossed the empty bottle into the weeds. "Five thousand."

I wasn't sure I heard right. "Did you say five *thousand?*"

"Not to mention the BLM land rights. You can add another five thousand on top of that number. He ran a small herd of cattle up until he died."

"Jesus, Hendricks. That's something like seven or eight square miles."

"More like sixteen with BLM rights. A pain in the ass, I know," he looked around, "but it's out here."

Five thousand plus acres. It would take a lifetime to find it and a ton of modern detection equipment to find it. "You said the Feds were out here?"

He nodded. "They were for a while. After Musgrave's murder, the Feds came out some months after, locked the place down. You remember Deputy Daniels, the guy who likes to come around the shop and bullshit about guns and hunting?"

I nodded.

"He told me they were all out here looking for the same thing and came away empty handed. They had all kinds of detection equipment but didn't find a damned thing."

"If they didn't find it, Hendricks, what makes you think we can?"

He fumbled for a cigarette and lit up. "Because we have two pieces to the puzzle no one else had."

It was a remote possibility Dave knew the value of the Chinese coin and wanted no one else to know about it. He must've known he was going down a bad road the night he was murdered. He must've known that fact along with the possibility he might not return. So he gathered up his belongings, including the coin and placed them where he hoped his daughter might end up finding them. But what was the significance of the coin along with the key? What was the connection?

I started thinking this was going to be harder than I had originally thought. I took out the small key and looked it over. "I think we need to find out what exactly this key is for and what exactly that coin you have is."

"Locksmith and a coin dealer?"

I shook my head. "No, we don't need anyone else involved. We can't let on we're even looking for the money."

He agreed. "Where else then?"

I stuffed the key back in my pocket. "I need access to a computer, none from work. The library will be our best bet but I need a card from someone other than you or me."

***

The quiet little village of Tijeras lay just off the I-40 freeway nestled within the surrounding rolling mountains and foothills some ten miles outside Albuquerque. There was nothing special about it other than the frontage road, the historic Route 66 highway, running through the middle of it. There were a couple of feed stores, a bank, a day care center, a bar, and a library. I just happened to hit the library on the day it was open, which was only a few days a week. I slipped inside and allowed my eyes to adjust to the dim lighting before moving toward the nearest computer terminal. I took a moment and looked around, seeing if anyone was watching.

Several people were wandering around, studying the vast collection of books on the massive shelves, another older woman was busy, falling asleep while reading some old romance novel. Other than that, no one was paying attention.

I logged on using Jill's library card. She was Hendricks's on and off again girlfriend. She had been kind enough to loan it to me and eyed Hendricks with a sly smile. I wasn't too sure on how their relationship worked other than it looked to be like friends with benefits kind of thing. He never elaborated but he did mention he had a weakness for slender-bodied redheads. She had worked at Duggan's in the past up at the C-store. She was a single mother with two kids. Her previous husband up and left her destitute. At least until Hendricks entered the picture and helped get her and the kids a roof over their heads and kept them fed. People said he didn't have a heart but Jill would tell you different.

I punched the keys on the keyboard, entering her name and ID number stamped on the library card. It took a few minutes before the computer loaded up the main library web page.

I began typing on the keyboard. My first search was a generic one about rare keys and came up with several from the eighteenth century. Another search revealed nothing even close to what I had on hand. I quickly remembered the letters stamped on the key loop and dug it out of my jacket pocket.

The key tumbled in my fingers as I looked it over with keen interest and hammered in the letters 'NNRR' and '*key*' into the search engine. I nailed a hit and scrolled through an auction listing for a key and lock set. It was an older key set and as I looked closer, I saw the letters on the rounded end.

NNRR.

I punched the keyboard keys and came up with a couple of hits, one of them held my interest for a long time. Nevada Northern Railroad. The railroad company operated from 1905 through 1983 and the lock was a spring-loaded front key drop marked *ADLAKE*. The lock system was invented and produced by one Andrew T. Hagerty who filed the patent for this system sometime in 1935.

If what I was looking at was correct, Dave could have locked up his ill-gotten goods with a vintage ADLAKE lock and carried the key around with him. I was still unsure why he would tape up a key under his desk though. That was puzzling. I could only conclude he felt the key would be safe there. He might've been paranoid about having it on him in the event he was ever arrested or being killed by his buddies in the Dixie Mafia.

The average price of five hundred bucks was the going rate for the lock at auction. Why use an antique, expensive lock when you could go to any hardware store and buy a cheap-ass padlock for a few bucks? I pondered this for a few minutes, remembering the property itself was an antique collector's dream. Also, there were still some old railroad paraphernalia lying around. Musgrave must've been into collecting railroad material.

The only conclusion I could conjure up was Dave used whatever he had on hand. He had this lock on hand. It was functional and would serve its purpose so why buy a new one? I was sure it had to be the key to that particular lock but the final question was, where was he hiding the stash of bucks?

I gave up on this thought and carried on with a new search.

I punched in Google Earth. It took a few minutes to locate Musgrave's property south of Willard and zoomed in on satellite mode. I found the map to be a little over a year old and going over several hundred acres was a pain in the ass. If I zoomed in too much the image became pixelated to the point of being unreadable and would flash an error. If I went too far out, you couldn't make out anything. I kept the image about centered on the screen and studied the images, occasionally scrolling over from one point to another. There were plenty of trails indicating heavy use at one time. I concentrated on those first, following along the thin trails with interest.

There was what looked like remnants and foundations of older buildings Hendricks and I had not noticed before in our earlier excursion but we hadn't walked the entire property either. The ruins looked to be crumbling foundations, some rusted cars, and a few old livestock corrals.

This was going to take some study time and the use of a detailed map. I would have to stop by the State geographical office and pick up some topographical maps of the area. Having those on hand might come in handy.

I punched out the print button a few times and waited for the printer to finish. The resolution on the printed pages was not all that hot but it was better than nothing. After close to an hour, I had narrowed down our search to a few possible locations but nothing more. The one area that really held my interest was a lone shack looking like it had fallen in on itself. It had what looked like footpaths that lead up to one single point and not any further beyond this point. The ground also looked disturbed with its square shape like something had been buried there. A pit where Musgrave might've had cleaned out this part of the property by burying the garbage? It wasn't uncommon for ranchers and farmers to gouge out a hole in the ground and pile their garbage in it. It was hard telling and Hendricks and I were going to have to go out for a few reconnaissance missions for a look see.

I realized if the money was still on Dave's ranch, it was going to take a long time to find it.

I punched in information pertaining to the coin Hendricks had and found it was indeed of Chinese origins. Using the phrase '*Chinese coin*' and '*New Mexico*' in the search tab, I tripped across an article on the University of New Mexico website about Chinese people working on railroads in the Land of Enchantment. My heart skipped a beat when the article had an image of an identical coin to Hendricks own coin. It had been excavated at a Chinese work camp and the dig site dated back to the 1880's. The Santa Fe Railroad was working on laying track from El Paseo, through Cedarvale, Willard, Moriarty, and further north into Santa Fe. There were several work campsites found along the long-forgotten railway tracks.

I hit the print button and the printer hummed and slapped out pages. I continued reading for information and found a map dated from the turn of the previous century pertaining to the population centers for the Chinese. Most of the areas were further north of Santa

Fe and the western part of the state. But there were a couple of areas around the southern and middle sections of Torrance County where Chinese families had lived and worked laying track for the railroad. Since the Chinese had been ostracized from living in any nearby towns because of the color of their skin, they had built work camps and moved from site to site as each point of the railroad was completed.

Dave's property fell in along the pathway for the railroad tracks that were put in years ago. After studying a few other maps of the area, I found there were no indications of those railroad tracks left in the region. I knew there had been old tracks running out of Moriarty. There were dirt berms running alongside highway 41 south of town. These ran all the way through the Estancia Valley but soon disappeared after the town of Estancia. After that, all physical landmarks associated with the railroad had long since melted back into the natural formations of the surrounding landscape or had been destroyed by the local farmers and ranchers.

I exhaled a deep breath and leaned back in the chair. The clock on the wall told me I had an hour to go before shift change at Duggan's. I still had to stop by the State office for a topographical map but would do that tomorrow. Amy would also be working the counter tonight and I felt my heart swell. I gathered up my printed pages and maps, checked out at the counter, and rushed out the door. I felt it was going to take a while in figuring out where Musgrave hid the money but I had at least made progress.

I was closer to the truth of the matter but still unsure of the final outcome. The bottom line was the Chinese coin Hendricks had and the key I held, were connected only by two facts. One fact was the railroad system that had once weaved its way across the Estancia valley those long years back. The other was Musgrave was a collector of railroad antiques.

I paused outside the library door, fumbled in my shirt pocket for a cigarette and lit up one of the crumpled smokes. I looked up and spotted a Dodge truck with dark tinted windows idling in the parking lot.

I could barely make out the bulky outlines of two men seated inside. The hairs on the back of my neck rose up. The window rolled down and the men inside took shape into massive bodybuilder types. The driver lowered his sunglasses and looked right at me. His massive arm dangled down the side. The Dodge rumbled out of the parking space and slowly rolled by. Both the men gave me the evil eye and I wondered why until I saw the license plate stating they were from Mississippi. They made a right turn on the main drag back towards Albuquerque.

I felt a twinge of fear for a moment. I might have to start carrying the .45. I shook off the edgy feeling, telling myself it was a coincidence, went to the Ford, fired it up and hooked a left turn back to Moriarty.

ELEVEN

Conversations with Amy came and went just like the days of the
week tumbled into months. Before I realized it, I was a few months
away from working at Duggan's for a year. Amy was always there and
we talked about things in life whenever time permitted. We didn't
speak about our encounter in the filter room but the tension between
us grew.

The shop was a busy blur of activity. Late summer was in full
swing and the early September mornings were much cooler than the
previous months. We were thankful for the change. Throughout the
summer months, our dark blue uniforms became sweat soaked around
the neck and armpits that left white rings in the fabric where the body's
salts had accumulated. Tires, oil changes, electrical problems, air
conditioning, overheating, anything that could make money, rolled in
through the shop. Even with the change of seasons, the summer heat

carried over into the early fall.

The one thing I noticed about these conversations between Amy and I was that she seemed to be careful in what she spoke about. She never divulged too much about her current or past life and I got the impression her marriage to Thomas was none too rosy. The fact she was married to a member of the Dixie Mafia never once deterred me. I did think about asking her about it but never got around to it, and when I did, I didn't bother. It was fine, though perhaps there were things she just didn't want to discuss or couldn't.

I continued stock-piling my paychecks and splitting my time between working on the El Camino, and Duggan's. I was earning an average of three to four grand every couple weeks and it was pounding the hell out of me, but I kept going. The high dollar checks though came to an end when my evil bitch ex-wife began soaking me for alimony. Her blood-sucking army of attorneys had tracked me down and began garnishing my checks. I would take half of what was left over and stuff it away and before too long, I had a few thousand more saved.

I began putting the 427 back together in the enclosed carport. I assembled the engine, and satisfied it would run, I turned my attention back to the El Camino. I wasn't going through any more issues once I took to the highway. I pulled the TH400 transmission and tore it down to rebuild. Even though it still worked, I just didn't want any problems in the future.

Hendricks and I made excursions out to Musgrave's place when time permitted. We scouted the area for any sign of the missing money. We beat the brush looking for anything out of the ordinary or any outbuilding that might be locked with a padlock that the old railroad key might fit into. We found nothing in terms of an ADLAKE lock.

We had been careful each time we went out on these

excursions but it was apparent other people had not taken the same precautions. A few times we had seen fresh tire tracks and even some footprints in the soft ground. We came to the conclusion other people might be hunting for the same thing. We started packing our pistols.

We kept up with the search and working the shop grind through red-rimmed eyes and in a constant state of sleep deprivation. The missing money and dreams of things that could be, kept us going.

Amy would always talk about anything. There was just something about going to work and seeing her there that washed away the sleep factor. As in all things, we finally get what we ask for, what we crave regardless of consequences.

I watched her at the counter as we made small talk. The tension between us had grown in a small amount of time. We both knew it. I could sense it. We had talked about things we never talked with others about. The soft touches, the long looks, we both knew what could happen if we were left alone. I didn't want it to stop.

We both knew the moment would arrive sooner than later.

Sometimes we all get what we want.

We made small talk about some fuel filter and the applications. I had been telling her about the different common filters that were used. On one quiz I was giving her, I asked which motors a particular filter was used on. She claimed it was this type of filter, but I knew she was wrong but I wasn't listening nor did I care. I wanted to hear her voice and be with her more than anything else.

The graveyard shift arrived and Amy finished up counting the drawer. Hobart sat by his toolbox munching on chili-flavored chips and sipping on his oversweet coffee. He eyed me once, grunted and went back to reading the *Albuquerque Journal*. I had made enough money for the day. I looked back through the side door. I could see Amy occasionally looking up at me.

I shouldn't have waited but I went back inside and found she had just finished clocking out when I took her by the hand and we quietly slipped into the filter room.

"Which fuel filter are you thinking?" I asked.

She smiled and went to the shelf with me behind her, watching the gentle rolling of her hips, well aware I was taking her in. She went to one shelf and slowly started to pull one down. I shook my head and she smiled wide and allowed me to watch her. She knew I was observing her physical body and she was happy to oblige. I could see that she wanted me to watch her, to take in her physical looks and admire her. She shifted her hair to one side and her body twisted to expose a small glimpse of her red bra through the gaps of her buttoned shirt. I felt a need to be with her, something urged me forth and damn the consequences.

"This one then?" she took ahold of another filter.

I stepped up behind her and took in the faint aroma of her perfume.

She turned and faced me, filter in hand. We were silent, only our breathing could be heard but our eyes spoke volumes about what we actually felt.

I took the filter gently from her hand and set it aside and held her gently.

We couldn't have cared less about the filter.

I pulled her in close. It was the first time I felt just how firm, but frail she seemed under my touch. Our eyes locked onto each other. I caressed her cheek. I just hoped I wasn't offending her by the stench of my sweat and grease.

"Logan..." she made a weak attempt to push away but melted into my arms instead and quit the fake resistance. I took in her beauty. Her stunning eyes and lips and I kissed her ever so gently, ever so slowly. She gave in to my lips as I slid my arms down to the small of her back and pulled her in.

She was breathing hard when she pulled back and shook her head slowly. "Logan, I…."

I cut her off. "Amy…we need to quit playing games. We need…" My voice fell off to a whisper.

She looked up into my face and after what seemed a long time, nodded and took my hand and pulled me toward the back door. She took up her handbag and jacket. With the shift ended, I wasn't sticking around for overtime.

"Wait, I gotta lock up." I ran to my toolbox, locked it and grabbed my gear and started for the back door.

By the time I managed to grab my clean set of uniforms, she had left quickly out the back door. I heard the door slam and I watched as she drove across the parking lot in her black Chevy.

"Son of a bitch," I whispered and realized I had perhaps stepped over the line. I shook my head. I started up the old Ford and threw it in gear and pointed the nose to home.

I cursed all the way home.

But there was a surprise waiting as I pulled up through the thick junipers. Amy was standing by her black Chevy. I didn't waste time and quickly killed the ignition and stepped out and took hold of her. She wasn't withholding anything either.

We stumbled inside and took our time slowly undressing each other between gentle kisses of urgent need, and marveling at the perfectness of our passion. The only sounds to be heard were our heavy breathing. The whole outside world had slowed to this moment and nothing else mattered.

***

The morning came and I watched her. She slept lightly, stirred and felt her breasts rub against my chest. She opened one eye then another and we looked into each other's soul for a long time.

"Morning," she said.

"Best one ever."

"What time is it?"

"Time for another round I think."

She smiled. "You think you have that much in you? I thought you were running out of gas on the last one."

"Probably not."

She kissed my cheek. "Next time."

"I'm looking forward to it."

"I'm sure you are."

I lit up a cigarette and blew out a plume. "Today's going to be a long one."

"It's just you and Hendricks again and me of course," she gently took the cigarette from my fingers, stretched across my chest and dropped it into an empty bottle of Heineken on the bedside table. "You need to quit."

I didn't object. "Getting tired of that, not you or Hendricks but I wish they would give us a third guy on the floor."

She laid her head down on my chest. "Do you think he'll say anything? He's seen us...in the filter room." There was genuine concern in her soft voice.

I thought for a long time. I doubted it. Hendricks didn't seem the type to say anything to anyone for any reason. I didn't think he would. Besides, he was more focused on the hunt for the missing dough rather than pay attention to Amy and I. "No."

"How can you be sure?"

"I don't think he cares one way or the other but there's nothing to gain out of it for him."

"I hope you're right."

"I am."

"You realize we have to stay quiet right?"

"To be honest, I want to scream out to the heavens about

this."

"You better not," her eyes narrowed to slits and lightly punched my stomach.

"I'm joking but I'm serious about seeing you more," I reached over and took up a Heineken, then on a whim looked at her. "Move in, we got something."

She smiled and ran a thin finger across my chest. "You would like that wouldn't you?"

"Yes."

She set her chin on my chest and looked into my eyes. "What then, Logan? We play house for a while then you get tired of me or my husband finds out and decides to commit double homicide?"

I snorted. "Better than being apart from you. Or we move on, get out of here and head somewhere to start a life."

She was looking into my eyes for what seemed forever. "Are you serious about that?"

I looked straight into her eyes. "As serious as anything else in my shambles of a life. If you would care to join my chaotic, disorganized life as a diesel mechanic, we can make a go of it."

"How about I think on it," she smiled.

"I do plan on leaving eventually."

"Is Moriarty that bad?"

I took up another cigarette but decided not to light it. Here recently I had begun chain-smoking and mentally had to tell myself to stop. I set the lighter and cigarette back on the bedside table. "No, I like the smell of cow shit and dead grass. I think a touch of greener pastures would be in order."

"But you're making money here."

"I am but it's not going to last forever." I didn't have the heart to tell her I was looking for Musgrave's money…but if I did find it maybe she would have a change of heart. "Maybe I'll look for that money everyone keeps talking about."

"It's a rumor, Logan."

"It is but what if I tripped across it?"

"What if somebody else already found it?" She gave a good impression of a shocked look.

"You're mocking me aren't you?"

"I don't think you need to be chasing imaginary things like the missing money."

"What if it isn't a rumor though?"

"It would be blood money, don't you think?"

I stood up and she watched as I stood before her. "Yeah, maybe you're right."

"I wish we had more time, Logan."

"We will again. I'll start the shower."

She smiled, nodding and sat up in bed and shook her long hair. "Be there in a moment."

I went into the bathroom and fired up the shower. The water ran for several moments before I was satisfied it was turning warm at least. I stepped in and began washing, letting the waters cascade over my head to wash away the grit and grime of yesterday.

I was finishing on washing up, wondering just where she was at when I heard what sounded like a door opening and closing suddenly. The air pressure changed for a second and I thought maybe another late summer thunderstorm had cut loose with a lightning bolt nearby.

I cut the shower off. "Amy?"

I stepped out of the bathroom, towel in hand, scrubbing the greasy crap out of my ears and saw she was gone.

TWELVE

It's not very often I wonder on the mysteries of women, but with Amy leaving, I began to. God must've had this cruel sense of humor while He was in the process of creating them. I was sure He had installed this mysterious vindictive streak deep within their DNA. Most of them are strange and mean and use a thick guise of syrupy sweet to try and leverage something out of a man. I was starting to think bedding her down was perhaps a bad idea.

With her leaving so abruptly, was that her way of telling me to pound sand?

Christ. What the hell was I thinking? She was married for God's sake! *And not to just any man, a member of the Dixie Mafia,* I thought. I quickly dressed and stepped outside the front door. Her black Chevy truck was long gone and I didn't even know the reason why. The sex was good, so good in fact I wanted her more, but had she felt the same way?

I threw my arms up to the heavens and wanted to scream out in frustration but the only thing I managed to do was mutter a silent curse and felt the swelling of my blood pressure.

There's a saying and I don't know where the hell I heard it. God had decided it was time to make a perfect woman. This perfect woman would be good, faithful, cute as a button and forever obedient. Once He was done creating these perfect superwomen, He told himself *'I will place them in all the corners of the earth.'* Then He made the world round and laughed and laughed at his own cruel and twisted joke.

Then there was a serious religious aspect, which terrified my soul. I could hear my dearly departed grandmother lecturing me on this *'filthy'* topic. She was known for being a stout Baptist, and I wondered what fates would await me in the afterlife. She had always been one to say to remain faithful, find a good woman but, I knew she would definitely not approve of Amy. *Why this married woman? Why would you bed down this harlot?* Damnation and fires awaited the unclean, impure of faith.

I could envision demons jumping up and down on my balls with sharp talons, ripping my guts open or ramming spears up my ass upon the mocking orders of Satan himself. From there I would be lifted up by the pole, still skewered in my ass, and set upright like a crucified Jesus. The demons would next set about flaying my genitals open with razor encrusted whips.

Either way, my thoughts were just not where they were supposed to be, but it was a good feeling. I wanted her just as much as she wanted me physically and emotionally. We fit all too well together. By God, she felt so good, so right even though it was all wrong. Her tight, perfect body, the glisten of sweat from our passion, our…lust, it was all perfect love-making. Everything about her was just so…good.

And now she was gone.

All kinds of things start playing on your mind, like was I good enough? What did I do wrong here…besides this being an extra-marital affair kind of thing. Maybe…it was a penis size thing? I wasn't getting that impression, nor did she give me any kind of indication it was an issue, but Jesus! Gone? Why? Maybe all of it was just a one-time gig, get the heart out of it kid. It was too late though. I was all in.

Or maybe I was thinking too much on the matter.

I tried calling her a few times but her phone went straight to her voice machine. I did my best to forget the whole thing. I was ready to chalk it up as a bad lesson that had left a sour taste in my mouth. I renewed my efforts to focus on the primary objective: getting the hell out of New Mexico.

I went to the kitchen, tossed down the remnants of a cheese stuffed bagel on the plate and got the mind ready for war with busting wrenches and making money while the coffee maker gurgled out black liquid caffeine. I could sit here all damned day thinking about this and the million reasons, but it wasn't going to fix a damn thing. Maybe she would explain it later. I waited most of the day for the phone to ring, hoping she would call, but the call never came.

It was late afternoon when I threw my hands up and grabbed the keys to the Ford, along with a few other things, and drove out to Duggan's. Either way, Amy would be there tonight and maybe help clear up this thing. The radio was belting out the tune *Saint of Me* by The Stones. I drove across the cracked and pothole infested parking lot, swerved into an open parking space next to the shop before cutting the ignition.

Trucks were stuffed in the bays and plenty more were piled up outside. Business was just getting started and as pissed as I was, I planned on cleaning up the floor and tossing the money in my paycheck.

The place was hopping. Several new guys were working the

floor. A guy whom Hendricks called Cueball, was working a turbo job. Another new guy, Chuck, was hammering on a Horton fan clutch assembly, getting it ready to toss a rebuild kit into it. Hal was airing up a tire in a cage while mounting another. Hendricks was running the air conditioning machines on a couple trucks and pounding a tire off a rim.

I went to the computer, clocked in and grabbed the first ticket available which happened to be troubleshooting some engine noise. I then checked the roster list of who was working and saw Amy's name was crossed out for the shift. I asked Big Mac about Amy and found out she had called in. Now he was looking at pulling a double. He didn't mind but he had to move his home schedule around. My alarm levels shot up a notch. I called for the driver in the mini lounge and had him pull up on the front side of the shop and began to work off my thoughts.

"Logan!" Johnson came out the side door.

I looked up just as I lifted up the hood on the Century Class.

"Dwayne paged for you. Get your ass up there, do your business and get back here!"

"Dwayne?"

"Is there another Dwayne around here? Get going!"

I looked for Hendricks but he was buried under the front end of a Freightliner. I tossed the tools in the box, locked it and wandered up front. I stopped off at the C-store for a coffee refill before heading to Dwayne's office in the back of the complex. I paused at Dwayne's door, exhaled softly and rapped on the wall of wood. A muffled response said to enter.

I entered and Dwayne sat behind his desk. Another man sat in another chair in front of him.

My heart froze.

Dwayne smiled. "Hello, Logan," then seeing I was looking at

the other man seated in the chair, "This is Thomas Hauser. He is filling in as a complex manager until we find someone else."

I nodded slowly. "Complex manager?"

"Assistant anyways, and he will be checking up on things back in the shop from time to time, well, the whole complex anyways."

"*Ahh huh.*"

Thomas stood up to a full six foot six. His shoulders were as broad as some of the biggest linebackers. The dark blue suit, as large as it was, draped over a heavily muscled framework that told everyone he worked out and ate well. He extended a large paw and noted the scars across the knuckles. He was not unfamiliar with violence.

He looked down with hard black eyes, smiled a wide grin that projected fear more than a sense of comradery. His southern tones were articulate and calculating. "I've heard a lot about you, Logan."

I took his hand and was met with a hard grip that could crack granite.

"Thomas is married to Amy…the counter girl back in the shop?" Dwayne quipped in.

"Oh?"

Thomas' smile widened further. "She's the light of my life."

I nodded, not knowing what to say. "Well, that's good."

Thomas's handshake didn't quit. He held a firm grip. "Yes sir, I don't know what I would do if she ever left my eyesight."

"Everyone in the shop thinks highly of her, sir."

He released my hand, sensing my discomfort. "Amy and I have spoken and I find it fair to say she has had nothing but good things to say about you, Logan." He seated himself.

I shifted the weight from one foot to another and my pulse quickened. A strong sense of distress oozed from the opaque pink walls. *Just what in the hell did she say? Maybe this was the reason why she left so abruptly this morning.* I thought.

He looked up at the ceiling. "Nothing but good things," he rubbed his chin. "Well, keep making us money back there, Logan. I just wanted to visit with an all-star mechanic. You keep going like you are with the numbers, and you could well be running a shop over at another Duggan's location."

I didn't have the heart to tell them, I had other plans. I kept a straight face. "I'll try my best, sir."

A long silence followed. Thomas looked me over for a long time. I could tell he was studying me like a predator taking a keen interest in its next meal. My eyes fell across his gaze and we locked in on each other.

Dwayne broke the silence. "You're free to go, Logan."

"Yes, sir." I turned to leave, but Thomas asked a question that stopped me dead in my tracks.

"One more thing," Thomas spoke. "Have you heard anything or seen anything…unusual back in the shop?"

I felt my heart being squeezed and my blood ran cold. Silence fell across the room. I wasn't sure I understood him right. "Sir?"

"It's a straightforward question. Have you seen anything strange while working back in the shop? Strange as in maybe, people stealing tools, maybe tires, or even money, or perhaps anyone carrying on secret liaison relations?"

"Secret liaison relationships?"

"Sexual. There is company policy about carrying on a sexual relationship with other employees here at Duggan's." Dwayne added in.

"We've had problems in the past with sexual relations between employees, especially if they're married." Thomas continued.

I thought about Dwayne and Andrea having their fling but I didn't think he was aiming for that. I tried to give him my best poker face. "I haven't seen anything."

He looked to Dwayne. What do you think? Lying or not?"

Dwayne shrugged. "Hard to tell, and we're off topic."

"I'm going with lying."

"You realize it's just business at this moment?"

He gave me a wide smile. "I just know if someone's lying."

"What kind of…" I was stumped on what to say.

Thomas held up a thick paw and smiled. "It's not a big deal, just kidding around, but if you hear anything, you'll come and talk to us, right?"

I wanted to say something else, but Dwayne spoke. "You can leave, Logan."

I wasn't sure if I could. My feet felt like they had been welded down to a slab of lead. I fumbled for the door handle, opened it, stepped through and closed it. Thomas followed with his dark eyes but remained silent. There was an evil hidden within his casual gaze, so dark, so loathsome, that it could penetrate and kill the souls of most men. I stood outside the door for a long time, thinking just what the hell Thomas was aiming for but deep down, I already knew. I was sure he knew something was amiss between Amy and me. But did he know just how far we had gone in our relationship?

I shuffled away from the door. Concern etched across my mind and thoughts as they drifted from one topic to another. I planned on making the mountain of money and the sooner I got the dough, the sooner I was out of here. But there was this nagging thing about Amy that kept gnawing at the back of my brain.

I didn't want to leave, not without her.

Had Amy confessed our affair to Thomas? The thoughts were endless but she had called off work for the day and that raised alarms. Anything was possible and I was beginning to think about lugging the .45 around. Who knew what would happen at this point. It was strange of her to call off for her shift and that left me wondering what was happening. I took out the cell phone and thumbed in her number. The phone rang once and went to her message machine. I mumbled a curse and closed the phone.

I went back to the shop, told Johnson I was tired and done for the day. He objected and argued but relented. He knew we were all tired and it was rare if I took off early or called in. I locked up the toolbox, hopped in the Ford and fired it off, then aimed it for home.

Dusk had settled over the land and distant stars poked through the thin veil of bluish-hued darkness. As I turned up the dirt road leading to the house, I noticed something out of place. Another vehicle was parked up in the driveway near the house. My instincts went into overdrive and mentally I was searching for a weapon. There had been a couple break in's lately, mostly by dope addicts looking to steal anything for their next high.

Amy. Her truck was parked in the driveway. I saw her jean-clad legs move away from the side of the truck and move towards me.

I opened the door on the old Ford and stepped out. Was Thomas waiting in the shadows with a pistol or rifle? Maybe a shotgun…shotgun can make a helluva bunch of holes, shred the chest and internals, a headshot would be worse. A buckshot blast to the head would be like popping a pimple. The next moment, I could well be looking at God. I was sure He would be asking some rather pointed questions.

"Logan?"

"Yes, God?"

"Was it worth it?"

"God, You created her and she's perfect in every way, damn right it was."

The hairs on the back of my neck stood up on end.

"Logan…"

"Amy, you sure took off quick this morning."

She nodded slowly. "I'm sorry but I got a call about something important that had to be taken care of."

God, she looked so beautiful, so sexually appealing. I took hold of her and drew her in close to me. "I can think of other things at the moment."

She pushed away gently. "I haven't much time," she took several steps back. We watched each other for a long moment. "Logan...what we did..."

"It was beautiful." I injected.

She gave a thin smile in response and pushed her thick hair back from her eyes. "It was, it was great, but I'm thinking we made a mistake. We rushed it a little."

Here was the bomb. "A mistake?"

"If I was a single woman, I would have no problems with this but I am married and my husband can be...a little unappreciative of all of this."

"What do you think he would do?"

She shrugged. "Well, I'm sure it would have something to do with the physical demise of a graphic nature to both of us."

"I got the same impression."

"You know then, he is in town?"

"We met. He's the new assistant complex manager." There wasn't any point in volunteering any further info. I didn't want her concerned any more than she was.

Her mind was thinking and she was silent.

"He took a keen interest in me for some reason."

"You have Dwayne to thank for that. Ever since he saw us talking up at the restaurant, he's been suspicious about our involvement with each other."

"What about us? Is there even an '*us*'?"

"There is, but we need to take this slow okay?"

I held up a hand. "When then? I can see something

here…between us. Something different…something real."

"You are sounding desperate."

"Do I? I'm not meaning to but I see something between us."

"Like something you saw in your ex?"

"No, you're nothing like her. You have something. You have the looks, you're smart and for some reason, I trust you. I can't quite put a finger on it, but something is real here. Not that fake nonsense you see on TV or my own failed marriage, but something tangible."

She crossed her arms and looked toward the house with a saddened face. "I'd like to stay."

"Then stay."

"Logan, we had a one-night stand. I can't just up and move in. I shouldn't have gone this far. Things have gotten complicated as it is."

I took a deep breath. "It's not complicated at all. Let's talk, let's do something about this thing we're in."

She shook her head. "It's not all about me and we're rushing this thing a bit fast."

"What then? Thomas? Why worry about it."

She looked up to me. "If he finds out, and pray he hasn't figured it out yet, he'll kill us both."

I've had my ass kicked on more than one occasion. My grandfather had said, *son, if you can't do the fighting thing right, you have no business starting nonsense to begin with.* Words of wisdom had never been so true. But I was willing to chance it this time, for this woman, for some reason. Somehow I had found myself in another dilemma but with a potential jealous husband in the mix. "We'll work through it."

She looked at her wristwatch. "I have to get going."

"What is the problem then?"

She looked up. "There are some things you really don't need to know at this moment and perhaps I hope you never find out," she looked away. "It could....change how you feel."

I reached out and pulled her in, looking into her eyes, I spoke with sincerity. "I doubt there is anything you could say to change my mind."

She took a long look and was silent again. We looked into each other's eyes, no words spoken between us, no sounds other than the sounds of the nearby trees gently swaying in the early autumn breeze. "I hope that's true." She pulled away and returned to the truck and hopped inside behind the driver's seat.

"I mean it, Amy."

She started up the GMC. The quiet purr of the motor rustled through the silence. She narrowed her eyes to beautiful, wonderful slits. "I believe you. Can you do something for me, Logan?"

I jammed my hands in my trouser pockets. There was a twinge of cold air blowing in the wind. "What is it?"

She gave a thin smile. "I have to stay quiet about this. I don't need additional problems, especially at work. Can you stay the same? At least until I get things worked out?"

"When can we see each other again?"

"Soon, I promise."

"Sure, Amy. I can stay quiet on this." I really wanted to shout to the heavens my disdain for cursing mankind with this thing called '*love*.' Or was it more sexual attractions and desire? God knew I hadn't been with a woman since my ex, which I reminded myself, was one of the problems for my divorce. It was the first time I felt this way about someone and was unable to do anything about it.

A raised eyebrow and a small smile. "Promise me?"

I nodded slowly. "Yeah, I can keep it."

"And one more thing....You know the missing money thing is just a rumor right?"

"Yes," I lied.

"Ignore it, Logan."

"You want me to promise?" I wondered why she was concerned.

"Say it - now."

I wondered for a moment what she meant but for the sake of conversation, why not? "I do promise."

She gave a smile and a wink, placed the truck in drive and slowly rolled forward. She looked back once and blew me a small kiss.

I watched her drive off kicking up a small dust cloud in her wake. The taillights disappeared around the juniper tree-clogged bend and she was gone. I was the schmuck in the bunch with shit on my face and standing here with sore balls.

I lit up a cigarette with a match and inhaled deeply of the acrid fumes. The stench of burning phosphorus from the match tip lingered in my nostrils. I was stupid to keep going after her.

There were the whispered warnings from Hendricks floating into my brain, the warning about Thomas being affiliated with the Dixie Mafia. If true, Thomas was sizing me up, studying a future adversary. Why else the questions he had asked? I hadn't the nerve to ask Amy about any of it.

I would just have to take my time, enjoy the 'scenery' as it came around. I was stupid in not getting out of here fast enough. The best solution would've been to ditch the whole mess and start a new life somewhere else. Lord knew I had plenty of cash on hand and the only thing lacking was getting the El Camino running. I shook my head and looked up into the cool evening skies and cursed. It had to be something in the local well water that made people stupid.

It just had to be.

The cell phone vibrated. I took it out, flipped it open and saw it was Hendricks.

"Hey," he answered.

"You busy?" I flicked the burning butt down the driveway.

"I said to hell with it and took off from work. I'm at home not doing a damned thing but waiting." A pause and then the sound of a clicking lighter. I could picture the cloud of cigarette smoke. "The Dunes?" he asked.

We couldn't mention Musgrave's name or ranch in casual conversation, so we resorted to using the nickname The Dunes. It was a precaution in case anyone was around listening however remote the chances, someone hacked our phones.

I watched Amy hook a right and drive off down Martinez Road. I was thinking about why she was concerned about the money. "Sure."

"You don't sound too much into it."

"I am Hendricks. I was just visiting with Amy."

After a brief pause, I could tell he was thinking about what I said. "Well, throw on some panties, bring some brews, flashlights, the map, and I'll meet you there in an hour."

THIRTEEN

I jabbed a thick finger on the well-worn map as a cold breeze picked up and ruffled the edges. The grease-stained finger slid across one crease to another, tracing several jagged lines that appeared to be man-made paths cut through the prairie lands of dead grass and thick clusters of twisted Juniper. I munched on a plain bologna sandwich pondering on which path to follow next. I took a look up making out several landmark features to coincide with the map to gather my bearings. I finished the sandwich, gathered up the backpack, and moved off down the chosen path.

Hendricks had left hours ago for his scheduled shift working the noonday rush. It was a sure bet he was up to his ass in broken trucks right about now. We had shown up just as the early creases of day cracked across the horizon lines, each in our own separate vehicles. We had been out here for the better part of the morning, searching for anything resembling anything close to where Musgrave had hidden his ill-gotten goods and found nothing of value.

I decided to stay behind and keep on with our quest, but in reality, I was bumming around and doing a half-assed search. My mind wandered from one problem to another, searching for soul-shattering solutions. The ex-wife was still soaking my paychecks for alimony payments. I had gotten my own lawyer but the rotten bitch had gotten her father's law firm in on the action and there was a looming court battle. My paydays were still being garnished by a third and there was nothing anyone could do. After finding no solutions, I refocused on my search for Musgrave's fortune.

We had been out here off and on for most of the summer and on through the fall. The first whispers of winter clung to the early November mornings and up through early afternoons. A breeze kicked up and I exhaled a cloudy mist of warm vapor and shivered. I forged a path through a patch of dead junipers. Moving was the only way to keep warm. I was beginning to think it was turning into a damned goat rope. We had poked and prodded, searched and busted up more junk in this search for the money and we were nowhere close to it. But we were looking over five thousand acres of land. According to my math, we were lucky to have searched five percent total.

At this rate, it would take another ten years.

Even Hendricks was starting to have his doubts and I had to convince him we were looking for a needle in a haystack. If Musgrave had stashed his dough out here, he wasn't going to make it easy for anyone to find. At the least, the hiking around, poking at sagebrush gave me time to think in this half-assed search. The cold was sucking the motivation from my soul.

I had to be sure Amy didn't catch wind of what we were doing. As far as she knew, I was working on the El Camino or chasing parts in my spare time getting the old warhorse up and ready for the highway one day.

The 427 was sitting in the bay compartment of the El Camino. So far, I had been told the motor could pump out an easy five hundred horses, but I needed to upgrade some things from the vintage 1970's stuff it had ran with for years now. The TH400 transmission was in place, having gotten a fresh overhaul with a stage two shift kit. I had installed a high stall torque convertor, a serpentine belt system, high flow water and oil pumps, a four-row radiator, a transmission cooler and finally an upgrade in the rear gears to 4:11's. Then there was still the two and a quarter inch exhaust system needing to be installed and then the fuel pumps needed to be upgraded still. The El Camino was falling into place and soon Moriarty, New Mexico would be a distant memory. I just hoped Amy would tag along for the ride.

I hadn't figured out what was keeping her rooted here.

Thomas would show up back at the shop from time to time. Each time looked more volatile whenever he spoke to her. The problems between Amy and Thomas looked to be mounting. She never spoke to me about these disagreements but their conversations were tense in the privacy of the shop office. I tried not to pry into it. I figured when the time was right she would tell me. I had witnessed her standing her ground with her arms folded, and Thomas towering over her with a mask of rage. You could tell he wanted to say or even do something stupid like hit her but she wasn't having any of it. She returned the glare of hate, spoke a few words and he would remain silent. He left the office in a cloud of bitter resentment. It looked like a divorce was in progress.

As she had promised, we did hang out from time to time. It wasn't just about the sex so much as we were developing a true relationship and I found it all appealing and interesting. Sometimes we met at the house, or made special excursions to Santa Fe or rented a cabin a few times at Lake Heron. I looked forward to those moments and lamented a bit more at her parting. I enjoyed waking up in the mornings and admiring everything about her. I wanted to find something special for her.

I go to flea markets every now and then. It's a habit passed down from my grandmother, who loved going on weekends when I was a boy. When I got to be a teenager, I hated going with her but when she passed away, I took a renewed interest in the ventures. I guessed it was my way of staying connected to her memory. Sometimes I never bought anything, other times I came home with some small trinket.

I came across an old woman selling off some antique jewelry. A ring with a green emerald stuck out from the rest of the jewelry. Ever since our time in the storage room, I felt green was her color. I paid fifty bucks for it and wrapped it in a small box.

When Amy opened the box and studied the ring for a moment. "This is Jade and the diamonds look…real."

I shrugged. I didn't know anything about gems or emeralds. "It's green and that's what I liked."

"This is expensive." She narrowed her eyes. "You didn't go into debt or anything for this did you?"

"No, I saw it at the flea market and liked it."

"Are you asking for something?"

"One day I will," I was serious.

"I might have an answer one day," she chuckled. She opened her left hand and removed one ring from slender fingers. She held it up and handed it over.

I took the ring from her fingers. "Your sister's ring?" The only thing I knew about her sister was that she had passed away. Amy never said anything about the how's and why's other than it was a house fire. I believed it was a personal loss that hit her hard. It surprised me she would give me something that had belonged to her sister.

"I don't think Lorraine would mind."

"I guess this means we're engaged?"

"Hardly, but you never know, Logan." She slid the Jade green ring on her index finger, gave a wink and a smile, leaned in, and we kissed.

To be honest, I wanted to be. I had thought about asking but thought better of it. There would be time enough for the big question at some point in life. There was a fit to our personalities that made life tolerable. I drank less, cut the cigarettes down to half a pack a day and we never argued about anything. There was a balance and for all the time I had wandered the earth, I believed we provided the necessary anchors in each other's life. I had put her sister's ring on a necklace and wore it. I didn't want it damaged while working away on broken trucks at Duggan's.

Cresting a small rise, the daydreaming came to an abrupt end when I heard the sound of an approaching car. Looking out far to the west, I saw a dark sedan cutting through the dirt road leading up to the property, trailing a giant plume of dust in its wake.

I knelt down, making sure the nearby shrubs were enough to camouflage my ass. It might be someone was lost, or cruising around looking at real estate or, maybe they were nature freaks going around snapping pictures of some elusive form of wildlife. There was no point in getting worked up, and I assumed it was one or the other.

The four-door sedan approached the gate and the passenger door popped open. A man hopped out, walked up to the gate, flung it open, then reentered the sedan and drove up to the main house. The engine idled for a few moments before the driver killed the engine. Whoever was in the sedan didn't move for close to half an hour before both the driver's door and the passenger doors opened and four men stepped out.

The odd part was the four men were eyeballing the nearby outbuildings. One, the larger of the two, entered one and began tossing stuff out while the other went to the main house. Soon you could hear more stuff being thrown around within. The other two men stood near the sedan and talked, laughing casually.

I had a sudden bad feeling things were centered on finding the money. We had other players involved and I had no idea just who the hell they were. The number one pick off the top of my head was Dixie Mob. It was their money after all. Why else come up here and begin tossing stuff around? Hell, the place had been gone through a fair number of times by law enforcement, scavengers and a host of homeless guys, all looking for what goods they could salvage and sell. I doubted the money would be anywhere near those buildings. I knew. I had searched through those buildings with a fine tooth comb and found nothing.

Jamming a hand into the backpack, I pulled out a small pair of binoculars and focused the dials for a clear picture of what was going on down below. The black sedan came into view as a Crown Vic and the blue lettering etched across the license plate screamed law enforcement. The two men came out of the buildings. One wore a grey polo pull-over with dark blue slacks. A black semi-auto pistol hung from his belt. With Oriental features, he was tight and clean in appearance with a muscular build. The other man was older with half his hair thinned out and missing. His scalp glared in the cold sun but he was just as clean in appearance.

I lowered the binoculars and swore. I recognized them right away and my pulse began hammering in my veins. *Richardson and Nguyen, but what in hell were they doing out here? And who are guys number three and four?* I peered through the binoculars and focused in on the remaining two men. The third man I didn't recognize but the fourth man scratched on the layers of my memories. The rose tattoo on his right hand jumped out. He pivoted and a skull tattoo was on his left hand. I caught my breath and remembered the State cop offering to buy my El Camino when I had broken down. I struggled to remember his name but suddenly it rose up from the matter of memory. *Fernandez, that's it, Fernandez. What the hell is he doing here?*

After a few minutes, Richardson entered the main house. Nguyen entered another shed, tossed a few things out before exiting, cursing, and kicking some of the boxes he had thrown out, before moving away to the next shed. He began tossing stuff out in a pile while Richardson exited the main house empty handed. He walked back up to the Crown Vic and the trio conversed for some time until one pulled out a paper and they began studying it intently. Richardson called out for Nguyen. He kicked his way through a pile of clutter and walked up to the three men. They spoke over the paper laid out over the hood. It had to be the same kind of map I had, a topographical one any Joe-blow could pick up at the New Mexico Geographical office in Albuquerque.

Wait...

If they picked up a map of their own...

A sense of panic began washing over me.

Several minutes went by. Nguyen leaned up against the hood of the Crown Vic. Richardson began pacing slowly nearby. Fernandez exchanged words with Richardson. I could see their lips moving and they appeared in deep conversation. Another sound whispered in my ears. I lowered the binoculars, snapped my head to the road as another vehicle approached. The Black Ram truck scratched on the memory layer of recognition.

The Ram pulled up beside the Crown Vic and the engine cut out. Two large men exited slowly. They were tall, thick with muscle that threatened to bust the seams on the clothes they wore. I aimed the binoculars at the license plate. Mississippi. My fingers tingled as the blood drained from my limbs. Months had passed but I recognized it as the truck from the library those long months ago.

Hendricks had said Thomas' cousins were named Robert Lee and Cleeve. The two of them together were known as the Devil's Dog Pound. They were twins and the only way to tell them apart was by the clothes they wore. Hendricks warned they might be floating around, he had seen them around Moriarty. Robert Lee liked to dress formal, suit and tie kind of guy, while his brother liked to wear jeans and t-shirts that stretched across the thick muscles of his chest and arms. They were both huge and thick with muscle. I was sure these were the cousins.

What the hell?

There were six men in total now and I swore for not bringing the .45 along for this venture. Robert Lee buttoned his suit jacket and did most of the talking. The conversation went on for several minutes. Richardson appeared agitated. He pointed a finger at one of the Mississippi guys and his muffled voice carried out over the breeze but I couldn't make out anything. Cleeve stepped forward and held his hands out. The sun glared off a large pistol hanging from a shoulder holster. They were all quiet for several minutes.

I wasn't sure what they were discussing but it had gotten heated. I was positive it had something to do with the money. If what Hendricks had said before about Thomas' cousins held truth, what were these cops doing talking or associating with known members of the Dixie Mafia? Was it possible the cousins were collaborating with the police? At this point, I wanted to forgo searching for the cash indefinitely.

After several minutes it appeared they had come to a mutual conclusion. The six began walking toward the base of the hill I was on top of. They fanned out and looked to be searching. I had searched this area enough to know that in a matter of minutes, the six men would be bounding up the trail and be right on top of me. I grabbed everything and moved back slow at a half crouch, my heart pounding in my throat. Once I was behind a large patch of Juniper trees, I turned and began running hard trying to avoid making any noise.

Heavy footfalls began pounding the earth. I snapped a look back but no one was there.

Of course, running has never been a forte of mine. Hate it, but with two large individuals running through the bush, you learn it'll give anyone positive motivation to catch gears getting out of trouble. I jumped a ragged washout, crossed down over a shallow ditch and then faded behind another cluster of skeletonized Junipers. I dropped down in time to see the cousins bouncing into view. Their heads bobbed right then left. There was a ledge just behind me.

I dropped my pack down first before jumping over the edge. I landed flatfooted and sharp pinpricks of pain shot up the balls of my feet. I rolled back on my haunches, stifling a groan, looked right, left and saw no way to escape out of eyeshot.

Quickly looking behind me, I saw a dark opening under the ledge, grabbing the pack, I dove in, snakes and all other living critters that might be waiting in there, be damned. It was a chance to take. I remained still for an impossibly long time before I heard thick thunder like footfalls raining from above. Small tendrils of silt cascaded down in front of the opening.

"You sure you saw something, Robert Lee?" a muffled voice whispered.

"Sure did, Cleeve, be quiet a moment."

Silt pillars cascaded down on my face. I suppressed the urge to sneeze or move and clutched my pack tight against my chest.

Another voice. I was sure it was Richardson. "Anything?"

There wasn't a reply.

Another man's voice. "I don't see anything."

Robert Lee spoke. "I as sure as the sun sets, I saw something."

"Wait…is that a deer?"

"Musgrave's ghost perhaps," an unfamiliar voice chimed in.

"Shit ain't funny, Arturo. Yeah, it's a deer," Cleeve replied.

I rolled my head over and saw the lone deer far off down the rolling lands of dead prairie grass. It was a young buck and it stood watching the men standing above me, curious as to why these humans were standing on his domain.

Richardson spoke. His voice sighed and sounded weary. "I don't think that deer is going to talk to anyone about us being here. As much as we like looking for ghosts and wildlife, we need to make the most of this discussion."

"It would be hell if the FBI was watching us right about now." An unfamiliar voice chimed in.

"To hell with the FBI," Cleeve replied.

"Yeah, they could fuck us hard if we're seen together," Richardson said. "Let's move on shall we?"

"You think I can hit that fucker from here? That buck is still a witness." The voice belonging to Arturo spoke.

Richardson snickered. "Shit, that's at least a couple hundred yards and all you got is your nine millimeter."

The sound of metal clearing leather followed by the metallic slap of an automatic chambering a round really focused my attention. Then a series of sudden thunder shots exploded and my senses jolted and cringed. Empty brass casings tumbled in front of the opening where I lay hidden.

"Shit, you missed and your deer took off."

The deer turned and was bounding away.

"You need a gun with distance and power." There was another sound of a gun being pulled from a holster. "Alright, no witness' even if it's a deer." A sudden series of rapid explosions followed and sounded like a battleship firing off a full broadside salvo. Several larger brass casings fell in front of me, landing on the hard earth.

The deer kept bounding away but with much more rapid maneuvering. A few dirt geysers exploded up close to it but it was still running until it bounded over a small rise and disappeared. "Shit, it's gone now," Robert Lee said.

"Are we done comparing dick sizes? Let's put away the guns and finish this discussion," Richardson said.

The sound of a gun being slid back in its holster and then Robert Lee spoke. "Our uncle says we wait."

The cold wind kicked up. Gold dust particles blew into my eyes and I held my hand up to shield out the worst of it. The men above must've shifted away from the edge. Their voices became garbled and patchy. I could only catch bits and pieces of the conversation. It sounded like they were moving away from the ledge above.

"Wait...we...Duggan's...fucking shop...FBI. How...act?"

Robert Lee's response was muffled. "Rainmaker...mutual problems...wait."

"...bullshit...We're just pounding our dicks...nothing," Arturo said. He sounded closer to the ledge above where I was lying.

Cleeve mumbled a response.. "Uncle says...your merchandise...inconvenience. What...want?"

"I want that FBI...whoever...is! If...cops...here, we're...I want no part...you understand?"

"...prison, Richardson," Robert Lee's voice carried away in the wind. "All you got...problem. Soon...won't be...either...us."

Silence and Richardson muffled a response but I couldn't make it out.

Robert Lee's low voice rumbled on for a few seconds.

Richardson spoke but his words disappeared in the wind.

More sand showered down. The sound of footfalls faded and their voices sounded distant. I silently exhaled a deep sigh. There was no reason to take a chance in leaving my position just yet. I was going to wait a long time before leaving the safety of my sanctuary. I thought about what had been said but none of it made sense. It all sounded shady as all hell and all I wanted to do was go home and drink a beer in the safety of my own home and never speak of it to anyone. The main part of the concern was it sounded like the FBI was somehow involved but I couldn't figure it out and gave up. Maybe they were looking over the accounting books. Duggan's had been raided by the Feds before for possible tax evasion.

I stayed under the rock ledge until the setting sun hovered just above the horizon. Thick, dark clouds were rolling in overhead before I decided it was safe to make the run back to the truck. Lying under the ledge for several hours had about crippled me. With stiff legs, I rolled out, careful to stay in the shadows, well aware the cousins and their four buddies were nowhere to be seen but that didn't mean they weren't roaming around. They looked the determined types.

Clambering back up the ledge, I paused and listened. For once I was glad the Ford was parked further down in the gulley out of eyeshot. The thing I was praying for was none of the six goons had tripped across it.

After several minutes, I pushed on, quickly running off into the thick shrubs, paused and listened. For several minutes, no sound existed except the sounds of the gentle breeze rustling through the cold thick trees. A few minutes more and I heard a car or truck fire up its engine near the house. I dropped down and crab-crawled toward a large outcropping of large rocks and boulders overlooking the ranch house below.

Down below, I saw one of the men open the passenger door, hop in and the sedan sped off down the dirt road following the black

Dodge truck. I waited several minutes longer until they had crested the small rise leading back to the asphalt highway before standing up.

The late afternoon shadows stretched across the hilltop and off in the distance thick, grey clouds were rolling in. The news had said a storm was rolling into New Mexico from the south. The worst kind of storm to have, and it was slated to hit in a few hours. The temperature had dropped. My teeth chattered and shook. All it meant was I hadn't the testicular fortitude to endure poking around the property looking for any more clues. It would all soon be under a couple feet of snow.

There was a cluster of tall dead juniper and pine trees at the top of the small hill. The skeleton branches swayed in the wind with the exception of one. That single thick branch looked out of place tangled up amongst those branches. I narrowed my eyes and walked up through the underbrush to it. A light pole materialized out of the trees and brush, old, bleached, and weather-beaten to the point of useless. Lord only knew how long it had been out here but it was slowly rotting away under the New Mexico elements. The pole stuck out above the tree line by a good ten foot, the tip was splintered to a jagged point. I hadn't seen it before.

Over the decades past, settlers of old had tried a hand at homesteading the land. Many tried, many more failed before moving away from the Estancia Valley. At one time this spot must have been an old homestead, perhaps even Musgrave's family of old times had settled out here and the land had passed down from one generation to the next.

I moved away, back down and circled around and looked again to see the pole from other vantage points, no one could see it even if they were looking for it or right at it. I moved back to the spot where I could see the pole. Something peculiar struck me suddenly and the adrenaline began pumping.

I took the short hike up the incline to the pole and began

searching. There were old remnants of an adobe foundation off to the side along with a pile of splinter timber and scrap metal. The place looked like it had been out here for a hundred years but there were indications that told me someone had been up here recently, maybe months ago. A discarded Budweiser beer bottle lay nearby in the weeds. It looked too new to have been out here for too long. The paper wrapping on the bottle had yet to bleach out under the New Mexico sun. The area was thick with overgrowth and dead prairie grass. Poking around through the rotten wood and foundations revealed nothing. It must've started life as a small house at one time.

The pole gathered my interest. I spent several minutes breaking and tossing the dead branches blocking my passage aside. Standing at the base, I looked up to the tip and saw a broken porcelain insulator. Looking at the base, there was a rusty nail, more modern in appearance. Tied to it was a piece of baling wire that ran down into the tan earth. I took a hold of it and pulled gently but the ground was hard enough to keep hold of whatever was tied to it. I spent another few minutes breaking away the soil until I saw a small purple disk come into view. Brushing away the loose soil, I saw the wire was tied off to a small jar.

The jar was modern as well. An old Smuckers jelly jar. I took hold of it and tugged it free from the soil and something metallic rattled around inside. A single item rolled round in the dirt-encrusted glass jar. I twisted the lid off and dumped its contents into the palm of my hand.

A single Chinese coin with the same square hole.

A gust of winter wind kicked up and sent a chill up my spine.

Hendricks had said Musgrave had told him long ago.

"My retirement is under an old pole."

FOURTEEN

The cold night air was sharp and bitter. I killed the ignition and the heater motor whined to a halt. We could feel the breeze seeping through the rotted door seals and soaking our bones in the cold. The nearby piñon tree branches swayed in the cold winds and raked against the metal panels of the Ford. We had taken off on a dirt path behind the ranch house and parked off the main road, hidden within a thick cluster. Even if someone happened to drive by, they wouldn't see the forest green colored Ford.

My teeth chattered. Our breaths turned into clouds of vapor.

The old verbiage *'cold as a witch's tit'* held truth. The clouds hung thick, low and heavy and all the small shrubs of piñon and salt cedar trees looked like acres of darkened tombstones littering the rolling lands for as far as the eye could see. I wondered how many bodies were buried out here from the beginning of time from conquistadors to the present. I also wondered if we were next.

I had tried to call Hendricks but cell phone service sucked out in the middle of nowhere. I made the mad dash back to Moriarty, swung by Duggan's shop and pulled him off to the side and showed him the coin. He told Big Mac he was feeling like shit and going home. We took off, swung by my house, grabbed the .45 and then to Hendricks place to grab his guns. We were on edge and spoke little on our way back to the ranch.

I did tell him about the Crown Vic, the black Dodge truck and the four cops and the cousins poking around the property, he remained steadfast in getting the money…if it were there. He was stubborn and I just wanted to wait until the time was ripe for another excursion after the storm had passed but he wasn't having any of it. He wanted to strike now before the storm rolled in and covered everything.

Hendricks opened the door, stepped out and mashed the cigarette butt with his boot tip. "Ready?" His breath mixed with cigarette smoke hung in the air in a thick cloud. His own teeth were chattering. It was hard to gauge if it was from the cold or the prospect of finally locating the money.

Nerves. They were kicking into overdrive. If what we thought was true, out there under the pile of rusted metal by the lone telegraph pole was an entrance of some kind that would lead down to a buried cargo container. I wasn't sure what we would find, but it was worth looking. I nodded, popped the door and stepped out. The cold ground was as solid as concrete. The news said it was going to snow and the low clouds agreed. I felt a glistening sprinkle of something cold and wet hit my cheeks. The air was thick with the coming moisture.

"Over there," I pointed.

Hendricks looked once in the direction, nodded, pulled out his Taurus .357 revolver from the holster strapped to his hip. He checked the cylinder and clasped it shut. He took a few speed loaders from his backpack and stuffed them into his jacket pockets. I tucked the .45 in the waistband of my trousers and checked it multiple times already, mostly out of nervous reactions. He leaned inside the cab, flipped the bench seat forward and took out a Mossberg 12 gauge pump. We didn't know what we were going to end up finding so it was better safe than sorry. He racked the slide, loading a buckshot round into the chamber. "Let's move."

Like apparitions, we moved down the long overgrown path. The only sounds were our footfalls on the cold, frost-encrusted gravel scattered along the trail. Musgrave was long gone, to angels or demons, but somewhere out here, his money was hidden. We hit the gate and waited silently, listening carefully for anything sounding out of place. Musgrave's old mobile home stuck out as a distant dark shadow nestled within the trees and overgrown dead weeds. With no further sounds, we moved through the gate and slipped off into the shadows offered by the clusters of scrub oak and Chinese willows.

We stayed on the overgrown pathway until we saw the tip of the telegraph pole stuck out above the dark tree line like a thin pencil stabbed into a corpse. Hearing nothing but the wind, we moved off the trail and disappeared into the dark shadows. Hendricks halted every once in a while, listened for several minutes for any strange noises. When nothing was heard, we moved on until we came to the narrow rise with the rotted telegraph pole jutting out of the ground.

As we approached, the ground softened, shifted into silt sand and Hendricks paused mid-step and fumbled in his jacket for his flashlight. He flipped it on and studied the ground with interest. "Someone has been here."

I looked down and saw the footprints in the soft soil. "You sure it wasn't us? Or the six dudes?"

"Did we ever pass through here?"

"Not that I recall, not ever." I pulled the .45.

He didn't say anything but he continued studying the ground. He knelt down and felt the ridges and outline of the footprints. "Large-footed mother came up here a few times," he pointed toward where the telegraph pole jutted from the earth. "All tracks lead right past that hill. The same person I think. Everyone's walked around here but no one's seen the pole, including us."

"The cops and the cousins were running around up here."

The night chill was soaking me to the bone and the shakes were rippling throughout my body. "We're overthinking here, let's get going and get this done."

He stood up and looked around a few times. "Yeah."

We moved off the trail, well aware we didn't know who was running around up here. It could be we were being watched this very moment. Could well be nobody or somebody, but the fact was we were treading on private property and perhaps Musgrave had relatives checking on the place from time to time or perhaps one of the nearby ranchers passed through. A million reasons and people came to mind.

The telegraph pole was bare. The exception was the stub of broken porcelain perched on top. Hendricks took out a mini mag-light and kicked it on. The round beam pierced the night and I began walking around the base of the pole, kicking at the ground for anything out of place. Other than what I had found earlier there was nothing.

"What're we looking for you think?"

"Something like a trapdoor, storm cellar door...something going down underground."

Hendricks walked slowly along the thin, overgrown path when he felt the ground sag under him. He took a step back, and using his booted foot, kicked away the topsoil. He looked up and waved me over. "It looks like a plate of some kind, not sure though, obviously something's here."

I helped clear the edge of where he had found something and

saw after several minutes of clearing away the thick growth and topsoil, it was a large metal plate. The both of us quickly cleared away the loose dirt, looking for the edges. Once it was cleared off, we found ourselves looking at a twelve-foot long and ten-foot wide piece of 5/8's thick diamond plate. There was no door access.

Hendricks looked around and found a long metal piece of thick rebar from the nearby pile of rusted scrap metal. He stabbed an end under the plate. We heard the metal scraping against concrete and he lifted up. He grunted and swore out loud. The dark crack opening resembled a leering corpse. I quickly dropped down and took my flashlight and held the beam down the gap. "We got something. We got a ladder and what looks like a pair of doors at the bottom of a hole. Looks like a shipping container, cinder block walls wrapped around the edges of the hole."

"Look like anyone been down there?" he grunted through strained lips.

Peering down, there was nothing that said anyone had been here for some time. "No, just cobwebs and dust."

He dropped the plate down. A cloud of dust exploded out. He leaned over grabbed his knees to catch his breath. "Has to be it, give me a hand."

We made the vain attempt in moving it but found this was taking up too much time. Not only were we fighting the weight of the plate, we also found that the nearby tree roots and thick underbrush had grown over it. Even Mother Nature was making a grab for the money and the earth was refusing to give up its grasp. We resorted to propping the metal plate up on the nearby smaller pieces of one-inch rounds of rebar from the pile of scrap. The gap was large enough for us to squeeze through and it was the best thing we could hope for. It was dangerous, but if the money was down there, it was worth the gamble. Small plumes of dust rose up and thin rivers of dirt cascaded down into the hole.

I aimed the light over to the double doors of the buried cargo container and saw the lock. My jaw dropped, adrenaline shot through my veins. It was a lock very similar to the one I had found on the internet.

"Hendricks."

He shined his light over and grunted.

"Key?"

"Is that the lock?"

I couldn't take my eyes from it. *ADLAKE* was etched across its surface. "It sure as hell looks like it."

He quickly fumbled around his pockets and pulled his hands out. "Shit!"

"What?"

"I must've forgotten it!"

"You forgot it? How in the hell could you forget it you damned twat?"

He smiled wide, a soft laugh erupted out and he held his hand out. There, within the clasp of his fingertips was the key. "Relax. I got it. You think I'd forget it?"

My heart was racing, hammering hard. "You ass," I whispered and reached over and snatched the key from his fingertips.

"You have the honors, sir."

"What? Me go down there? Alone?" I took a long look down the hole. *What about spiders or snakes?*

"I'll be on watch. Remember we're dealing with mob money and we can't take any chances at this point. We could get a visit," he took a look down the hole and switched the Mossberg's safety off and, as if he was reading my thoughts said, "It's too damned cold for spiders or snakes so, move your ass." He looked into my face and nodded for me to move on down.

I knelt down swearing then slid under the plate and made a grab for the ladder. I swung a foot down slowly on each wooden rung and settled there until I was comfortable they weren't going to break. I hit the dirt floor and turned to face the large double doors and took the key from my jacket pocket. Looking up, Hendricks's face was looking on. He nodded. "Hurry the hell up," he whispered.

The key fit the slot and carefully, ever so slowly, I turned it over and the large clasp swung open. I looked up. Hendricks smiled and I could see the excitement etched across his face. I leaned over, took hold of the door levers, lifted and swung the large rods open, then peeled the doors back, which took some effort due to the timeframe the container had sat under the ground. The hinges had about seized up and the doors squeaked and moaned. I could see rust flaking off of them.

The door was open enough so I could slip inside. I poked my head in, jamming the flashlight inside first. From my viewpoint, I saw one side of the container lined with shelves and what appeared to be a bunch of boxes piled up on the end. Along the other wall, a large tarp covered something all the way the length of the container itself. A thin layer of dust had settled over everything. The doors must have not been fully sealed when Musgrave had placed the container in the ground.

Shelved racks lined both sides of the container and each shelf held a massive collection of junk of all sorts Musgrave must've found important enough to horde away in case the world came to an end. The shelves were packed with boxes of MRE's, a generator, cots and other odd assortments of military gear anyone could get from military surplus stores or online outfitters. I moved a section of tarp aside and whistled out loud.

A large gun rack and every slot held a rifle, pistol, or shotgun. I knew the shotguns were cut below legal limits or military grade. There were multiple AR and AK rifles, which I wondered if they were full auto or just the civilian versions. Judging by the sawed-off pump shotguns, I assumed they were all illegal in nature. Dave must've thought the end of the world was coming soon or he had deals in the mix to move these weapons for extra dough. I touched the barrel shroud of one of several M249's and wondered how he had managed to even get those. The whole wall was a large gun rack and there were several rows of composite plastic and wood crates stacked up under the tarp.

Markings from the crates ranged from explosive projectiles, a Model Barret, M4 along with a host of other weapons. All were marked US property. Whatever Musgrave was into, it was serious.

"Hey, most of these guns look like military grade stuff!" I shouted.

"We ain't worried about those. Any sign of the money?"

I dropped the tarp and focused on the shelves.

Rummaging through the shelves had produced nothing and was beginning to think this was nothing more than a goat-rope session. I opened all of the boxes, containers, anything that could possibly have held a quarter million in cash and came up empty-handed in the search so far.

I shined the flashlight to end of the far wall, eyeing more shelves and saw the ammo cans stacked up neatly and began opening them one at a time. There were .223 and a wide assortment of handgun and shotgun rounds but when I hit the bottom row, I popped open a can. Several thick bundles of Benjamin Franklins were looking up at me. My heart skipped a beat. I took out a handful of bundled hundreds and yelled out for joy.

"Hendricks!" I shouted. "Holy God! We found it!"

He muffled a response but I couldn't make out what he said.

I frantically searched the remaining ammo cans until I had nine of them laid open. All nine cans were packed with hard cash. The other ammo cans, I stacked back up in their place. We would have to cover up our tracks as best we could. Hopefully, time and the elements would cover up our ever being here before the money was discovered to be missing.

I took one of the cans up to Hendricks who knelt down shotgun at the ready. "Hendricks," I whispered, holding the ammo can up for him to see.

He took out his flashlight and shined it downward. "Jesus."

"We did it!" I hissed.

He looked away. "C'mon, we got to haul ass. How many?"

"Looks like nine ammo cans. All packed with cash! Hundreds, fifties!"

"Bring 'em up, c'mon, let's go!" He was watching with keen interest in case anyone or anything was moving about. He flipped the safety on the Mossberg as I began handing them up to him. The first snow began to fall. Small particles of frozen moisture sprinkled across my face like cold pinpricks. Soon, the snows would bury this place. After handing up the last ammo can, I slammed the doors shut, struggling for a minute with the latch before it locked into place. Slapping the padlock back into place, I flew up the ladder and slid out from under the plate cover and out into the open air.

It was easier now to drop the plate back into place. I felt like Atlas holding the world and could've moved the damned thing by myself at this point. Hendricks found a busted bucket off in the brush and began scooping silt sand and covering up the edges, then, breaking off a tree limb, he brushed over the area. We took a look at our handy-work and decided it was close enough to see the area still looked undisturbed. We were hoping for a good wind to help cover up things or maybe the incoming snow would help matters, but either way, we were going to get away clean as long as we covered our tracks.

I took the rope from our bag and cut a couple pieces long enough to loop the ammo can together and each of us to carry out. I slung the make-shift sling over my shoulder carrying the first five cans. Hendricks took up the other four and we made our way slowly back to the truck, carefully hugging the shadows from the nearby trees.

The .45 shook in my hand, shadows shifted within the rustling trees as the few lights from Willard danced like broken gems off in the distance. Hendricks kept the barrel of the Mossberg pointed out in front of him. He had no intentions of letting anyone get the money if he could help it. The tracks back up by the pathways still had him concerned.

The Ford sat beyond the fence. We approached it carefully, splitting off and moving slowly towards it. We were both reading each other's minds that maybe somebody could be waiting for us there, but once we popped the doors open and pointed our guns inside, we were greeted with nothing more than an empty bench seat. I unslung the ammo cans which had begun to dig an angry furrow into the shoulder muscles and started up the Ford. The 390 turned a few times and fired off into a low rumbling idle.

We tossed the money in the back of the truck storage box. Hendricks kept an eye open pointing the muzzle off into the darkness, in case we were seen or there would be some kind of movement from people or a vehicle but there was nothing but the cold wind and the rustling of the trees. I slammed the storage box closed and listened for anything, an engine starting, running footsteps, anything and was met only with the sounds of our beating hearts and the soft crunching of the gravel under our feet and the idling Ford. We jumped in the truck and slammed the doors and pulled out leaving the headlights off.

I found myself eyeing the mirrors, looking for anything and anyone who might be following but found nothing but empty trails leading out of the Dunes. The further away we got, the softer my grip became on the .45.

We hit the paved highway at fifty just as the snows began falling in a heavy sheet. It was perfect timing. Even though we had left behind some signs of activity, the snows would cover anything of our being there. Within minutes, the wipers struggled to keep up with the fast falling snow.

We looked at each other, smiling and then howls of success and laughter erupted from our lips. Hendricks hammered the dash in delight. For the first time in a long time, I felt like a king among men.

***

The early morning had bought more snow and the sun was trying to break through the thick clouds over Moriarty but it wasn't having much luck in doing so. The sounds of chirping birds nesting up in the rafters greeted me when I walked into the shop. I found Hobart sitting in his usual spot sipping on his coffee mug. We greeted each other as I unlocked my toolbox.

The night had been long. Hendricks and I had gone to his place and divided up the money, not stopping until every dollar was counted. The surprise came when we calculated that instead of the original quarter million, we had counted out three hundred and eighty-four grand. Our cuts were more than enough to see us through any hard times ahead and build a better life for ourselves.

I stuck to my original plan on where to hide the money. I had barely enough time to stuff the backpack with my cut of the money and head home, cram it under the water storage tank located in the well house behind the house and head to work. I peeled off five grand and hid it in the El Camino for back up money.

I had just opened the toolbox when Hobart smiled. "Nice boots."

I looked down at my boots. The mud from the ranch was still encrusted over them. Even though the ground was hard, I had picked up enough muck that, when the snows fell, they had gotten the mix wet. "Just mud around the house," I went back to unlocking the toolbox.

"You don't see that kind of mud around here. More like further south."

I looked up and smiled. "You a soil expert?"

"No, just know that red clay on your boots is from down south, say Willard? Maybe further down."

My heart froze. Just what did he mean? How would he know the mud on my boots came from down south? Did he know, somehow figure out I had been out on Musgrave's ranch last night? I shook it off. No damn way he could know. No way could anyone know. He was here all night. No one around the shop could possibly know anything about what Hendricks and I were doing. "It's mud from around my house."

His eyes narrowed to slits as he sipped on his coffee mug. He said nothing more on the subject. He looked up and saw it was close to seven. In his usual manner, he stood up, smiled and took up his lunchbox and walked silently out the open shop bay doors. I looked down at my boots and thought nothing more on it. Going to the computer, I logged in and found there was nothing pressing on the wait list and went and poured a cup of coffee from my thermos.

As the dawn began to break open to reveal a snow-packed landscape, I had decided to make the break despite Hendricks warning to hang on here for a time. We had discussed this point in depth. It would be better to stick around if we found the money. This was a precaution and a valid one. It would look strange if we both up and quit and disappeared, especially with Thomas and his cousins hanging around. It would look really suspicious and set off alarm bells.

I wanted out and away. Hit the road and disappear. Never to be found or seen again. The question that remained was where? Texas might still hold the answer but I was wondering if I could even find work out there at this point. The word was mechanics from all over had flooded the region and very few were able to find work.

North to Montana was another option, or even to North Dakota. Political word was oil companies by the droves were dropping wells into the Bakkan Basin. It was the start of a new boom and it would be nice to hit the ground floor on that gig.

I watched the clouds begin to let loose another onslaught of fresh snow. The lot was packed with parked rigs as word came in I-40 was closed from Santa Rosa to the Texas border and from Albuquerque to Moriarty. I downed the last of my coffee and flicked the butt of my smoke out into the snow-covered lot.

And then there was Amy.

I knew I couldn't leave without her. Deep down inside, I felt it, knew it. One way or another, I was stupid for sticking around but I was going to wait, money in hand be damned. I was going to wait for her to finish her business here before shoving off this dead desert for other places unknown. I wanted a life with her in the picture and there was no other way around it.

"Damn it," I whispered.

FIFTEEN

The only good thing about 2008 was when the El Camino rumbled back to life. It took a few cranks, checks and rechecks to make sure the firing order and timing was set right before it coughed and went into a loping idle. After several minutes, I shut it down and readjusted a clamp that was leaking off a small puddle of coolant.

I spent the early spring morning placing the hood back into place, installing the new four-row aluminum radiator, rechecking the wiring hookups, double-checking the transmission bell housing bolts, all while letting my thoughts drift. Mornings like this were rare.

The phone went off a couple times. The number was from the Duggan's shop. It was my scheduled day off and I ignored the persistent ringing. There had been a rash of people quitting and Johnson was pulling what hair he had left, out by the handful trying to fill schedule demands. For once I had time and money and no real need to keep killing myself at the truck stop.

I cranked the motor over again and it fired back to life. I let it idle and watched the gauges reach operating range before sliding the selector through the gears to make sure each one was functioning. After a final check for leaks, the El Camino rolled out down the gravel driveway to the asphalt road below for its maiden voyage.

I'd spent the last few months of winter putting everything back together. Even though Hendricks and I had found the money, and we were willing to leave, we stuck to the plan of continuing to work at Duggan's shop. I was fine with that, even though I fought compulsions to leave in the dead of night. I figured I could have Amy convinced it was time to leave during this time frame, and she would eventually agree. But she didn't. I focused on the El Camino. Working on the war horse was easier to do than to keep hounding her about leaving New Mexico, and Thomas, far behind. She wasn't hearing me on anything related to those subjects and I couldn't figure out why.

The transmission shifted through the gears. The engine roared down the road and didn't miss a beat. I kept going for an hour, remembering Amy and the times we had. The last couple of weeks were hard, perhaps harder for her due to my persistent demands we leave. We still hooked up but she was elusive as to where she was staying. In all the time throughout our relationship, she never once told me where she was staying. I asked her to move in but it was persistently shot down. Maybe she feared Thomas would find out and thought it best not to. Maybe it was best not to provoke the beast with a sharp stick while he was locked in a cage. Eventually, the cage door could swing open. I relented on the subject after seeing her point, but I continued on asking her to leave New Mexico with me.

She had stopped by a couple of days before. For once, she began talking about leaving New Mexico and spending more time together. She was anxious though, but happy, like she wanted to tell me something but held it in. After a long shift, she was waiting out in front of the house as I pulled in. She wore large sunglasses, a red leather jacket that fit snug over her small frame, she looked good under the early springtime sun. I felt everything was finally moving off in a better direction. It was just a question of where we wanted to go. Alaska was an option but she wanted somewhere in the northwest on the table. Either way, I really didn't care where we went as long as we were together.

She continued working the counter, but Johnson was moving her and my schedules around. It was rare we worked together on the same shift anymore. I figured Thomas had a hand in that. There was hatred in his eyes whenever we met like he wanted to beat my ass, but he never acted on those impulses. I wondered about that. What was keeping him from doing so? I had a hunch he knew about Amy and me. I figured Amy had something to do with keeping him in check but she never explained anything when I asked. Surely she knew Thomas held a quiet grudge against me. She would smile, kiss me and tell me I was reading too much into things or change the subject.

Some things went along normally. Life resumed with some quiet tranquility and we would watch the sunrise out on the back deck. I still worked my ass off at Duggan's but once the shift was done, and Amy said she was waiting for me at home, I punched out and left before anyone could say anything. It was good to see her waiting at the home front and I lamented the silence and the residual scent of her perfume when she wasn't.

But something changed and I couldn't put a finger on it.

She would get phone calls and said she and a friend were going shopping. It seemed legit but when the calls came in the middle of the night, she would disappear to another part of the house and whisper. Then, a week ago, she left for several days and never answered my calls. That had me concerned to no end. When she did call me back, she said she had to leave town for business. What business it was, she never said.

I guessed it was Thomas.

Everything changes at some point or another. Was she trying to decide on what to do?

Besides the problems with Amy, there were the growing problems looking forever larger at Duggan's truck stop. Everything looked to be falling apart.

I let the El Camino carry me to I-40 and I turned east and floored the accelerator, my thoughts drifted like a careless soul on a vast ocean. I had seen mechanics come and go. Some were quickly forgotten, just nameless faces in an ocean of employees revolving in and out of Duggans. Then there were the few guys you carried around in your soul. Like it or not, you are part of one large family and you are friends forever. But then there are those in your happy little group, who fall off the earth.

That was just the start.

It was within the last couple of weeks when the rumblings of change began to sweep across Duggan's truck stop like a brush fire out of control. The days that had often finished with big dollar bangs, began to grind to a halt with a whimper measured in pennies. Something's you see coming, but you're too tied up trying to make the dollar and ignore or miss what's going on around you.

It was 2008 and the money wagon had come to an abrupt end. The only good thing was Hendricks and I had our mountain of cash.

Fuel prices had started an upward tick, ever so slowly at first, before turning into a runaway freight train rolling up to fifty cents to a buck a gallon at a time. Unleaded gas shot up to a bit over five bucks a gallon while diesel, the lifeblood of the trucking industry, shot up to almost eight bucks. In some places, such as Needles, California, I was hearing gasoline was something like nine bucks and change a gallon for unleaded while diesel was over ten bucks.

All the politicians were assholes about it. They were elated at the high gas prices due to the fact their investments in the oil industry were making them millions. The American oil companies acted like drunken whores looking for a good time with the political elite. They planned on keeping the money train rolling in for as long as they could. They sent their skilled team of lobbyist whores to Washington, giving out blow and hand jobs to any politician wanting to cash in.

Trucking companies began to fold up. Owner-operators began parking their rigs, hoping to wait out the worst of the rising fuel prices. Theft of diesel in the parking lot became common practice. There wasn't a day that went by where a half dozen rigs, who had fueled the night before, were found the following morning sitting in the lot with empty tanks. We found these had been drained out by other drivers parked next to them, who, armed with electric pumps, would drain their neighbor's tanks in minutes. The price of fuel soon hit the seven dollar mark and there was no sign of it slowing down. The jobs rolling into the shop became non-existent. The bays that had once been packed with customers and easy payoffs, now stood open and desolate with nothing but the occasional tumbleweed blowing through the large bay door openings.

Many people across the US started getting laid off at their jobs. Businesses started closing down or made the move to Mexico. Some people couldn't even qualify for unemployment benefits due to rules and bullshit red-tape. We started seeing more people living in their cars, trucks or bumper pull campers who had begun parking around the truck stop because there was just nowhere else for them to go. Some came from other states, and just like me, became stranded when the money ran out and gas was just too expensive to keep going.

Sometimes, I went and gave what money I had in my pockets

to the stranded motorists. It wasn't much, but I could see the desperation in their eyes. It was reminiscent of over a year ago when I was stranded myself. Some of these guys came in, looking for dough and selling off what stuff they had on hand. Most of it wasn't much. Maybe a few cheap name brand tools, multi-meters, dishes or whatever they had. You could tell they were on their last leg. I gave what money I had. I could afford such nice acts since finding Musgrave's fortune months ago. I even cut a few coupons for free dinner and showers up front. I wasn't supposed to, but I did it anyway. What the hell could management do to me? Fire me? Word around the campfire was Duggan's was being looked at for a buyout.

The winds of change continued.

Big Mac, after several years of getting hammered behind the counter, decided enough was enough. He came into work, took a long look at the empty counter and walked right back out the door without uttering a single syllable. He went to work at the gun store down the road the following day at full time instead of the usual part-time. He was more into guns anyway.

Mongoose disappeared and never did return. His toolbox sat in the bay, collecting dust and his father came and retrieved it some months after his son disappeared. He didn't know anything about the whereabouts of his son and was worried about it. Last I heard, he was in jail down in Tucson for wandering the streets butt-naked while on an acid trip.

Then there was Derek. It was still fresh news floating through Duggan's entire Moriarty complex this morning.

He hadn't shown up at work for several days but everyone back in the shop didn't think too much about it. There had been a rash of people quitting anyway and we just assumed he had done the same. His toolbox sat untouched during that time and we wondered when he was coming to pick it up.

But he never did and never would.

His body had been discovered in the early morning hours out in the middle of some rancher's field. The rancher had been out rounding up his cattle when he tripped across a corpse dangling from a thick branch on a lone Chinese elm tree like rotten fruit. From what I had heard from Torrance county deputy Frasier, who frequented the shop and had responded to the call, Derek had committed suicide but some things didn't add up in my mind. One being was the question of why? Derek just didn't seem too depressed when I last spoke to him. He mentioned he had plans set for a vacation somewhere in Europe, having paid for tickets and hotels in advance. He had plenty of money from my understanding. He was also too clean cut and methodical and never raised up any warning flags. The troubling part was why go out in the middle of nowhere and hang yourself? None of it made sense.

When Hendricks called to tell me the details, he mentioned that Derek's employee picture was being mounted on the Wall of Remembrance up in the main complex. His photo would hang beside Dave Musgrave and Lonnie Blondes photographs for all time.

The young guys like Cue Ball, Chris, Chuck and the rest of the lot soon fell off the rosters one by one over a course of several months. Some never even let anyone know they were quitting. They just up and left. Most of them wandered back to school and were working towards a degree of their choice. Some began working towards an engineering degree, others drifted into welding jobs, government jobs or something other than busting their knuckles at some shit job for some shit outfit for shit wages. I envied their youth and enthusiasm. Busting wrenches was all Hendricks and I knew. We were too far along in life to quit now. As in all things in life though, the ride would end eventually but we were set money wise thanks to Musgrave.

One day, I looked at the schedule rosters and noted in over a year's time, I had climbed up from the bottom of the pile to being the number two man, Hendricks being in the number one position. Everyone else under me was all new faces and the wave of new guys was shaping up to suck donkey nuts. I didn't try to help or train them. The ambition and drive weren't there so why bother?

Some things though, never change.

Dwayne the complex manager was still messing around with Andrea, the busty, long-legged blonde up in bookkeeping. He was slipping away from the everyday realities of what was Duggan's Truck Stop life. He never came back to the shop and could've cared less about why the shop employees were dropping like flies.

Something's, as I've said before, I should've seen coming. Like my divorce. I should've seen it coming when I kept seeing the next door neighbor spending more time with the ex-wife than I was. The day the doors closed at Consolidated Express, the day I broke down here in Moriarty, New Mexico, knowing the old El Camino was just not up for the task of a road trip. Some things you see coming and can prepare for it, other things one just can't for no matter what.

It was also the year the grumblings of Duggan's selling out could be heard all across the lands. It was whispered at first, some unsubstantiated rumor that occasionally made the rounds, except this time, there seemed to be some legitimate truth. I also heard a soft whisper that Duggan's had bought in some troubleshooter who was known as the Rainmaker. It was said he could turn any facility into a money-making machine but so far, we hadn't seen any evidence of financial improvements.

As a cost savings measure, Dwayne and Johnson shut down the graveyard shift. Hobart was moved to swings much to his annoyance. We all figured it was part of this Rainmaker's way of stemming off the bleeding of wasted wages with nothing rolling in overnight. Johnson had issued me a key to the shop, making me responsible for lockdown at midnight. Even though Hendricks had been here the longest and held seniority, he just never trusted him.

I had thought I could trust Hendricks to make smart moves. He had done so up until the day I saw Jill driving a brand new Dodge Durango across the parking lot. I felt a twinge of betrayal.

Hendricks walked out of the shop and up to Jill who stepped out of the Durango. They kissed and she took hold of his hand telling him something she was excited about. After several minutes, they hugged and she took off in the Durango.

I watched her leave and Hendricks stood there watching. He was still watching when I walked up and nudged him. "What the hell?" I whispered. "Tell me, please tell me, that is not a new Dodge."

He looked me in the eyes. Anger flashed for a quick moment. "What's it to you?"

"You broke your own rule. You said stay low," I jabbed a finger at the Durango, "*That* is not low key."

He shrugged. "She needed a new car. The van was junk, it puked a motor."

I closed my eyes and exhaled. "So you paid cash for it."

"It's none of your business, so butt out."

"It is if it gets us caught, you dumbass."

"We're leaving, Logan."

My rage was suddenly swept away. "Leaving?"

"I turned in my two weeks' notice a few minutes ago. Jill's got family in California, so we're going there for a while."

Months had passed since we had found the money. We had made plans to leave New Mexico, each going our separate ways, but it wasn't until then I realized this was the end of a good thing. "It's time then?"

He nodded. "I stuck around too long as it is, Logan. I guess I got tired of waiting for you to make your move with Amy. Jill and I are engaged."

"Engaged? You mean as in married soon?"

"What else does it mean?"

I sighed. It was hard to believe things were moving on in life. People come and people go. Life at Duggan's continued to change and evolve. "Well....Congrats?"

He looked out across the parking lot and around to the shop. "I've been here for almost six years, hard to believe I'm actually leaving, but my woman's got a hold of me." He lit up a smoke and changed the subject. "You got your plans in place?"

I shook my head. "I can't leave without her."

"Funny...money and women are our weakness."

There was a twinge of truth in Hendricks words spoken several days before. I allowed Amy to get too close to the heart of matters. I had over two hundred grand stuffed away and had yet to convince her to leave with me.

The El Camino rumbled down the highway. The speedometer slipped past eighty and the fuel gauge bounced to under an eighth of a tank.

Maybe it was time to leave New Mexico and just leave Amy behind. If she were serious, she would follow. Or would she? I pulled over at the 240-mile marker and glided into the Flying C Travel Center, and up next to an open gas pump before killing the ignition. On the other side of the gas pump, a mini-van with several kids gawked at the El Camino. The man behind the steering wheel took a look but pivoted his attention back to the windshield. I pulled the Com Data card and topped off the gas tank before going inside to grab a green chili cheeseburger.

I moved away from the gas pumps and parked at the far edge of the parking lot away from everyone. Leaning against the fender, I ate the burger and looked out over the vast, rolling prairie lands to the east. Iron grey clouds swept the plains on the distant horizon and I admired the view. I was feeling the sudden urge to leave, right now, today, and put this barren place in the rear view mirror.

I was feeling on the edge of burning out, a bright torch flickering wildly in the torrential winds of change and about to be extinguished. I started feeling the ravages of time and my profession. I felt the knees giving out, back muscles sore, the effects of cold on joints, wrists and the fingers, every now and then, my back muscles would cramp to the point where I had to take a knee until the pain subsided. Every day was becoming an increasing battle with time and the wear on the body. In ten years, I might not be working as a diesel mechanic anymore, let alone thirty.

By this point in my life, I had been busting wrenches for the better part of nineteen years and didn't have anything to show for it. I was thinking maybe retirement was out of reach since I hadn't funded any kind of 401k or anything else for that matter. My bad some people will say, but when you got bills, a whoring ex-wife who wiped you out in a divorce and a crap economy, there's nothing left but burnt intentions. I did have a small pension I was going to receive from the union when I worked at Consolidated. But I wasn't going to see any money from that until I hit sixty-five, and who knew if it was even going to be there when I got to that ripe old age? Sure, I had thirty years to go to get there, but ten years fly by fast and it didn't look like anyone was hiring for anything and one never knew if today would be their last among the living.

The only consoling thought was I did have the two hundred grand. If I played it smart, maybe invested some of it, I would have a nice fund built up by the time I hit retirement age.

Amy was my anchor and I hoped we would eventually move off together into the distant horizon leaving this god-damned truck stop to burn. I tossed the burger wrapper to the ground, slid behind the wheel and fired up the El Camino. I took note of the gauges and found the oil, electrical, and coolant gauges in good order before sliding the gear selector into drive. I hit the gas pedal on the interstate on-ramp, opening it up the four-barrel Holley in a throaty roar. The El Camino rumbled its way back to Moriarty.

I thought I might as well head into work and make a few extra coins. God knew that evil bitch of an ex-wife needed a new Lexus, house, or something else to pay for with my money. What else would I be doing anyway? The El Camino was finished and ready to roll out and all I had left to do was wait on Amy. I had nothing but time to wait for her. The closer I got to town the worse I felt. I knew then I had overstayed my welcome in Moriarty but the thought of Amy was keeping me grounded.

But she damned-well better hurry up…

***

It was late afternoon when I arrived at the shop and found it dead. I decided to haul ass to the front and grab some grub. The dining hall was loaded with drivers, all talking or playing with their phones. Some had laptops and were using those to talk to family across the far reaches of America.

I stabbed a fork into the mystery meatloaf and crammed in a slab into my maw. I wondered about the new cook frying up everyone's grub. I had heard he was Chinese guy, some high-roller cook who went to some big name culinary school back in New York. Rolling the meatloaf around my mouth, I had to admit, the meat tasted pretty damned good. I just hoped it wasn't cat meat.

Amy was at home having been scheduled off time. God knew what she was doing. We had talked some about leaving but she didn't want to talk about it right then.

I took up the company newsletter and began reading through

the mini-articles. I had swallowed another bite of the loaf when my ears picked up something foreign, unnatural to the surroundings. A couple of men seated themselves across the table from me.

Looking up I stopped chewing.

Richardson. My eyes slid over to the man sitting across from him. *Nguyen.* I lowered my head, eyes went back to the badges.

I raised up the newsletter, hoping to hide my wandering eyes. The waitress glided up to my table. "Anything else you need *shug?*"

"No, no thanks." I leaned back, dug in my greasy pocket and handed her a crumpled twenty.

She took hold of it.

"Keep the rest," I started to get up out of the booth.

The cops eyed me for a second but went back to talking to themselves. Nguyen looked up again and eyed me cautiously while stirring a spoon in his coffee. Richardson followed his gaze. I walked away, sweat beaded up on my forehead. I could feel their eyes boring into my back as I walked away.

I exited the complex and made my way through the lot, glancing behind to see if they were following. No one was. To be sure, I wound my way through the maze of parked rigs and the trash-strewn parking lot. Drivers moved in and out of the shadows, going up front to feed or wash or buy fuel and junk food.

Large shadows moved, flickering in the open sun. Heavy footfalls and rolling tires from passing trucks vibrated across the broken asphalt. I felt hairs stand up on end, every sense and nerve tingled like they had been singed with an open flame. I stayed close to the shadows, fear balled up into a tight knot deep in the gut. Someone had to be following, or at the least, watching.

The shop was some thirty yards away still. I felt like I was in the crosshairs of a hunter's rifle sights. Or was I panicking? I knelt down, breathed deep, and exhaled slowly. I stood up, walked out across the remaining expanse of the parking lot and entered the shop through the bay door. No one followed.

I popped open the toolbox, opened the drawer to toss my keys in when I noticed the envelope. A large manila with metal clasps folded out to hold the lip shut. Written in a large black marker was my name.

I looked around and reached for it and bent the metal ears together and opened the envelope. Carefully peering inside, I saw there were a handful of photographs and I wondered who had placed them there.

Fear gripped my gut.

The photos were of me and Amy, one kissing in front of the house. Another showed us together up at the restaurant, another showed her truck parked in front of the house, and yet another with us kissing again with my hands in her jacket.

I looked up and around, feeling the tingling sensation etching up my spine.

Someone knew but then again who didn't? Just about everyone knew about Amy and me.

I looked out the bay door and saw a glimpse of the large dude disappearing into the shadows by the storage building. I felt the hairs rise up on the back of my neck.

Cleeve or Robert Lee? I couldn't tell from this distance but I was sure it was one or the other. For several minutes, I felt eyes boring into me from the dim darkness of the shadows by the storage building. The afternoon sun was still a few hours off from turning dark. I stood there shaking with the photographs in my hand. I could feel and knew, something was coming, something evil, and something surreal.

SIXTEEN

Things can shift in the blinking of an eye. You don't expect anything to happen but when it does, it all goes up in flames and you're beating yourself to death trying to get the fires to quit eating your flesh.

I told Johnson I was sick and needed to get home. He quickly responded with a booming fuck off home comment. He didn't argue since the shop was empty and overstaffed. I drove the El Camino hard and fast, watching the rearview mirror for anyone who might be following but no one was. The manila envelope was on the passenger seat and my gut was a twisted knot. The feeling of numbness washed over me when I saw the black Chevy truck parked up in the driveway. Amy stood by the door. I waved but before I could kill the ignition and open the driver's door, she slid back inside without any acknowledgment.

"Shit," I whispered. Had someone given her a stack of pictures also? I walked up to the front door with the manila envelope. She stood inside, arms crossed, back to me. My eyes glanced over to the coffee table. Stacks of green bills were stacked on the table. I knew what she was going to be mad about. I kicked myself mentally for taking any of the money out of the backpack. I had gone to the pack and pulled the five grand from it and hid it in the El Camino's spare tire compartment behind the seat. It was labeled as my just in case money. I then had stuffed another five grand up in my closet. "I can explain."

Amy reached down, grabbed a handful of the money in her hands. "Please tell me this is not what I think it is?"

I blinked, unsure how to respond. I reached for her. "Amy…"

She flinched, drew back her hands. "You bastard, do you realize what you've gotten us into?" She threw the fistful of money at me and the wad of currency exploded across my chest and fluttered to the floor. "I hoped, prayed it was money from your job."

"We found that." I instantly flinched realizing what I had just said. If I had played it cool, I could've passed it off as money earned from Duggan's.

She whirled around, eyes full of rage. "We? Like Hendricks? Is that who else is in on this?"

I held up the photos. "I think we got bigger issues right now."

She took the photographs and then let them fall from her shaking fingers once she saw they were of us. "Oh my God!"

"Who?"

"Who? What do you mean 'who'? Everyone knows!"

"Someone knows."

"Who? Hendricks? The whole shop? Thomas?"

"I don't know. I found these in my toolbox. Someone put them in there."

She began pacing and folded her arms. "Oh my God…oh my

God...I should never have..." she whispered over and over.

"Let's get out of here then, Amy. I don't think we have much time left." I was sure of it. I couldn't think who would place the pictures in my toolbox. Hendricks knew about me and Amy, and maybe a few other guys in the shop suspected it, but I was banking on Thomas and he was giving a shot across the bow, letting me know he knew and was coming.

"You," she pointed a finger, a tear cascaded down her cheek. "You are going to get us killed, Logan. You have no idea what you're doing." Her voice was cracking and angry tears formed in her eyes. She knelt down and began raking the money into a small pile with her fingers. "Where's the rest of it?"

"This is all of it." I lied but it was a weak lie and she knew I was lying. I wasn't going to tell her about the rest of the money.

She jumped up. "This is only maybe a few thousand, you're lying!"

"Okay," I kept my hand up. She was going to be really mad and I had a hard time lying to her. All she had to do was twist the truth-knife a bit deeper. "Okay, maybe a little bit."

Her shoulders sagged and she turned her face upwards with eyes rolling. "For the love of God, Logan, where is the money then?"

"Why? Why do I so desperately need to give you the money? Can you give me an answer?"

"I don't have to explain anything to you, Logan! Right now lives depend on it."

"That's not good enough, Amy."

"God-damn it, Logan!" She stormed forward and punched my chest several times, hard. I deflected the blows, slapping them away.

"Okay, we...me and Hendricks found the money. It was out on Musgrave's ranch. We found it several months ago, right before the first big snow storm. If I didn't care about you, I would've left then but here I am, waiting for you."

"Hendricks," she pointed her finger at me. "You need to call him, right now, and tell him to bring his cut of the money back!"

I knelt down, scooped up the pictures. "I'd say we have bigger problems."

"You idiot! The money is the problem!" she screamed.

I had never seen her upset before. I held my hands up hoping to calm her down. "Hold on, Amy, really I do understand. But I think...it's time for us to get out of here. We take this money," I pointed at the stacks of money on the table. "And we get the hell out of here...right now, together."

She held her hands over her face. "Oh God."

"What? Why are you so damned afraid? Why? Has all of this been about the money with you?"

"A couple of mechanics manage to find this money," she whirled and made for the bedroom.

I was taken aback and followed after her. "Mechanics? You make it sound like a dirty word."

"You don't understand," she was grabbing any box or bag from the closet, dumping out its contents on the floor and looking through the jumbled mess searching for the money.

"God-damn it, Amy! How about making me understand!" I grabbed her.

"Let go!"

I wasn't buying her weak attempts. "We can leave, right now, but every time I beg, you shoot it down. Every time I talk to you about a new life and moving to a new place, you blow it out of the water. Why? Why are you hell-bent on staying? For months now, I've been asking, begging you, to get out of here with me but you won't!"

I didn't realize I had been yelling at her and she stood surprised, shocked. "I..."

"'I' what Amy? Damn it! Why?"

She remained silent. Tears began flowing from her eyes. I wasn't sure of anything anymore and I was thinking I was a retard for staying to begin with but love had its hooks into me. "I just can't say anything. I promised and I care a lot about you. You just don't understand."

"Promised? For fuck's sake, Amy, promised who?"

Her sides heaved, worry etched across her face. "I can't say, Logan. There's more to this than I can say but you and Hendricks may well have gotten yourselves in deep trouble and the bad part is, you don't realize it."

I snorted. "Give me a break, Amy."

"Let go." She looked into my eyes. She wasn't going to say anything for what reason I couldn't fathom.

I shook my head and let her go. "I was stupid to stay, Amy. I should've left a long time ago. No woman is worth this."

Her jaw dropped open. "Oh! Now you tell the truth! You prick!" She lunged forward, hammering me with her fists.

For the first time, I felt pained by what I had said. I felt the grip of once had been love slipping off into a burning crevice of burnt desires. I let her keep hitting me. I didn't fight back and began apologizing. "Amy…please, I'm sorry, I didn't mean to say that."

Breathless, she staggered back, rage filled her eyes, and her hair was a tangled mess. "Keep the money you asshole! That's why you stuck around anyway!" She turned and stormed out of the room, feet hammering the floor. I felt the vacuum of love being sucked away in her wake and the sudden chill of loneliness settling in its place. I followed her out and into the living room, grabbed and spun her around to face me. "Damn it, Amy, listen to me."

She struggled, trying to pry my hands off her. "We're done, Logan, now let go! Fuck you and your fucking money!"

"We're not done by a long shot. What's this with Thomas being an enforcer for the Dixie Mafia? You," I pointed at her, "you're married to a God-damned mobster."

She blinked, the rage suddenly washed out of her face, shocked that I knew something about her. Her mouth contorted, trying to search for excuses but nothing came out.

"I knew for a while in case you're wondering," I whispered. "So what's the story with the Dixie Mafia, Amy? Huh? What? Why hasn't Thomas done anything about me and you? He has to know, right? What about the money?"

"There's more to that than you know, Logan."

"So, all of this is about getting the money then? Is it all for you? Were you playing me all along?"

"No," she whispered.

"God-damn it then why?" I was about to give up. I let her go.

She slowly shook her head, tears welled up. "I can't."

I clasped my hands together and put them up to my nose. I was going to have to try another angle. I looked into her eyes. "I do love you, please believe me when I say that, and I'm sorry, but you're being so damn secretive. Please...please, look at it from my point of view."

She looked into my eyes, pleading. "Please, the money? Where is it?"

"Has this all been about the money? Is this why you and I are together? The money? I give it to you and then you run off into the sunset?"

She shook her head. "No...not the money. There's more to us than anything, I just...don't want to see you get hurt."

"Then please...make me understand why. Why do I have to give you the money? Is it Thomas? Are you afraid he'll kill us? Did you make him a deal to spare our lives in exchange? Explain that it is something along these lines of thoughts I have."

She shook her head to each question and tears began falling again. "You don't understand…"

"Make me."

She looked into my eyes, took hold of my shirt with shaking hands and her voice fell to a whisper. "It'll change you, it'll change, how you see me and I really don't want that," her voice shook.

"Not in the slightest, Amy."

"Are you so sure, Logan?" her eyes narrowed, more tears began falling but her tone was resolute, firm.

"Try me," I whispered.

For several minutes, we looked into each other's eyes. The only sound to be heard was that of our breathing and her sniffling. I sighed, turned and walked into the kitchen, opened the refrigerator and pulled out a Heineken. I popped the top and took a long swallow before lightning up a cigarette. The last remnants of the day sparkled through the kitchen window, casting a small rectangular patch of multi-colored light across the linoleum floor. We looked at each other and for the first time I saw her as something small, frail but there was a strength I hadn't realized before. The front door swung lazily in the breeze and she moved to close it. She could've left but she didn't. She moved into the living room and sat down on the edge of the sofa. She placed her face in her hands in an attempt to compose herself.

I handed her the Heineken. She took hold of it with shaking fingers and took a swallow. She then asked for a cigarette and I gave her one. She lit the cigarette and inhaled deep of the acrid smoke and closed her eyes.

Finally, she looked up and slowly began talking. "It starts with the money."

SEVENTEEN

Sometimes the truth hurts and in some cases it kills. You have to be careful what you ask for. I demanded the truth and Amy started off slowly, anguish poked through those tear-soaked eyes. She occasionally would look into my eyes, perhaps looking for signs of retribution or rejection. I held on to her words, neither interrupting nor condemning her.

She had been there.

She was high on Mexican Valium or Flunitrazepam along with a few lines of coke. The concoction was boiling in her system and she felt like vomiting. The Chevy truck's air conditioning had stopped working and the heat was unbearable with four people crammed in the extended cab as it rolled to a stop up at the Musgrave's ranch. She didn't want to be here but Thomas was insistent. They had other plans later that night. Some judge in Las Cruces had wanted Amy to meet him at some high-class hotel. Being part of the Gold Coast Flyers Club had its perks. She was an escort but only for the high-end clients willing to pay top dollar for her services. Thomas made sure on that part. As always he video recorded the encounters via hidden cameras and would later use the footage to blackmail some of the clients. It was all expenses paid for the judge but it would cost him later.

Dave Musgrave came out of the house, shirtless, holding a bottle of Bud light in his hand, and a big smile. The little blonde, Lonnie Blonde, stood on the porch, holding the overhang support, drunk, stoned, and wearing a pink and black dress that looked to have been thrown on. Amy knew her by reputation as being a swinger, partier and loved her drugs and drink. Amy had bought some of her drugs of choice from her whenever she visited Duggan's in the past.

"Hey all!" Dave had yelled. "Surprised to see you here." He looked into the truck as Thomas stepped out, his joy quickly turned to real surprise once he saw Dwayne and Arturo stepping out of the truck also. "Oh shit...I guess...?"

Amy had slid out the open door and lit up a cigarette. She didn't want to be here.

Thomas frowned and pulled down the sleeve on his shirt. "You know why we're here, Dave?"

He took a pull of Bud Light. "Not really."

Thomas looked up to the dark skies. It was going to rain soon. The smell of wet mildew hung thinly in the air. "The money and the guns and we're gone."

"The guns are being dealt with, Thomas. I thought that's what we agreed with. I buy them, store and then move them across the border."

Thomas thumbed back toward Arturo. "You knew about the change in plans."

"And fuck over the Juárez Cartel? Screw the bosses back

home? C'mon Thomas we already made a deal with them. Now you want to sell them to this," he pointed at Arturo. "...this fucking cop?"

Dwayne stepped forward. "Things always change, Dave. Look, before we get too rowdy here, you hand over the guns to Arturo here, since he already paid for them, and hand over the money. Not the money Arturo here gave us but the other money. We know what you've been doing these last few years and now you got to make things right."

Dave smiled through thin lips and snickered. "Like what? If you're calling me a cheat of some kind..."

"No one's saying you are, Dave but we know. The folks back home know. Thomas here knows." He stepped forward. "You've been skimming money from Duggan's for a long, long time. We came out here for you to make amends. You hand it over, no harm, no foul."

"Bullshit."

"You call it what you want but you know why we're here and we're not leaving until then." He waved a hand. "It's better than having the Devil's Dog Pound show up. At least it's us, right? We're all friends here."

"Nearly a half a million in cash is missing, you fuck," Thomas snarled.

"The Cartel is supposed to get those guns next week and I'm the one left holding the bag? I'm the one having to explain this shit to them? You know what they're going to do to me?"

Thomas stepped forward. "Where Dave?" A few fist thumps to the gut. Musgrave dropped to all fours puking out his dinner and beer. The beer bottle dropped to the ground and shattered against a rock.

Lonny Blonde screamed out from the porch and came running. Arturo grabbed her, swung her around and a pistol materialized in his free hand. The skull tattoo flexed, the leering jaw opened as if to swallow Lonnie Blond. The pistol cocked and the barrel pressed against the side of her head. She struggled but Arturo held a firm grip. He smelled along her neck, and then with the tip of his tongue, he licked behind her ear. She screamed, crying out into the night. Thomas' low laugh made Amy's skin crawl. She stepped back further into the shadows unsure what to do.

Thomas held up his hands. "Now that we have your undivided attention, Dave, we want the guns and the money." He grabbed him by his thick hair and yanked hard. "You see, Arturo means business. Hell, he might fuck her then kill her…while you watch."

"Let her go, Thomas, please let her go."

Dwayne looked at his fingernails. "Money?"

Dave nodded. "Okay…okay, just please."

Dwayne smiled and looked to Thomas. "You have such a way of words and actions. Now Dave here's what…"

No one saw what happened next. Even now, Amy didn't know what really happened. She didn't know where the shot had come from at first, but the explosion rang out, a blinding light and the ground boiled up a small angry geyser. Lonnie Blonde held a pistol but the shot went wide, Arturo, surprised let go of her and fired off several shots, Lonnie Blonde fell to the ground with a yelp of pain and then nothing. No movement, no nothing. Amy's ears rang out, she found herself screaming in surprise, Thomas produced the .500 Smith and Dwayne fumbled for a small chrome automatic from his suit pocket.

Dave rolled away, was up on his feet and running towards one of the outbuildings. Thomas shot off a round but missed. Arturo began blazing off more rounds but Dave had flung himself behind a battered Lincoln. The bullets impacts blew out the windows and thumped across the panels. Within seconds, Dave had pulled out a shotgun from the Lincoln and fired off a round. Everyone scattered for cover.

The night-time air snapped and buzzed with flying lead. Amy screamed and threw herself to the ground where she found herself staring into Lonnie Blondes flinching eyes. Blood speckled from her thin lips. She moaned in agony and held out a shaking hand. Amy slowly took hold of it and flinched when the gunfire picked up in tempo. Amy saw Lonnie Blonde's lips move and whisper something but at first, she couldn't make out anything she was saying. Amy leaned in closer and heard clearly between the gunfire.

"...*buried...under the old pole....*"

A scream grabbed Amy's attention.

Dave had been hit, he screamed and his shotgun blast went wild into the nighttime skies. Thomas shot again and the screams stopped instantly.

Dwayne held his gun in shaking hands. "Is that it? The fucker...."

Thomas rose up and moved forward with the barrel pointing out, Dwayne followed close behind with the chrome pistol trembling in his hands. He looked around the bumper of the Lincoln and swore out loud. He reached down and flung the shotgun away. He stood up and screamed into the night. Everything had gone wrong in an instant.

Amy looked back to Lonnie Blonde and found her staring off into eternity. A thin red ribbon of blood began pouring from the edge of her mouth and dripping to the dusty earth.

Thomas laughed. It was so horrible of a laugh. "Jesus!" He shouted. "You ever seen so much brains splatter out of a head?"

Dwayne looked horrified, shaking his head, leaned up against the Lincoln and tilted his head back to the skies.

Amy, horrified, ran back behind the truck, pukes.

Laughter.

She then pushed herself off the truck and ran off down the

road and into the dark night.

She wanted away, away from the horrors she had seen. She didn't care where she went just not there, not with Thomas, not with anything mob related.

Arturo caught her, tackling her to the ground. In a flurry of dust, she fought him but she was too stoned to be effective.

Thomas walked up casually. The .500 revolver hung heavy in his hand.

Arturo held her up.

Dwayne leaned over to Thomas. "This was not supposed to happen."

"Yeah? No shit?" Thomas replied.

"And to bring Amy along? We got big problems."

Thomas looked her over. "Alright Arturo, let her go will you?" He looked at Dwayne. "I figured this thing with Dave would go another way, not this way." He waved a paw in a sweeping motion indicating the carnage around them. "Then we were all supposed to go to Las Cruces for the other gig."

"The guns?" Arturo queried.

Thomas nodded. "Somewhere around. I'll find them, don't you worry."

Arturo looked at his fingernails. "My associates might not agree."

Thomas looked hard, eyes narrowed to slits. "What the hell you mean by that? If I said I will find the god-dammed guns then I'll find them."

"You better hope so."

"You cops are all the same you know that? Idle fucking threats!"

Dwayne shook his head in disbelief, stepping in between the two men. "Look, guys, this is not going to sit well with a lot of people from all sides of this, I can tell you that. Let's let cooler heads prevail and we'll work through it right?"

Arturo shook his head. "What do you propose?"

Dwayne stuffed the chrome automatic in his jacket pocket. "I call the Rainmaker."

"Rainmaker?"

"No problem too big that can't be solved."

"You know once you call him in, he controls everything." Thomas frowned.

Dwayne looked at him. "You got a better solution?"

Arturo nodded. "Alright, we call Rainmaker. He's better to deal with anyways." He looked at Thomas with hate in his eyes. "I can respect that."

Dwayne looked at Amy. "What do we do with her?"

Thomas looked at her. "She's stoned. She's seen worse and done worse." He walked over and grabbed her. "Right honey?"

She had never seen people dying. She nodded, fear etched in her face. He smiled, kissed her on the lips before shoving her to the truck.

We go onto Las Cruces, he had said. They had a meeting with the big shot judge. He claimed to be a Christian, a regular church-going guy but he also had a weakness: whores…escorts. That's where Amy came into play. They would record everything and use it to convince the judge he was prosecuting the wrong guy, who also happened to be a member of the Dixie Mafia. After that, back home to Mississippi to smooth things over within the ranks. The higher ups would want to know details of events and would want their money and the guns found.

You are a whore Amy, he had said. *And whores do what they do best. Being a whore.* He had slipped a hand into his coat pocket, pulled out a bottle, popping the top. He forced her to take several pills. Said it would calm her down.

While they drove away into the night, away from the carnage, away from the wet bodies that had already begun to rot under the nighttime skies, she pondered a single question:

Was it for love?

In all of the three years of marriage with Thomas, Amy couldn't remember a moment of tenderness, a moment where she felt she would protect him. The marriage had been wrong from the beginning. The drugs, alcohol, and sex were for Thomas' own personal gains. She didn't feel like a wife, more like a personal tool to be utilized at his whim and in any way he saw fit. He had told her she was the best whore he had.

Lonnie Blonde, on the other hand, had done something worthwhile. She was protecting her man. She had done something for the love of her man, of this Amy was sure.

Amy vowed she would quit the drugs, quit screwing all the men so Thomas could get his kicks. She wouldn't play along anymore. She would leave, run as far as she could.

She made for one attempt once back in Biloxi. She gathered up a handbag full of dope and disappeared. The running was the easy part. It was kicking the drugs that was going to be a problem. She didn't know where to go and found herself high on coke, drunk and having taken some pills she had in her bag. She had gone to her sister Lorraine's house. She went to her and explained she wanted away from Thomas. Lorraine listened and plied questions. Amy wasn't sure, but she was coked out of her mind, and maybe said things she hadn't meant to. Lorraine took a business card from her desk, scribbled a number on it before handing it to her. "I'll call tomorrow but we have to be quiet about this, you understand, Amy?"

She looked back and found Amy looking at her through tired slits, head lolling on her shoulders.

"Damn it, Amy. I asked if you heard me."

She nodded she had.

"You can sleep here tonight," she said. "Does Thomas know where you are?"

She fell off into a drunken sleep before she could answer.

Tomorrow never came. Amy awoke, grabbed a few things, including a bottle of vintage whiskey Lorraine kept in her study desk. She disappeared in the early morning hours and found a dump of a hotel on the east side of town. She was down to her last bottle of bourbon and a small rock of crack-cocaine. She heard a car door slam, several shadows clouded the window. The door shattered and rough hands grabbed her, dragged her outside. At first, she thought it was the police or some thugs but saw it was the cousins Robert Lee and Cleeve. They took her back to Thomas who told her Lorraine was dead. She wasn't sure if she had heard right.

"Dead?"

"There was a fire, Amy. Do you understand what I told you?" Thomas leered. The smile made her question what had happened.

She was too stoned to think about what had just been said. "When?"

"Yesterday."

"Yesterday," she whispered. She hadn't realized she was so stoned as to lose track of time. "A fire?" She went to grab her bag but Thomas grabbed and shook her.

"You're staying, Amy, you understand?"

"My sister..."

"Dead." He laughed.

She started thinking of ways to kill Thomas and escape.

Several days went by and Amy began to realize going to Lorraine was perhaps the worst idea she had. She tried to escape once more, but Robert Lee was waiting and dragged her back into the house.

More drugs, she wasn't sure what they were but Thomas kept her sedated and supplied.

With Lorraine's death, she felt she had nothing to lose if she killed Thomas. The drugs had taken hold and sunk their claws deep into her brain as a scattered plan came to mind. It wasn't much of a plan, just pieces and fragments of ideas, but it was better than nothing. She took up the .357 revolver Thomas always kept in the living room desk. She didn't know how to use it, but she figured out how to open the cylinder and found six bullets within it. She knew who was responsible. She had done a few lines of coke to calm her nerves, perhaps a few too many, and cradled the revolver in her shaking hands and waited.

His truck pulled into the driveway.

It was raining. Low rumblings of thunder sounded off in the distance.

She slipped beside the front door and waited with the heavy revolver in her trembling hands. The lock turned and the door swung open. He stepped in from the rain.

He turned to close the door and faced the muzzle of the gun. The muscles in his jaws were working. He slowly closed the door. "You don't have it in you, Amy. Put it away."

She sniffled, eyes bloodshot from tears and drugs. The gun shook in her hands.

"Alright, go ahead," he grinned, "do it. Show everyone you got what it takes." Seconds clicked on. He leered. "I'll make it easy for you Amy. Your sister, is this what this is all about, you gutless bitch?"

She thumbed back the hammer. "You...*fucker*. Did you...?" she whispered.

The raindrops pattered on the windows, seconds went by. "I did you a favor, you gutless whore," he whispered. "Coincidence, all coincidence, you feel better now? Now put away the gun." He turned away, walked into the adjoining living room. He tossed the keys down on the desk, lifted the bottle of Jack Daniels and poured a tumbler full. He eyed her as he drank. She didn't know what was worse, when he turned away or the statement of being a gutless whore. The words hung thick in the air.

She pulled the trigger. The explosion and the power of the recoil shocked her and the gun tumbled from her hands and hit the floor with a thud. Thomas turned and saw the bullet had missed him by a foot or better. He laughed and set the glass down on the desk and stormed towards her.

She dropped down to her knees to recover the pistol but Thomas was on top of her. She fought back, screaming, balling her fists and hammering anything on his massive bulk that would hurt him but it had no effect. She might as well have been pounding a brick wall.

He howled in laughter. "God-damn, a wildcat, I didn't know you had it in you!" He grabbed her, a hard slap and she felt blood pouring from her nose and lip. She tried jumping up but he settled the bulk of his weight down on her and slammed her head on the floor. He reached over and grabbed the stainless revolver. He shoved it against her forehead.

"Fucking whore," he whispered. "You like that? You like the feeling I'm going to kill you, Amy?" He slapped her again and stars bounced across her eyes. She felt her eye swell up, stinging and more blood. One of the rings on his hand had cut her just under the left eye.

"I'll kill you, you bastard!" she spat and kept hitting him across the chest. She reached up in an attempt to gouge his eyes but all he did was lean back and swat her arms away and laugh.

He slapped her again, the hit was harder but the punch to her gut took all the fight out of her. She cringed in agony, choked and quit trying to hit back. He stood up and kicked her in her mid-section. She gasped out a loud moan, eyes going wide. Her breath quit and he kicked her again.

"Don't you ever do that again, you understand?" He leaned over and grabbed her hair and yanked it hard. She screamed through hysterical tears. She wanted the pain to stop. The blood from her nose dripped on her blouse and mixed with her tangled hair.

"Look at you now," he sighed and let her go then walked away with the pistol, leaving her lying there withering in pain and crying tears of anguish at her to kill him.

He poured another drink and still held the revolver. He looked at the wall where the bullet had burrowed a tattered hole in the elegant rose print wallpaper. "We'll get through this." He downed the shot and poured another.

She had caught her breath, gasping in pain, she eyed him with rage. Blood continued to run from her nose and lip and dripped to the floor. She rose up on wobbly legs, using the wall to help steady the world from spinning. "I'm leaving, and to fucking hell with you!"

He pointed the revolver at her, took careful, deliberate aim and eased the hammer back. The barrel was steady, unwavering. A flash of lightning followed by a distant rumble of thunder made her jump. "No, Amy, you're not," he smirked, "I love you too much."

She had hoped he would've pulled the trigger. Her brains splashed all over the floor and walls but he didn't. How she wanted this pain to end. "Do it….do…it!" her voice was hoarse.

He stepped over slowly, holding the pistol to her forehead. He grabbed her by the chin. "Get on out of here, Amy. Go get cleaned up." He walked back to the desk and drank another shot while watching her cry in pain as she slowly turned and walked away, clutching her stomach, and still holding the wall for support. "Make sure you get back in here and clean this blood off the floor. This is God-damned two hundred-year old Tobacco Pine you're bleeding on!"

Days went into weeks. The swelling had all disappeared and the cut at the bottom of her eye had scabbed over into a small, thin pale two-inch line in the shape of a crescent moon. There would never be enough makeup to cover that up. At least he hadn't broken her nose.

Thomas said hardly a word to her during this time. She had gone on a cocaine and wine binge hoping for a heart attack but the gods on high had denied her. She stayed in the house, never leaving, just brooding and planning. Thomas made sure she stayed home. She couldn't go to Lorraine's funeral. There was the black Dodge truck parked just down the road with one of his cousins sitting inside. The truck would show up whenever Thomas left. When he came home, the truck would disappear.

He had said if she left, he would find her. He had the resources at his fingertips, so what was the point of running? Was this love? No, she realized, not love, not ever, not after everything. Three years of marriage had produced nothing but misery. The good times had passed away. The drugs, alcohol, and sex with other men for some unseen gain had all left a bitter taste in her mouth. She knew Thomas was seeing other women, especially those at the strip club in downtown Biloxi.

It was time to change.

Thomas left one early morning, as usual, demanding she move her ass to clean up the house, and herself. She didn't respond. She didn't want anything more to do with him, loathed him, wished her hands hadn't shook pulling the trigger and wished the bullet had magically found its way through his skull. She finished her shot of bourbon, feeling the liquor settling into a burning glow deep in her gut.

"Did you hear me, Amy?"

She looked up, a look of contempt etched across her face. She poured another glass full of bourbon. The wine and cocaine had run out days ago. Thomas refused to buy any more. "Fuck you."

He smiled. "Maybe later, I got business to take care of. You know business that keeps this roof over your cute little head." He opened the front door. "Move your ass and get to cleaning yourself up. You really put a spell over the judge from Las Cruces. He wants to see you again." He tugged the jacket sleeves down. "He's here for a legal convention or some shit. We got a nice hotel picked out for the two of you, so dress nice and sexy." He left, slamming the door behind him.

She wandered to the front window, watching him, hating him. He strolled so casually, so sure-footed like nothing had happened, like a dedicated employee dashing off to work with purpose and stride while the loyal wife waited for his return. She felt a weight lift when the engine to his Chevy truck fired up and pulled out of the driveway. He sped off and disappeared over the small rise. The black Dodge was nowhere to be seen.

Late? she mused.

She let the drape fall back over the window. She went to the bedroom and began packing, only filling a small pack. She wanted nothing from this house and everything in it could burn. She could keep trying to kill herself with drugs and alcohol or do something else.

Burn and run. The words played in her mind.

She floated from one room to the next, silently, arms crossed and peering into each one. There was a stench of hate and sex lingering within. When she reached the garage she saw the cherry red 1967 Corvette. The Corvette was what he treasured the most. Big block, rare 427 original with tri pack set up, perfectly tuned and maintained. He changed oil and filters regardless if it needed it or not. He took better care of the car than...*than me*, she thought.

It had been one of many things that had attracted her to him in the first place. He had promised waves of good times and a happy life, but it was nothing more than waves of drug-fueled orgies and violence.

The keys dangled from the ignition.

She went to the living room and looked out the curtains once again. The black Dodge truck was nowhere to be seen. That was odd. She looked up and down the street and the truck was still not there. She hustled back to the bedroom gathering up everything in a small travel bag. There was another .357 revolver. A Smith and Wesson model 28-2 she had found in the closet. Thomas had done his best to remove all the firearms from the house but had missed this one. She had no idea where to go but anywhere was better than here. She quickly grabbed her things, tossed them in the Corvette before throwing the garage door open. She slid behind the wheel, lit up a cigarette, fired off the Corvette and backed out just in time to see Thomas walking back to the front door. He must've forgotten something and was returning to the house.

They locked eyes. She slowly flipped him a middle finger.

His eyes went wide and he lunged forward just as she punched the gas. The rear tires boiled off in a cloud of smoke and dust as she flew out of the driveway backward and slid sideways onto the main street knocking over several trash cans. The elderly neighbor across the street was watering his bushes in a bathrobe. His jaw went slack watching all the commotion. She jammed the forward gears and floored the pedal. The engine roared out thunder and again the tires screamed and took off in a cloud of dust. In the rearview mirror, Thomas had ran into the street but stopped running. She maneuvered the Corvette down back alleys and side streets. If Thomas was back there anywhere, he was going to play hell in catching her this time. She floored the pedal and hit the interstate at a hundred and twenty.

Amy made one stop on the outskirts of Biloxi to a known competitor, bought eight grams of blow and had finished snorting two of those just before passing over the Mississippi State lines. Traffic disappeared in her rearview mirror, and then the Louisiana and Texas state line rose into view. She drove straight through, not daring to stop except for gas and maybe a soda. On through the night, she drove straight into Texas and finally stopped when the trees melted away to vast open deserts.

Where?

Where could she hide? Thomas was sure to try and find her. The exception this time was he would kill her. The Corvette was his most treasured car. She had no doubt. Plus, she knew too much and had become a liability. Thomas' bosses would demand something be done to put her away forever also.

She pulled over in a dirt town, bought several pints of bourbon, topped off the small gallon gasoline jug in the trunk before pushing onwards several miles before turning down a nearby dirt road. The road turned to a dusty trail with deep ruts that ran between the edges of a large swath of cotton fields that had yet come into season. She killed the ignition and watched the western skies while downing a whole pint of bourbon. She came to a sudden realization she could end all of this. The .357 lay on the passenger seat.

She slumped over the steering wheel, broke down and cried. She had failed at avenging her sister, had failed in her marriage and failed at everything. She became things she had never wanted to become. A drug and alcohol soaked addict, the worst was being known as a whore.

She took out the coke and snorted a little more, envying the finality of death and the forever bliss of eternal silence. Crying was not going to fix the problems. Death would eventually come around.

She emptied the Corvette of everything, namely her bag and purse, took the gallon can of gas and began sprinkling it over the red paint and interior. She lit up a smoke and pondered her next move. The choices were limited. Take the .357, blow her brains out or keep moving. She had some money left, but not enough to see the long haul.

She flicked the cigarette into the Corvette. After a few seconds, the interior burst in a flash of flames. She grabbed everything and began the long walk back down the trail, leaving the Corvette burning on the edge of the field. After a couple hours of wandering, she stopped alongside a ditch bank of running water and took another hit of coke and bourbon.

She rummaged through her purse, took out the .357 and tossed it to the ground and found the business card her sister had given her. One phone call would be all it would take to end it all. She studied the card and had a sudden realization.

Lonnie Blonde. She had said something with her dying breath.

"...Under the old pole..."

EIGHTEEN

I leaned back and took in her story.

Amy rocked back and forth on the sofa edge, looking away to the floor. Her mascara had run down her face, tears still ran, sniffling, she wiped away at her nose.

I didn't know what to say. In reality, I didn't know much about her but to hear this slice of her life gave me pause to consider just what the hell I had gotten myself into. Hearing her talk about being an escort, a prostitute, raised concerns but I withheld judgment. People go into prostitution for various reasons. I figured Amy's reasoning was drugs and good times and placed blame on Thomas for that. I couldn't fathom why he would pimp out his own wife other than personal gains and illegal motives. We had never talked about her growing up, I didn't know what high school she had gone to, and I didn't know anything about her. I knew she said she had gone to Mississippi State for accounting but that was about it.

I stood up, stepped into the kitchen and took up my third Heineken before lighting up a cigarette. I stared at the green bottle for a long time.

She looked over, watching, concern was etched across her face. "I know this changes things."

I popped the top, took a slow swallow. "It is a lot....to digest."

She leaned back, sides heaved, but her face changed to one of resolute finality. "I'm sorry about all of this, Logan. I truly am, but whether or not we make it, I need you to give me the money. Your life and Hendricks's life hinges on it."

I handed her the bottle but she declined it. "Look...I...asked for the truth, you gave it. Drugs? I never thought..."

"Six months sober before we met."

"Six months?"

"Rehab."

"And Thomas knew?"

"We talked, but I refused to tell him where I was, and he still doesn't know where I went."

I finished the Heineken and set the empty down on the table.

"It wasn't supposed to go this far, this fling between you and me. I've ruined so many things but the money...you have to understand, I need it."

"I was a fling then? A means to an end?" That hurt to hear.

"Yes," she took out a cigarette and lit it up. Her fingers trembled.

"Revenge against Thomas?"

She nodded. "It wasn't supposed to go on like this but as time went on, my feelings changed for you, please believe that. I didn't think these feelings could..." Tendrils of cigarette smoke filled the void between us. "...could really exist. I've never lied to you, Logan.

Our hearts just got tangled up."

I couldn't imagine what she was really going through, the mangled mash of emotions that had all smashed together at this moment. I had thought she was just this lonely woman who was looking for something more out of life but she was a woman bent on revenge against her husband.

"This Arturo, is he a State cop? He has a skull tattoo on his left hand, and a then rose on his other?"

She nodded. "How would you know?"

"You mentioned tattoos, and I remember a State cop with the same ones you mentioned. When I first broke down outside Moriarty, this State cop, Fernandez was on his name tag, he helped me out."

"He's an evil bastard, Logan, and there's more than just him involved. There's a whole group of dirty cops, just like Arturo, looking for those guns and money."

"And Thomas?"

She furrowed her eyebrows. "What about him?"

"He knows about us."

She looked at the pictures on the floor. "Evidently, he does, but I don't think he would do anything."

"You're sure?"

"I can't say for certain, to be honest. I know too much and he wants me back under his thumb, he wants his whore to go back to work."

"Don't say that you're not a whore, Amy." I let it go. Thomas maybe still loved her but it was in such a way that his viewpoint on the subject was for his own personal self-gratification. It had nothing to do with building a life together. It was focused on the destruction of people's lives for profit. I shifted the subject. "The guns, the money, you wanted to destroy it or something?"

She shook her head. "Not exactly."

I waited for the explanation.

She shook her head, sides heaved. "I can't, but you have to trust me. For everything that we have left in this relationship, up to this point, you have to really place your trust in me."

Trust? Like my ex? I wanted to ask but didn't think it would be fair at this point.

The silence between us grew. I studied her face through all the tears and smeared mascara. It hurt to see her like this. The only sounds to be heard were the rustling of trees outside as the gentle winds pushed through them. If I told her the whereabouts of the money, what was she going to do with it? Run? Was that the end game motive?

We both had kept secrets from each other but she hadn't lied to me up to this point. Maybe hiding things, but she never lied. If I kept the money, at least we had a chance at a new life but…it was blood money and the Dixie Mob wouldn't stop in their search. It would only be a matter of time before we were both killed. It was all headed to a futile end.

"Is there even…an *us?*" I asked.

"If you want it to be then it's a yes."

Everything in life is a gamble. I sighed. I ran my hands through my hair and took a deep drag off my cigarette. I really needed to quit. "Alright, it's out in the well house out back, buried under the reservoir tank."

She slowly handed the bottle back, then with gentle hands, took hold of my face. "You are doing the right thing, Logan. I'm sorry…so sorry if this…what I told you, changes things between us? I mean…"

I took hold of her hands. "Nothing we can't work through. God knows, we all have our problems."

"I'm serious, Logan." She leaned in. "I love you."

The kiss was gentle, soft, and sincere. Nothing like I had

known before.

"Will you stay close to me?" she whispered.

I nodded.

"Where did you find the money?" she asked.

I found that question puzzling. "What's the point? We found the money."

"It's not just about the money, Logan. You and Hendricks had a map or something?"

I leaned over the sofa, looking for the backpack. It was there. I took hold of it and pulled the map out and laid it out. After a few moments, I pointed it out. "There's an old telegraph pole here." I placed a finger on the spot. "There are a few of those poles out there but this one is tangled up in a bunch of dead branches. It's hard to see it unless you're right up on it." I explained what I could in locating it and she listened intently. I told her about the guns still in the container and that they looked like military-grade stuff.

She listened to me finish while carefully folding the map and holding it. "Do you really trust me, Logan?" She tucked the map away in her jacket pocket.

"I do."

"This is just the start of things to come. If you are really serious about us," she squeezed my hand tight. "Will you come along with me?"

I didn't hesitate. "Anywhere, anytime."

"Even if it means leaving everything behind?"

I nodded unsure where she was going with that.

"Please call Hendricks."

I knew he had several days left to work. He had spent the last couple weeks helping Jill pack her things for the odyssey to California. I took up the cell phone and made the call but it went straight to voicemail. I shook my head.

"We have to find him and convince him to give up his cut of the money."

"That's going to take some effort." I didn't even want to mention anything about Hendricks buying Jill a new Dodge Durango.

"He's going to have to and you need to help me convince him." She fell silent for a moment, fidgeting with her hands before looking into my eyes. "I need to tell you something else."

I heard a noise from outside. Like a metal slap, the closing of an automatic pistol. Or was I being paranoid? Then the sound like someone stepping softly on the porch, boards creaking. I stood up. A shadow slipped by the window. Or was that just a car passing by? "Wait."

"But I need to tell you this last thing."

"Hold that thought." The .45 was on the coffee table.

"There's more though."

More? Like how much more? I wanted to ask but the front door exploded and Thomas rushed in with rage and murder in his eyes.

I started to yell out for her to run but she was already headed out the back door.

NINETEEN

Amy bolted out the back door and disappeared into the inky darkness. I couldn't blame her for not sticking around, not after all she had told me. Thomas was going to kill her and I was sure she was thinking I was just behind her. I was hell-bent on following but made a grab for the .45 instead.

It was a dumb move.

Thomas kicked the table and everything flew up in an explosion of fury. Thomas grabbed me by the shirt, then lifted up and slammed me up against the wall. I fell to the floor and ducked as a meaty fist smashed into the plaster wall. I countered with a hard right to the ribs and a left uppercut, but it was like punching a slab of frozen meat. He shoved hard and again I hit the wall before his knee caught me in the gut.

I roared out in rage, lunged forward and shoved him back into the kitchen and against the refrigerator. It teetered under the impact. With my left hand, I came up into a wild hook that hit him just under the rib cage.

Grunting he grabbed me with his free arm and flung me back up against the counter where I felt it crack and give. The counter flipped up when I hit the floor and a heavy boot hit me dead center in the chest. I rolled over, felt the wind knocked out of me but I bounced up, spun just in time to take on the full lunging of the bull. We both flew back into the living room and smashed into the coffee table, sending it scattering in a blast of wooden splinters.

I twisted him forward and gave him a hard left to his ear. He yelped, and then came roaring back with a right of his own to my gut. I tucked over, eyes going cross-eyed, but I lunged forward, screaming and both of us fell to the floor, knocking chairs to all corners of the room.

I grabbed his hair and began slamming it to the hardwood floor. I could see his eyes going cross, but he kicked me over to the left and managed to free himself. We both scrambled up to our feet and locked horns again except I was catching the hard end of the business. He managed to grab my hair with both hands, a couple of knee kicks to the face and I was seeing stars.

I punched his gut with a series of hooks, his belly shook from the impacts and he grunted but the shots had no effect. He slammed an elbow down across my back and I collapsed. A heavy foot came up but missed as I rolled back. I managed to launch back in, but he grabbed me in a bear hug that threatened to crush the wind out of my lungs. I reared my head back and slammed it into his jaw. He let loose, staggered back and toppled over the sofa.

I was far from done. I grabbed a broken section of table leg off the floor. There was no way I could keep this up. Thomas was in much better shape and had a life of violence and experience to back him up. I needed an equalizer.

I clambered over the sofa and grabbed him. I bought the table leg down on top of his head. His eyes glazed over for a second and I slammed the side of his head like a major league player hitting a grand slam. He rolled back and kicked out and caught my leg I felt it buckle. He slammed his meaty hand right into my mouth and I felt the stinging blow flatten and bust my lips open. I kicked out, hitting him the groin, he grunted in agony, knelt over and I charged forward, screaming and managed to shove his head through the plaster wall a few times and managed to knee kick him in the face. Blood began to ooze through the thick layers of plaster coating his face and he smiled wide and screamed a scream something akin to the Vikings of old.

I kept kicking and slamming the table leg down but he was deflecting the blows with his arms. He made a grab for the leg and gripped it like a vise. I started kicking him until he slumped and I stomped his face several times. He was still smiling, shaking off the hits and each countermove he threw, became weaker. He let loose of the table leg but I was winded. I was running out of gas though, my kicks were becoming increasingly weaker and soon we both collapsed from sheer fatigue.

I stumbled up to my feet. Gasping, I tossed the table leg to the floor and staggered to the back door. I had to find Amy and we had to run like hell. Thomas rolled over and was up on his knees grabbing my .45. I cursed myself for leaving it out.

"Hey!" Cleeve suddenly filled the front doorway with his enormous bulk.

I whirled, working the back door handle frantically. Shadows moved behind him in a flurry of activity but I wasn't having it. The door popped open like a hidden trapdoor from Hell into the Heavens of the cool night. I threw the door open, heaved myself out and took off running as fast as my feet could carry me into the surrounding thick clusters of juniper and salt cedar brush.

I wasn't sure which way Amy had gone. I was sure Cleeve and Robert Lee were supposed to catch anyone coming out the back door but Amy managed to get out and run before the cousins were in place. It was safe to assume then Thomas had jumped the gun and charged through the front door like a scalded bull in the proverbial china shop. If he had been patient, they would've caught both of us. As it stood, I was the only one left to catch. With Cleeve and Robert Lee closing in, I had little chance of escape. The odds were stacking up against me. I just hoped Amy would stay running.

I was running like hell, cursing and wishing I had the .45. I chose the better part of valor and took to running. Running and nowhere near where I wanted to be, slamming one lead clogged foot after another forward and not getting anywhere. I could feel the sticky, warm film of blood oozing from the throbbing cuts across my face and chest. Maybe running was a bad idea, but when your life depends on it, running away is always the best thing to do. I had other things to worry about though.

The hounds of the Devils Dog Pound were running and nipping at my heels in the thick darkness behind me. Their giant bulks crashed through the thin Juniper and pine timber like it was a minor annoyance. I looked back once, their Buick-sized frames smashing through and there wasn't a thing I could do about it either. Bile, fear and the twisted knot of adrenaline-soaked despair gnawed at my gut. Dying was not a forte of mine and I had plans to keep going, keep running, and the way I was going, I could've run back to Las Vegas nonstop if they'd let me.

Money. It all boiled down to the money. I cursed through thick, swollen lips, cursed Hendricks for talking me into looking for it. I calculated he was dead about now. Probably with his brains blown all over the living room walls with a cigarette still perched neatly between his fingers. *The bastard! When we're in Hell together, I was going to beat his ass for the rest of eternity!*

I hit a low spot in the ground, felt my foot slide out, my weight shifted and I slid to the ground face first amongst the thick layers of old and decayed pine needles. I rose up just in time to feel the meaty bulk slam into me from behind like a freight train. I felt my breath blow out of my lungs and together we fell to the ground with my face being ground into the pine needles with hard force.

I groaned, cursed again, and then felt the weight lift off of me. I rolled over and saw the two standing above me, one held a giant hand cannon. Southern boys like their guns big. I guess it makes up for lack of manhood or something, but I ain't saying that to their face...not right now.

"Logan..." The deep southern drawl spilled out from the giant shadow. The cocking of the hand cannon really bought focus into my eventual demise. The gun was steady, solid, and sure in its owner's hard hand. There wasn't a trace of fear in the business end threatening to swallow my soul whole. It was all business and business was about to be booming. The dim moonlight reflected off the stainless steel finish, the dark maw slowly opening to eternity. With a maw like that, you didn't dare talk shit to it.

.44? I mused.

I gave a small smile and felt the busted lip open up. I held a hand up, hoping to avoid getting splattered by a close-range cannon shot or the ass beating I was sure was coming. But money, lots of it, means people will bust your ass for it, kill you even. Amy was right. I realized too late that going for the money was a bad idea.

"Now guys...." I started to gather my feet under me, realizing running was going to be a fruitless effort. I'd had my hands full with Thomas and the winds of fighting were gone from my sails. I didn't have the strength to take on Pee Wee Herman let alone two steroid pumped hit men. These guys must work out…all the time. Running would be in their workout regimen right along with bench pressing hundreds of pounds of weights.

All I had was brains and some brawn from being a diesel mechanic, but nothing as compared to the sheer masses facing me.

"Now…I know we can come up with something better than this." It was all I managed to get out before the giant booted foot came swinging out. The blow to the gut kicked the wind right out of me. I was thinking of Amy in those last seconds. Life, I was finding out, usually ended with happy thoughts, or things uncompleted. Amy was all I thought about. Where was she? Was she alive or had the Dog Pound killed her also?

Robert Lee and Cleeve leaned down, took hold of a leg and dragged me back through the thick brush like two demons going about their duties of retrieving a sinner's soul from the winds of freedom. At least they hadn't knocked me out, or maybe that was a bad thing. Maybe they wanted to make sure I saw what was coming next.

I cursed and they kept dragging me along. The sharp pine needles and chunks of wood dug against the skin on my back. They stopped just outside the back door where Thomas was waiting. They dropped my feet just behind the El Camino.

Thomas held a handkerchief and wiped away the blood from his lips. He looked to Cleeve. "Where's Amy?"

He shook his head. "Nothing."

He swore. "She got away then?"

Robert Lee nodded. "We looked, but didn't see which way she went."

"You jumped the gun before we were in position, Thomas." Cleeve pointed a thick finger. "Uncle ain't too happy either."

Thomas swore then looked down. His eyes were full of hate and rage. "I'm sure lover boy here knows some of the answers we're looking for. Where's the money? We found some of it inside."

"Fuck you, Thomas."

He kicked out a booted foot deep into my gut. My breath exploded from gritted lips. "Not in a million years. Where's the money, fuck-stick?"

Gasping, I rolled over and looked up with my best expression of defiance. Robert Lee knelt down, grabbed my hair and slammed my face against the rear bumper of the El Camino. My nose exploded in a bloom of blood.

"The money, Logan."

"Out in the well house, under the storage tank." I hoped Amy was nowhere near the area.

Thomas nodded. "Alright, Robert Lee, go get the money. Cleeve…load up this piece of shit."

Cleeve grabbed my arm, pulled me up on wobbly feet. There was a sedan parked in the shadows some twenty feet off. I could see the dark shape of another man sitting behind the steering wheel. A plume of cigarette smoke rose up from the driver's window. Cleeve shoved hard and I staggered toward the sedan but Thomas held up a hand. "No, we're taking the El Camino."

I was curious about the fourth man seated in the sedan. The red-tipped end from the cigarette glowed bright but I wasn't able to make out any recognizable features. Whoever it was, he was watching as Cleeve shoved me in the back of the El Camino. He climbed in after me and slapped a heavy hand on my head. The other thick hand held the .44, the barrel end pointing down to my eyes. "You move, you die."

I couldn't argue with that point.

Robert Lee materialized out of the dark shadows holding the ragged backpack. "Got it."

"Money in it?" Thomas asked.

He nodded.

"Good. Put it in the car and let's roll." Thomas then leaned over the railing. "Well, looks like we got all of it now." He snorted. His smile widened. "I thought you would be tougher. Hendricks put up a better fight."

"Is he...?" Not really wanting to know the answer. After everything we had done and now it boiled down to this.

He frowned. "Escaped just like Amy. My inept cousins couldn't catch a house flying in a tornado," his gaze was smoldering dark coals. "But we have you and that's fine with me."

"Then why are you taking me anywhere? You got what you wanted. Why not end this now?"

"Amy. My wife, she is still my wife. I'll let you ponder that on our way to my house." He slid off the side and opened the door to the El Camino and fired it off. The sedan behind us then started its own engine, and together we took off down the dirt roads. We moved down the main road, hung a left headed west. We were taking the backroads to Thomas' house. Cops usually avoided the backroads. They were too busy working the main highways looking for drunk drivers or responding to domestic disputes.

I felt my gut sink. The night was going to be long and drawn out. I thought about the morning sunrise, Amy and how beautiful they had been. I realized at that moment, I was never going to see another of those days again.

TWENTY

Going down 217 gave me plenty of time to think and rethink my dilemmas and future. The El Camino headed down a bunch of back roads and dusty trails with the mystery sedan following close behind. We hit eighty before making the turn on Juan Thomas and accelerating into the inky darkness. The asphalt road faded into dust and rumble strips but Thomas kept the pedal mashed steady to the floor and Cleeve held the muzzle of the .44 pressed against my head. I just hoped his trigger finger wouldn't slip and plaster my brains all over the bed of the El Camino.

Several turns later and the El Camino slid to a stop. Cleeve jumped out and dropped the tailgate then motioned with the hand cannon to get out. The sedan that had been behind us drove by silently and continued up the trail to a house nestled within the trees. It was a Buick LeSabre but the windows were tinted to such a degree I couldn't see the driver.

Thomas shoved me forward. "You think you had her?"

I didn't say anything.

"Just wait." He slapped the back of my head. I reared back to fight but Cleeve slammed the butt of the .44 revolver across the side of my head. I stumbled and fell. Robert Lee held a .44 AutoMag and kicked my leg. "Get up."

Cleeve reached down and yanked me up to my feet. Thomas shoved hard from behind. He pulled a .500 Smith. "Nice necklace."

The necklace had slid out from under the shirt and now dangled in plain sight. He reached over but I reared back. Cleeve and Robert Lee held me in steel-like grips. Thomas clutched the necklace and with a quick tug, the links snapped. He held it up under the dull light of night. "She gave this to you?"

I refused to give him a response.

He smiled. "I'm surprised she did. That bitch would still be alive if Amy hadn't run to her and told her everything." He lifted the .500 and planted the barrel against my forehead. "I'm going to do the same thing to you."

"What? Set me on fire? Fuck you, twat!" I started to launch myself forward but was poleaxed by a sharp blow to the back. I hit the ground and staggered up to my feet. "You gutless fuck!"

He lifted the .500 and slammed the barrel down across the bridge of my nose, blood drained from my nostrils once more and I fell back to the ground. He stood over me and thumbed back the hammer. I looked up in defiance and gritted teeth. Blood drained from my nostrils. "Go on, you fuck....do it."

He smiled. "Not yet, but it's coming, and I'll make sure it's a closed casket. Get up."

I stood up on wobbling feet, wishing the world would stop spinning. Then the four of us moved up the trail. Up ahead, I could see the lights from a house hidden in the trees. A couple of cars were parked there, one of those being the Buick. The other was a Cadillac CTS and I recognized it.

Dwayne. I swore.

Thomas led the way through the door, carrying the backpack. "We come bearing gifts."

Dwayne's voice was unmistakable. "About time."

I walked in and the room fell silent. Dwayne looked up and stopped counting the stacks of money. I assumed it was Hendricks share of the missing money. The blonde bookkeeper, Andrea, slowed her count but kept going. "What the hell is he doing here, Thomas?" Dwayne stood up.

"Relax. We need the guns as well, and fuck boy here knows where they're at." He dropped the backpack by the table where they were counting.

"It's about Amy isn't it?"

He slapped Dwayne's shoulder. "And that too."

"We don't have time, Thomas. The Feds are barking up our ass and you make it a time for revenge."

"Business and pleasure sometimes mix."

"Damn it, Thomas. Really?"

Thomas motioned for me to step forward and when I refused, Cleeve landed a solid punch to my lower back. I fell to my knees and cursed.

"Where's...?" Thomas asked.

Dwayne shook his head. "In the den."

"Andrea?"

She looked up from counting.

Thomas produced a small pistol from his jacket pocket. "If he moves, shoot him in the balls or kneecaps."

Andrea nodded, took the pistol and flipped the safety off. She pointed the muzzle within inches of my face.

Thomas motioned for Dwayne to follow and the four men moved off to an adjoining room. He took the necklace and Amy's ring and tossed them down on the heavy granite kitchen counter as he passed by it. I was thinking of angles to get the ring back but was drawing a blank. After a few minutes, voices rumbled off from the room. Shadows dancing, weaving in the dim light cast from within. There was a Hell in there and I had no intentions of being sucked into it. I eyed the front door.

Andrea sat on the edge of the sofa, puffing gently on her cigarette. The small frame automatic pointed in my face. She eyed me with narrowed slits and gave a thin smile. Right about now I was craving a smoke but she wasn't offering.

Thomas could be heard in the next room talking in low tones to someone. I paused, wiped away the blood from my nose until Cleve came out and grabbed me by the shirt and yanked me up to my feet. We walked by the counter and I saw the broken necklace and ring tossed there. I thought about making a grab for them but thought better of it. Cleeve shoved me forward hard enough to knock the wind out of a water buffalo. I entered the room.

Once in, Cleeve shoved again and I fell to the floor. Instead of feeling plush carpet, I realized a clear tarp had been placed over it. I felt the plastic crinkle under my weight. I was sure I was going to die.

"That'll be enough Cleeve."

The voice jolted memory and I looked up. Robert Lee and Cleeve had filed into the room. Dwayne poked his head up from the floor. There was some sort of access panel leading down under the house. He smiled and lifted a heavy bag up to land on the floor. I wasn't sure what was going on but Thomas looked to have had a stash of money under the house. Thomas stood in front of me. Another man was standing nearby but I couldn't get a good look at him.

The figure spoke with absolute authority. "Dwayne? Go take the bags in the living room and let's finish counting. We have a long road in front of us."

Dwayne climbed out of the hole in the floor and grabbed the bag and lifted it up and left the room where he was met by Andrea.

Thomas shifted and the man's face turned to me.

"*Hobart?*" I whispered.

He smiled, took his jacket and set it across the bed. A small frame .38 snub-nosed was stuffed into a tanned and well-oiled shoulder holster rig. The brass cartridges within the leather loops gleamed under the dull light. "You know, Logan, I always liked you. Never once did you ever treat me like crap or say a cross thing."

I went back through my mental files and remembered Hendricks warning me about the Dixie Mafia connection. Right about now I could kick my own ass for not running away then. I craned my head up, feeling the blood running in thick streams from my nose. "Mafia?"

He frowned and shook his head. "It is what you say, but we prefer 'business associates.' Mafia is such a strong and rough word to use these days." He looked at his fingernails. "Cleeve, would you be so kind and fetch Logan a towel for his nose?"

Cleeve left the room for a brief moment and returned with a pink towel and handed to me. I sat on my ass and placed the towel against my nose, wiping away the blood as much as I could.

Hobart continued. "You know Logan, hard work never hurt anyone. I admire people who work hard and have set goals in life, that's why I like to work back in the shop. Sure I could have done some plush office job, maybe even complex manager, but I liked being a mechanic as it has a certain romantic appeal to it."

I didn't move. The stinging salt from the nose soaked the towel but looked to have stopped for the moment. I was sure my nose was broken. "Rainmaker…you're the man that got called in to fix Thomas' fuck up."

Thomas bristled with contempt but said nothing.

Hobart smiled. "Well, he is my nephew, along with Cleeve and Robert Lee. Now, pray tell, how would you know such things? Let me guess, Amy."

I didn't respond. I could feel the walls closing in.

"It sounds fair to say, she may have spoken too much on delicate matters."

"She didn't have to tell me anything."

"Anyone ever say how bad a liar you are?" Before I could respond, he cut me off with a wave of his hand. "We have so much to discuss, Logan." He sipped his coffee and then leaned over to the table and picked up a stack of photographs. He held one up with me and Amy kissing, then another but a different angle. "I took an interest in photography at an early age. I liked to photograph people and the everyday goings-on in their lives."

"You took the photos," I stated.

"Both of you are very charming together." He looked up to Thomas and laughed. Thomas though wasn't amused.

"Why?"

"It moved you to action did it not? When Hendricks bought his whore a new Dodge Durango with cash, I knew the both of you had the money." Hobart set the photographs down gently on the nearby table.

"How long…did you know?"

"About the money or your fornicating with my nephew's wife?"

"Amy."

"For some time now. My nephew is quite upset about it as you can see, but I managed to hold him in check until we got what we needed." He leaned forward in the chair. "And then there's this mess with the money and such. What to do, what to do?" He rubbed his hands together.

"Keep the money," I said.

"Oh, we plan to, Logan."

I exhaled sharply. Blood dripped on the towel.

Hobart nodded and looked at his wristwatch, a Rolex from what I could tell, and not one of those cheap ones either. "We haven't much time, Logan."

"Time for what?"

"I know about Amy and you, it is rather obvious you two are carrying on sexual relations that would make the Bill Clinton blush. It rather provides a unique problem. On one hand, we have Thomas here, the jealous husband, and then there's you, Hendricks and the money and the Feds and missing guns."

"Where's Hendricks?" I demanded.

Hobart looked around the room before settling his gaze on Thomas. "It would seem he is not here for this gathering. He somehow managed to escape," his eyes rolled over to Cleeve and Robert Lee. "Along with Amy, it is such a shame we have only you, but, we will find them in due time."

"Feds?"

He stood up slowly, sighed and went over to the window and peered out. "Quite a mess indeed," he lit up a cigarette. "The FBI is wandering around again. Someone has tipped them off as to the going ons at Duggan's and we have yet to discover who would do such a thing, but we have a few ideas." He turned, blew out a plume of smoke. "What says you, Logan? Do you know what truly is going on here or have you not the faintest idea?"

"First time I've heard about the Feds," I swallowed hard. Something told me I better choose my words carefully.

He turned and faced me. The coffee cup in his hand tremored slightly. "Boy, something tells me different."

"I'm serious as shit, I don't know anything about any of this."

"You lying boy. I can smell it."

Robert Lee chuckled, which sounded like a couple boulders rolling down a hillside.

Hobart wasn't smiling though. "You see..." he set the coffee cup down on the nearby table. "Some things just don't add up. One being you and Hendricks just happened upon our money, then we got the FBI poking around again at Duggan's. I find this hard to believe but..." He knelt down in front of me, took hold of my jaw. "I think you're lying. I think Amy told you where this money was located. I think perhaps the three of you had dreams of grandeur about a life that could be. I find it so hard to believe just you and Hendricks were on a treasure hunt and just happened to figure out the puzzle of Dave Musgrave's misbegotten fortune."

I shook my head. Sweat was rolling down my forehead. "You got this all wrong Hobart, I swear."

He stood up. His face became a distorted mask of hatred with a wide leering smile. "A shame we have to go down this road, Logan. I had such high expectations of our conversation here but now I'm disappointed."

He nodded.

Cleeve stepped forward, forced me on my stomach and landed a hard knee in the small of my back. The air blew out of my lungs. Blood and sweat smeared across the tarp.

Hobart continued with a sick smile stretched across his face. "Where is Amy? I'm sure you do know, surely, you two made plans."

I gave an honest reply. "I don't know, Hobart, I swear to God!"

He nodded and Cleeve leaned in and grabbed my left fist but I wasn't having any of it and fought back. He cursed and slapped the side of my head with a hard, cupped hand. The response is immediate and he seized one of my fingers with a firm, hard grip. I knew what was coming and I scream.

Hobart plied the question again. "Where is she, Logan? It's a rather simple question to answer."

Breathing hard, I felt cold sweat wash over me. I know what's coming. The bubbles of blood from my busted nose tickle the nostrils. "I swear dammit! I don't know! God-damn it! Don't…!"

Hobart nods.

I feel a quick tug and wet snap. The pain was immediate and I screamed, slamming my head against the floor. Cleeve landed a blow to my ribs with a balled fist that resembled a hit from a sledgehammer and I balled up in pain. I was sure a rib cracked.

Thomas laughed. I wished to God I had managed to grab the .45 and blow his ass into the afterlife.

Hobart lit up another cigarette and blew a plume of dirty smoke in my face. "You doing this to yourself boy. This is not a game we be playin.' Now, I ask again, where is she?"

If I had known where she was, I might've given her up by this point, but I wasn't going to give in. I shook my head. There was no point in answering. I had hoped maybe Hobart would be satisfied with my mangled body. He had plied the question enough times with the same answer to hopefully leave me alone. My life was damn near at an end. I could feel the cold shadows of Death cascading over my soul.

"You're lying again. Why do this to yourself?" He sighed and gave a nod.

I immediately felt Cleeve grabbing for the finger next to the mangled joint and I resisted, bucking and fighting back to keep him from getting a firm grip. He had a fight grabbing the digit, so much so that Robert Lee had to help. He jumped in, landed a knee on the side of my head, pinning it hard to the thick tarp. Hobart nodded and another wet snap. I scream and stars bounced across my vision.

Hobart looked down and shook his head. "I don't think you understand what position on the field you're supposed to be playing. You do understand Amy is wanted by the Feds?"

Gasping, I let out a belch, feeling the thin fluids of bile rising up my throat. This was new to me, and I had no idea why Amy would be wanted by the Feds. "I don't know anything about the Feds."

Hobart was yelling, his face deep red. "Of course you do. You two were fuck-buddies last I heard. Surely, she told you these things whispered in dark shades of sweet passion, humping like two mongrel bitches?"

"Didn't say a damned word Hobart, I swear. I don't know anything you're talking about." The pain from the two mangled fingers shot wave after wave through my body and I was shaking from fear, rage and the future prospect of a slow death.

"The guns?" Thomas asked.

Hobart nodded. "Where are they then?"

"Under an old telegraph pole."

"Which one? There are many of those out there!"

I explained which one and what landmarks to look for. The only exception was I told them south of the ranch house, not north. It would be my own secret I would take with me to the grave much like Musgrave had taken his to his own. It would be my last act of defiance but I had to keep a straight face.

Hobart studied my face for a long time. He wasn't buying my explanation apparently or he felt I had served his purpose and chose to discard me much like a dirty tissue. "Make it look like suicide, Robert Lee."

He stepped forward, planted the .45, my own pistol, up to my forehead. Cleeve paused. "Robert, wait."

For a moment I had the fleeting thought someone had pity before realizing what a stupid thought that was.

Cleeve mulled it over. "If you shoot him in the forehead, the cops might think it's murder."

Robert Lee rolled his eyes. "What is it you propose we do?"

Cleeve looked into my eyes. "Under the chin, I think would be best. Maybe if we blew out all his teeth, cut the fingertips off and such, we scatter the rest of the parts."

Hobart laughed. "True, we make him disappear in pieces so even if one part is found it's unidentifiable."

Robert Lee stood up, held the pistol in open hands. "Well, why try and make it look like a suicide then?"

"Can I do this?" Thomas injected. "He was dicking my wife and I do have some say in this?"

All three looked over to Thomas. Hobart thought for a moment, sucking his lips. "True, Thomas does have that."

"Damn," Robert Lee muttered. He handed my .45 over to Cleeve and pulled his AutoMag to check the chamber.

All my life is down to this second, this sliver of time. My thoughts moved from when I was kid riding my bike with a baseball card rattling against the spokes. Blowing on a dandelion for the first time, my first kiss with Denise Dodd in the third grade, everything. No monuments would be erected in my memory, no library named after me, nothing. I would be washed away and lost forever in a vast ocean of countless unknown and forgotten souls. In ten years no one would remember my name or who I was. Thomas stepped forward, placed the .500 against my forehead. I looked him in the eyes. He gave a small smile, his eyes casual like he was examining a fine meal at some upscale restaurant. At the least, if I were going to die, I wasn't going to give the prick the satisfaction of showing fear.

Seconds. Life. It's going to end like this.

The hammer on the .500 pulled back ever so slowly, each click sounds like thunder. His smile widened.

The sudden explosion shocks me to the core. My heart froze but found it's still beating.

The drywall and the window explode inward. Cleve stumbled back, his chest opened and closed for a fraction of a second, his face scrunched up in sudden agony, the .44 hanging from limp hands.

Everyone was shocked, the sound of glass and bullets flying. Thomas spun the .500 around, pointing out and began firing through the window. Hobart pulled his .38. All hell cracks open.

More gunfire and my ears are throbbing and ringing from the sudden claps of rapid thunder. The bullets have no problem punching through the double-wide trailer. It's made of press wood, pressed cardboard, and thin sheetrock. We might as well have been crammed inside a cardboard box.

Am I dead? I still feel the broken fingers and realize I'm not. I made a mad dash for the doorway.

Screams of rage, gunfire sparking off like broken diamonds shattering the darkness and I realize we got new players in the mix.

TWENTY-ONE

Death was a new phenomenon, a learning experience. I had seen death but only as an observer from the outer edges of life. Flashback to July fourth of 2003. I can still see a nineteen-year old girl, dead with a white sheet draped over the driver side of what had once been a Toyota sedan. Images flashed of my grandmother gasping out the last of her life and my own father dying from cancer. This time I was in it, front row seats.

I crawled out of the room, past Cleeve gasping for breath on the floor, and grabbed the .45 lying near him. Wincing, I made it to the living room when another round of gunfire ripped into the double-wide forcing me back into the kitchen. Drywall dust and wood splinters blew through the air, glass shattered, stuffing from the sofa and currency from the table, exploded into the air. My ears rang from gunfire coming from the inside and out.

Andrea shrieked. The small pistol Thomas had given her spilled from clawed fingers. She stood up to run, but caught a ripping burst of full-auto across the back before dumping the table over and spilled out over the floor. The room showered in a cloud of thin mist of blood. Blood sprayed over the floors and walls, she tumbled, gurgled and twitched, her once bright blue eyes looking off into forever land.

Dwayne screamed at Andrea's quivering death spasms, his eyes fluttering wildly in terror like he had seen the Grim Reaper coming for him. He pulled some cheap looking chrome pistol and began blasting the room wildly. Everything around him exploded in a flurry of destruction. His gunshots weren't enough to counter the incoming carnage. He took off running for the front door only to be torn to shreds in a rain of hot copper-jacketed death. Blood exploded over the door jamb, his jaw hung open in surprise, before slumping over outside, his foot hanging just inside the doorway, twitching from sudden death.

The bullets were not giving up. Whoever was out there wanted to make sure everyone in here was dead and full of holes. Splotches of purple clouded my vision for a moment. Each shot jolted my nerves into spasms and my heart threatened to explode. The next swarming cloud of hot death must've hit the electrical box. The lights flickered, a bright pulsing flash of blue lit up outside. A curtain of darkness fell across the house. The only light left was from the rays of moonlight floating through the windows and bullet holes in the walls.

I took advantage of the sudden lull, gathered my feet under me, and took two galloping steps across the kitchen. Shattered glass and debris were all over the place. I suddenly felt my feet lose grip with the floor, sliding over the glass. I slipped and twisted sideways and slammed the floor hard enough to rattle my teeth and pop my jaw. I felt a sudden, sharp and agonizing pain of something ripping through my denim trousers and tearing through the thick muscles of the thigh. I screamed in agony just as the staccato of gunfire picked up in tempo. More debris exploded through the air. Looking down, I saw part of a glass winged unicorn. It was missing a large section of its wing. The broken piece was buried deep in my thigh, angry blood boiled around the edges. I groaned through gritted teeth and the ripping chainsaw of gunfire kept exploding around me.

Thomas pulled a twelve gauge from somewhere and shot belching flames out through the shattered window in the adjoining room. Hobart began firing back through the same window.

Robert Lee rolled out of the room with his massive .44 AutoMag. He narrowed his eyes to angry slits and started lifting up the hand cannon. I frantically crawled backward further into the kitchen, cutting my hands and arms on the shattered dishes. In the next second, I was going to see angels or demons. I whispered the name of God's son in a vain attempt at redemption. Robert Lee's massive bulk suddenly shuddered violently. Large, red splotches ripped across his gut and he doubled over screaming before cutting loose with his hand cannon, blasting the floor around me hoping to drag me to Hell with him in his last moments. He fell to his knees, groaned then twisted and fell on his side next to Cleeve. He quickly clutched Cleeve's hand, muttering something when another chainsaw sound swept through the house.

I ducked and felt the kitchen exploding all around me. Water lines burst, the kitchen sink and counter above disintegrated, cabinet doors collapsed. I looked up again and saw Robert Lee still clutching Cleeve's hand but half his skull was missing, blood and brains pumped out in a thick glob over the floor. I winced and gagged.

"We got to get out!" Thomas screamed.

Hobart said something but it was drowned out by all the noise.

Cleeve had the other magazines to the .45 and I crawled over to him. Gagging, I fumbled through his jacket pocket, found the two magazines, and slid back just as another wave of lead splashed across the corpse.

A shadow popped up down the hall in front of me, followed by a burst of lightning that shot lead all around. Whoever it was, was trying to breach the house and finish off everyone. The counter above exploded, splinters nailed my cheek. I raised the .45 up and emptied the mag. The slide locked back just as the shadow disappeared back outside.

Dumping the magazine, I gasped, adrenaline pumped hard through my system. I screamed like a bitch in the midst of angry shouts. Gunfire and bullets impacted and exploded through everything.

I wanted to live to see the morning light, see another sunrise, touch the trees, and feel the sun's rays of warmth wash over my skin. I loaded another magazine with shaking hands, hit the slide release and felt it slam home. I looked around quickly, looking for anywhere to hide. Then I saw it. Bullets had left deep impact marks in the solid oak kitchen table. It had withstood the onslaught so far. Leaning over, I grabbed its edge and with heavy effort, tipped it over and it slammed to the floor. I pulled myself behind it.

A shotgun blast tore the edge. I poked a quick look and Thomas racked the pump and blasted another round at the table just as I pulled back. I stabbed the .45 around the edge and pulled the trigger twice. Now, I was in a gunfight with Thomas and Hobart. The gunfire from outside paused. It was a sure bet the men outside were wondering what the hell was going on.

Hobart paused when he saw his dead nephews, screamed in rage when he saw I was still among the living. He reloaded his pistol, shot off a couple, turned and fired two at in my direction. We traded more shots before a new threat shadowed the front door. We quickly pointed our guns away from each other and at the doorway. For that fraction of time, we were unwilling allies. Our common enemy waited at the gates of our impending deaths. Our eyes darted from each other to the new threat hovering there.

"You a dead man, Logan," Hobart whispered hoarsely.

I didn't say anything, staring at the front door and keeping a wary eye on where Hobart and Thomas were pointing their own guns.

Thomas reloaded the twelve gauge, stuffing thick rounds into the tube. "When I find that bitch, Logan, I'm going to...."

He didn't finish. Another burst of gunfire from outside sent everyone grabbing for cover. I fell back behind the table and waited out the storm of lead. I popped up and fired off a few rounds at Thomas, but he managed to stuff his large frame behind a thick wooden dresser. The slide locked back and I ducked back down.

The rattling staccato of gunfire from outside began again just as I dropped out of sight. Bullets and lead angrily chewed on the overturned table. I muttered a curse while reloading the .45. Somehow, Hobart and Thomas had not been hit, not so much as a scratch. Hobart shot off the last few rounds from his .38 while Thomas banged off a few from the sawed-off pump. Hobart knelt down, rolled his head and began reloading. I hit the slide release, reared up and shot another round at him, but he had pulled back. Everything ground down to slow motion and the gunfire from outside seemed to pause. Maybe the bastards were reloading, who knew. At any moment, whoever was out there was going to breach and kill us all.

Hobart crouched low and began firing, the bullets digging into the tabletop, sending splinters flying. He rose up for a better shot, his frame fell into my .45's sites. I pulled the trigger and his chest opened and closed in a fraction of a second. Blood exploded out everywhere, splashing the doorway and nearby walls. Not only had my shot hit him, but the ripping death wave of spewing lead started back up again.

He stumbled forward and took a dive, hitting the counter with his face and slumped to the floor. A pool of blood began leaching out to mingle with the water.

Thomas heaved himself out of the room, the twelve gauge pump held tight at hip level, he craned his thick neck, and his eyes fell on me. He swung fast as I rolled away but I felt the searing heat of buckshot ripping and biting through denim. Screaming, I shot off a couple rounds only to see him fall away from view behind the wooden table.

The gunfire resumed from outside, more holes, more shit flying and I was on my last leg...literally. I screamed again and heard Thomas shooting out the back door. I lifted the .45 but he saw it coming, swung the sawed-off my way and banged off a round. The buckshot blast hit the overturned table. Splinters exploded blinding me for a split second, but it was all he needed. I felt the sudden heat slap my shoulder, agony rippled through the muscles then blood began running down my bicep. I quickly leaned over the table edge. The .45 weighed a ton in my hand. We locked eyes and he pulled the trigger on the shotgun. There was a loud click. He cursed, dropped the shotgun and flew out the back door leaving it swinging in the gentle breeze. I chased him with the last rounds of the magazine but hit nothing but drywall. The slide locked back on the .45.

I hoped the bastard would've gotten shredded but the gunfire fell silent. I found this odd and wondered how he even managed to accomplish not getting his ass shot off. Either the guys outside were either too shocked to shoot him or were possibly wondering what the hell was going on inside. It was a fair guess for the later. We were not only shooting back at the intruders but we had blown each other to hell in here.

Several minutes drifted by and I was in agony, wondering how to get out alive. I shifted my legs. Shattered glassware lay all over the floor and water stood well over a couple inches. Hobart's blood leaked out in thin rivulets mixing with the sludge and water.

"Who's all in there?"

My ears were ringing from all the gunfire. Should I even answer? I ejected the magazine and realized I didn't have any more ammo for the .45. I was in for the slow ride to hell unless something happened. I groaned through gritted teeth, blood ran from my shoulder, my damn legs and everything burned. Pulsing throbs of pain rippled through my body in waves with each beat of my heart. Slowly, I rose up, feeling the glass grinding deep in the thigh muscles, the buckshot tears in the other thigh opened and oozed blood but I was mobile. If I could stand, I could run but it was going to hurt like hell.

Throughout all the carnage, I spotted a glimmer of hope. The broken necklace and ring lay on the shattered countertop. I brushed away the debris and picked it up. The ring was all I cared about at this moment. I stuffed it in my pocket. If I was going to die or live, at least the ring was coming with me.

"We know someone's in there."

I stayed silent and moved my leg and then leaned over from behind the counter. Hobart lay just a few feet from me, his .38 just a mere foot or so from dead, twitching fingers. The money, the main bone of contention in this mess, blew about in the soft breeze that filtered in through shattered windows busted up drywall and open doors. His eyes had a dimmed, faded view of eternity beyond. He twitched once but I knew he had gone to meet his Creator.

I knelt down and fumbled for the .38 with shaking fingers. The glass sliced and ground its way further into my calf muscle, the floor under me was slick with blood and water. I stifled off a scream and moaned in agony through thin lips.

About this time, I was feeling pissed off. I had no idea who these bastards were outside but if I was going out, someone was coming with me down the yellow brick road to eternity. I cursed it wasn't Thomas. I grabbed the counter for support, leaned over, and used the remaining shreds of curtain flowing in the gentle breeze for cover and took a look outside. I could've shit kittens and fireballs.

Out in the dim moonlight, Richardson was reloading an AR. Richardson, the same cop at the ranch talking with Cleeve and Robert Lee, the same cop I saw in the restaurant the day before yesterday and who asked about the money so long ago when I repaired the tire on his cruiser. He whistled, waved a hand and was soon joined by Nguyen also armed with some other large caliber rifle machine gun. Another man joined them armed also with an assault rifle. His Hispanic features were twisted in anger, but the tattoos on the back of his hand told me it was Fernandez. The three of them conversed for a moment in the lull. I had the .38 and that was it. I could blast those last bullets into Richardson's cranium but I'd be dead seconds later. The shadows shifted and two more men joined the trio. They were all decked out in black tactical gear and armor. It was a safe bet they were all cops at their day jobs.

These cops weren't here for a social visit or to bust up the Dixie Mafia. They were here to settle vendettas. Dave Musgrave, a known Dixie mob member, was murdered over the money and guns. It made sense to think these five cops had come to rectify the problem of getting their guns. Since they didn't have the guns, which Thomas and Dwayne had promised them, they would go after the money, and if possible, the guns. These were bad cops, dirty bastards, who had pimped out their souls to gain a financial edge over others of their profession.

Fuck, fuck and fuck!

I looked back behind me. The back door swung lightly in the breeze. I calculated four, maybe five shooters waiting outside and then there was Thomas. If there was any hope in surviving this, it was going to be through the back door and hope to God nobody was out there waiting.

I heard additional muffled voices and harsh whispers. What they were talking about was out of earshot. I was sure they were debating what to do next. I flipped the cylinder open on the .38. I ejected the cylinder, feeling the empty casings, throwing these to the floor and found there were only two rounds left.

My Kingdom for a few bullets more!

I thought about Robert Lee and his damned hand cannon but it was nowhere to be seen. It was probably stuffed up under his three hundred pound carcass and I wasn't in any shape to move him and it would create too much noise.

"Whoever's in there, we just want the money!" Richardson yelled out.

I refused to answer. There were five corpses in here and I didn't have plans to be the sixth. I stuffed the last two rounds into the cylinder and cocked the .38. I grabbed the .45 off the counter and stuffed it into the waistband of my trousers. Any minute the bastards were going to make a rush. I was sure of it and two bullets were not going to be enough to hold back the pending slaughter. The back door hung open and nine times out of ten, the cock suckers outside were waiting. If I bolted out the door it was a sure bet I'd be shredded in seconds. A minute went by then the sound of something heavy landed with a distinctive thumping then a pop and a thick smoke began floating into the rooms.

Gas! CS!

I looked down in a panic. Water kept spraying out from the ruptured kitchen sink lines. The floor was slick not only with water but blood. I saw the tattered dish towel, grabbed it and rolled it around in the water then covered my mouth to filter out the worst of the CS and stumbled across the shattered kitchen.

I took a quick look outside the window again. None of the dirty cops were anywhere to be seen. Hobbling over to the back door, I took a quick look and saw no one was there. Fear gnawed at my gut. Once I took off from here, it was a wild shot if I was going to live to see the morning light or come face to face with my Maker.

I was faint from blood loss and didn't have time to spare and bolted out the back door without a further thought. It was all a gamble. I held the .38 up and out with my good hand. I was expecting gunfire to break out from everywhere but was instead met with silence. I hit the nearby tree line in time to see red and blue strobe lights flashing off in the far distance and knew instantly the cops were coming. I counted four Torrance County units hauling ass up the main dirt road but they were still miles off from my vantage point. There was no way I was going to wait for the cavalry. Right now, I was looking at spending life in prison just for being here.

Inside the house, a few shots of thunder echoed, bright diamonds flashed as Richardson's crew made sure the dead stayed dead. I kept running, slipping down a small slope and felt the jagged glass being driven deeper into the flesh. I bit off a howling roar from deep within my chest and rolled off further into the dark brush.

Looking up towards the house, I saw a man exit the back door, a rifle held up to his shoulder, sweeping the area from side to side. I held the .38 barrel end up towards him. If the son of a bitch moved my way, I was planning on planting the last two in his fat head. Seeing nothing though, he slowly lowered the rifle and went back inside.

I gave a mental sigh of relief, relaxed the grip on the .38 and rolled over on my back. I cursed. All that work and a bunch of dirty cops come and take it away. The money was gone now and there wasn't a thing to do about it. Every last bit of currency gone in a single night from my and Hendricks' hands, first by the Dixie Mafia, and now ripped off by Richardson and his crew of dirty cops. I rose up on my hands and knees and wretched and gagged. I wanted to vomit but nothing came out.

I crawled away from the shadows and further down the tree line. I slowly stood up, looked back once at the house. I could hear men yelling out in jubilation much as Hendricks and I had done when we found the money. The only difference was we hadn't killed a soul for it. I knew they were loading up and hauling ass and after several minutes, a truck started up, headlights kicked on and tires kicked up a large cloud of dust and disappeared down the dirt road. The terrain was crisscrossed with so many ways in and out. They probably knew the roads to take to avoid the incoming cops.

Time was short and Thomas was still running around out here somewhere but there was no time to worry about him. I was sure he had split sheets and had kept running from the hell behind us figuring Richardson's crew would finish me off. I was no longer his main interest. He would be concerned about his own safety. I realized it was time to shag ass and run. It was time to leave Moriarty and run like hell. At this point, I couldn't trust a soul and that meant anyone from the south, Mississippi especially, the cops, anyone. I was sure the Dixie Mob back in Mississippi was going to call down the thunder once they caught wind of me living. With the dirty cops here in New Mexico, those bastards would have friends in their network and could reach out and touch anyone with any kind of bullet for any kind of reason.

No. Hit the road, hide. Find the one rock nobody will kick over while looking for you. Hide deep.

The El Camino was parked down the hill. I slipped out of the tree line and hobbled my way down the pathway to the run-down barn dripping blood along the way. I held the .38 in trembling hands expecting Thomas to pop out of the nearby underbrush. If he did there were two rounds for his fat ass. I wasn't in the mood for any more brawling. The events of the night had sucked me dry of any strength and willpower to fight anymore.

Cresting the small rise, the pearl white beast faced me, its chrome grill dropping open as if in shock in what I had become. I staggered to it and leaned against the fender, a smear of blood left in its wake. I thanked God the keys were still dangling from the ignition. I slid in and fired it off, threw it in gear and tore ass out of there in a cloud of dust and flying gravel.

TWENTY-TWO

*Will I live...? **Bleeding like** a stuck pig...shot to shreds...you mother fuckers!*

  How much prison time? Fuck...my career is over!

  *Your **career**? For fuck's sake! How about your **life**? Hospital is out of the question....or is it? Bastards will be asking questions...then the cops will come running.*

  Always questions and never enough answers. I shook off the flashing images of bullets ripping into human flesh, blood pumping from gaping wounds, the dead, dying gasps, drywall exploding, gunfire...the screams...*I can't believe I saw...*

  I slumped forward screaming at the windshield, gripping the wheel so hard my knuckles turned white under the thin grime of cracked, encrusted blood. Pain washed over me in waves of agony. The steering wheel was slick with blood but dried quickly giving it a sick, sticky feel. I was shaking all over from the pain, rage…and fear.

All for the money and no one's going to live to see a nickel spent.

It's all gone to hell…

Another rippling wave of anguish hit with each pulsing beat of the heart and I hissed and moaned through gritted teeth. Link Wray is belting out a ditty about fire and brimstone from the radio. He isn't too far from the truth. I leaned forward to cradle the hand with two busted fingers. They looked like swollen, limp sausages.

The El Camino roared ahead, yellow headlights cutting through the thick darkness revealing a rolling, twisting trail of washed out grey ash. The tall trees of pine and piñon line the single path out of the hell I had come from. I'm expecting the cops to materialize out of the dark shadows with guns blazing.

My mind wandered. I'm feeling weak. I'm not sure if it's from the blood loss but I can only think of her. *Amy…the bastards know I was there…they'll come looking…to kill me, I'm sure…*

The El Camino began a violent dance over a long patch of washboard road. The buckshot in the shoulder sent out pulsing throbs of protest with each jolt. I struggled to keep the car on the road. I screamed again but kept the pedal down hard. The black asphalt road looms into view and I hang a hard left and floor it, the tires screaming out in protest. But I don't let off the throttle. The big block roared out a rumbling staccato of ripped-open hell. It was my faithful servant in my greatest hour of need.

Got to run, escape…find the rock where you'll never be found, that no one will ever kick over…

Slumping over the wheel, I cut off a moan of anguish, blood drips to the floor. It's all over the place, my blood and my life. My shoulder is ripped open exposing raw, torn flesh under the tattered and blood-stained t-shirt. I look down, the glittering edges of the glass, embedded in the thigh, gleams under the dull moonlight flooding into the cab. I clutched the damaged limb feeling the edges sticking through the blood-soaked jeans.

I've heard people say *'expect to get cut in a knife fight.'* I guess it applies to guns and glass also.

I make another hard turn, heading north on 217 and punch the gas hard. The blood-slick .45 slid across the seat and hit the passenger door with a dull thud before falling off onto the dark floorboard. The .38 digs into my gut and I pull it out with a moan of agony.

I took a quick glance in the rearview mirror. The pulsing auras of red and blue lights flash high above the dark treetops far off in the distance.

The cops are back there...they know now. Sure, they're scratching their heads wondering just what the hell happened, but they'll come searching before too long. It won't take much to add two and two.

I should've left New Mexico months ago. Fuck the money, fuck Duggan's and fuck everybody.

Amy...

She was the real reason I stayed. I should've listened to her. She was right from the beginning. Or had she played me a fool?

I shook off the thought. *No...no, she wouldn't...*

She said she loved me, just the one time, but it was sincere in her tone, I knew it then and I know it now. She wouldn't say something like that and not mean it. I felt it as truth. She never lied to me, not once.

"I love you." The soft whisper of her voice had said. Her slow, silky kiss was like cocaine to an addict. I wanted more. There was a chance she would be waiting at the house. It was a big gamble but worth taking. I had to find her and quick. With Thomas floating around, I was sure he was looking for her also but with bad intentions on his mind.

The radio started banging out the eerie opening twangs to

Montgomery Gentry's *Gone.* The speedometer inches up over a hundred and ten. I mash the pedal, the engines thunder picks up a beat, and the surrounding landscape of hushed shadows flash by in a blur.

***

I hit the brakes hard on the El Camino and slid to a stop just before the stop sign. Dust drifted forward, clouding everything. I had seen the strobing array of red and blue lights flashing off in the distance and about shit.

The lights were on up at my house, which meant cops were looking for me but which ones? Was it the dirty bastards or the genuine good guys?

I made a quick turn down the dirt road for a quarter mile before pulling in at a house that had been up for sale for the last several months. I killed the headlights. Leaning out the window, I verified there must've been a half a dozen cops up the house.

Fuck!

How in the hell could the cops respond so quick? They'd bust your ass for running a red light and when you really needed them, they were nowhere to be found, but this time something felt wrong in all of this. Why were they at my place? Several scenarios ran through my mind and only one made any kind of sense. I knew a few cops and they knew me. It wouldn't be hard for just one of them to put the finger on me.

The other thought was maybe the neighbors down the road from Thomas' house got a bit nervous when the gunfire set off. Maybe someone had seen me leaving, hauling ass out the back roads out to the main blacktop. Or...maybe Thomas had called it in? If he did it would be stupid on his part. He would have to explain why four dudes and a broad were dead in his house shot full of holes. Or maybe an anonymous phone call?

The answer was apparent and the only viable one.

Thomas was going to have to explain things to his superiors in the Dixie mob back in Mississippi. He would lie, of course, telling them Hobart and his nephews, Dwayne and Andrea had lured me up there because they knew I had found the money. I went up there with my buddies, the dirty State cops, and we all had a gay old time flinging bullets at each other. Of course, the money would still be missing, unbeknownst to the mob boys, Thomas would be in the clear. The Dixie mob would send out everyone and everything they had beating the bushes looking for me. They would want blood for Hobart's death along with his nephews, even if they didn't believe Thomas.

Someone or Thomas had called the cops and fingered my ass. They wanted to know about the five corpses. If I surrendered to them, those dirty cops would find out and would instantly know who I was and would figure out some ingenious way in getting rid of me. Shit, one of those dirty bastards could even be up there at the house right now. If I popped my head up, I was sure to get it blown off Elmer Fudd style just for resisting arrest. Dead men tell no tales.

Either way, I was royally screwed. Take the A-train to hell from the Dixie mob or the cops. A helluva choice.

I slid down my seat as a police cruiser, with lights strobing, floated by the road and steered up through the inky darkness before turning down the driveway leading to my house. I fired up the El Camino, placed it in drive and coasted out of the driveway. With lights off, I continued down the dusty road for several miles before kicking the lights on. There would be no way to haul the toolbox out of Duggan's shop without a trailer. The thought of ripping one off came to mind but I quickly dismissed it. It would be my damned luck I'd get caught in the act and shot dead by the owner.

There were too many different ways it could go but the end result was the cops were up at my house, possibly tearing it apart looking for clues, evidence, anything that would hint on where they could find me. I guess I could count my lucky blessings.

The main question that burned at the heart of the matter was where was Amy? If I had my phone, I would've called her, but it was up at the house.

She had bolted and kept running.

"Stay close to me," she had said but dammit, she was nowhere to be seen. At least Cleeve and Robert Lee hadn't got her. She had run and was she still running? With no money in the picture now, all she had was a handful of nothing. Duggan's truck stop? Was she at the truck stop, waiting to hear from me? That was a possibility.

I aimed the El Camino towards the truck stop. The .38 trembled in my hand.

***

Duggan's was a half-filled pint of ale drifting into oblivion as a drunk economy slowly began swallowing what was left of its soul. Out of the near two hundred parking spaces available, it was lucky to have maybe fifty or so trucks parked in the lot.

I let the El Camino drift to a stop just under a large willow tree to hide. So far I hadn't seen any cops on my way over here. I had no intentions of being seen if it could be avoided. Looking back towards the shop, I rummaged through the glove compartment, praying for a cigarette. My efforts were rewarded with a crumpled pack containing a single cigarette. Lord only knew how long it had been in there. I lit up and took a deep drag.

My thighs burned in agony, the shoulder wept sticky red fluid that screamed afire every time I moved it. I watched the shop and saw no one moving around inside, which was not a big surprise in that it was closed.

Going in was going to be a roll of the dice. There was the remote possibility law enforcement would be waiting in the shadows. I gripped the .38 hard. I had the five grand stuffed in the little compartment behind the seat. I wondered how long the cash would hold out. If I was careful it could last a long time but when it ran out then what?

I popped open the door and dragged the duffel bag behind me, my shoulder screamed. I was glad I had packed the bag into the El Camino. Blood splattered down to the asphalt and concrete. Hobbling up to the back door, I kept the .38 close to my gut. I unlocked and pulled open the door and poked my head in and saw no one was inside the parts room. I was fortunate the shop had closed down at midnight. I had a few hours left before morning shift began dragging ass in but for now, I had time to patch up what I could.

"Amy?" I called out but silence was the only answer. Maybe she was hiding in the shop office or the shop itself.

Slipping in, I let the door close and turned the deadbolt. Silence and darkness was all that greeted me. I leaned over and felt the wall and switched the light on. The element flickered and hummed to life, showering the room in dull light. The employee restroom was off to the left and in there was a medical box with basic supplies. It didn't have much to offer but it would help get cleaned and patched up for the time being. The shower was going to be a big help in cleaning up.

Looking around, Amy was nowhere to be seen or heard. I swore wondering where she had gone. I had hoped she would've been here but there was no one here. I didn't have the time to keep wondering. There was too much to do in the meantime.

I limped to the bathroom, flipped the light switch, and did a quick look over. The gunshots and glass injuries were swollen to angry, ragged tears. Blood leaked from the puckered, ragged edges. Looking through the medical cabinet mounted on the wall next to the sink, produced a wide array of bandages, wraps and a fresh bottle of hydrogen peroxide and a can of blood clotting spray. Dosing the injuries, I carefully cleaned out some to the loose debris and applied the peroxide and hosed blood clotting spray next. The shit stung and I didn't know what was worse, getting shot or the repair efforts. Cuts and gashes streaked across the face, the nose was slanted at a weird angle, dried splotches of blood were splashed across the face, neck and the shirt was a ruined mess.

And he ain't pretty no mo'

I went to my toolbox and rummaged around for a few moments and found what I needed. The pick set, thin needle nose pliers, a magnet and then I remembered Hendricks left his toolbox unlocked most of the time. His toolbox sat behind mine and he had yet to load it up as he still had a few days left to work before making the run to California. I doubted he would be working here anymore after this night. After the Devil's Dog Pound had paid him a visit, it was a sure bet he was on the run. I wondered where he was at this time. Surely he was in the same boat I was. I was just thankful he had decided to work out his two weeks. I rummaged through his catch-all drawer and found the Oxy and penicillin pills he refused to take from his dental visit months ago. They were a treasure to find. I also grabbed the bottle of Crown Royal from the bottom drawer of my toolbox.

I hobbled back to the restroom and mentally prepared myself for the upcoming pain session. I couldn't put it off any longer. With trembling fingers, I peeled away the torn and bloody clothing and found I was looking more like overripe hamburger meat that had been left sitting in the fridge too long. I trashed the clothes, turned on the shower thankful there was a handicap bench in it.

I spent the early morning naked, sitting on the shower bench, patching up the buckshot wounds, finally digging out the last of the lead balls with a pick. The skin screamed in protest with each probing prick and a stifled grunt of agony spat into a saliva-soaked towel clenched between tight teeth. The .38 lay on the toilet lid within easy reach along with all the medical supplies I had amassed. I had poked around the puckered edges and pushed the ball out of the wound. Sweat and blood ran in thin streams over the shower stall walls and bench. I doused the areas in hydrogen peroxide and finally used a thread and needle soaked in iodine to sew up the worst of the torn flesh.

Leaning back, I took a pull of Crown Royal, gasped and eyed the slit on the left thigh. One last dig out remained. The edge of glass gleamed under the bright lights, taunting, daring me to pull it out. Touching the swollen edges, a sharp pain shot through the tender torn nerves and the leg jerked in nerve reflex. I took another swig of Crown.

The worst part had to do with digging around the thigh and pulling out the remaining pieces of glass embedded deep down in the slit. I about passed out several times in the process, stopping only when the world filled with shooting stars and the dark edges of unconsciousness began closing in. I retched several times, breathing hard, the last of the glass fragments pulled free from the flesh and I let it fall to the shower floor.

I spat the towel out of my mouth, and leaned back against the shower wall, drenched in sweat and blood and moaned a heavy sigh of relief. The thing I had to be grateful for was both shotguns blasts were glancing blows. Even though I had been peppered, the majority of the shot missed. I let the warm shower water cascade over me to rinse off the worse of the bloody mess I was covered in. My whole body shook in pain. I hoped no infection settled in.

I was running out of time. As much as I wanted to stay under the shower fall of warm waters, it was time to finish. I was done digging out the majority of the mess and would have to deal with the rest later. Wincing, I patched up the areas as best I could with what was on hand. It wasn't much but it was better than having nothing. At least I had gauze wraps and pads. The two busted fingers were strapped into place and wrapped tight to keep them straight. I cursed Cleeve and Robert Lee. It would be a while before I could turn wrenches again.

I popped a handful of ibuprofen and a penicillin pill before slowly, with twitching, shaking arms changed out into the fresh clothes from the duffel bag. I had to get out of town. It was only a matter of time before the cops came looking. *And if the police or the Dixie Mafia has to come get you, they're going to bring a shit-ton of firepower for the next round.*

I looked over at the .38. I didn't think I could survive another shootout and didn't want any more ass beatings or getting shot. I just wanted to find a nice quiet place to hole up, sleep, and wake up only to find it was all just one big horrible shit-filled dream. The angry buzzing pain from my injuries reminded me it wasn't the case though.

I donned new clothes from the duffel bag and felt like a new man. I scooped up the old blood-soaked ones along with the shoes and tossed them in a trash bag salvaged from under the sink. The trash truck would be rolling by in a few hours so any evidence I had on me, besides the guns, would be disposed of.

Several minutes later I had emptied the medical cabinet of everything that might have a use but I was still going to have to find more peroxide and maybe some other stuff.

Slipping out the back door, I heard the early morning birds beginning to sing out the approaching day. I had a couple hours left before dawn. A sudden thought gripped me. It felt as if I was being watched, or perhaps paranoia from last night's events had made me aware. The El Camino sat under the willow tree, the edges of the branches sweeping lightly across the hood. I gripped the .38 in my waistband and began breathing hard. I waited several minutes until I mentally convinced myself nobody was there.

I tossed the trash bag into the dumpster and peered around the corner of the building. No one was there and the parking lot was still at half capacity with idling trucks. I stumbled for the El Camino, carefully glancing from side to side, looking into the dark shadows. After tossing the duffel bag onto the passenger seat, I fumbled with the keys for a minute, and then cranked the 427 to life.

I took a last look at Duggan's, threw the car into drive and sped off. I hit I-40 westbound at near ninety. One direction was as good as another and the faster and further I went, the harder it would be for anyone to find me.

TWENTY-THREE

I took to the road, heading west through Albuquerque and on into Grants only stopping once for fuel at some pull-through, backwater joint along the way. I limped into the gas station restroom after seeing the wound from the glass cut had opened up again and blood had seeped through my denim. Every time I moved the legs, pain shot through me like a wave of electrical current.

The fear of infection was my greatest concern. I popped a penicillin pill and fired up the El Camino, hit I-40, holding it down until I reached Grants just before creases of dawn began cracking across the land.

The Walmart was a twenty-four-hour store. I hobbled across the street and began searching for bandages, gauze dressing, ice packs, hydrogen peroxide, iodine and thread and needles along with anything dealing with killing off the pain in my arm, hands, and legs. I looked longingly beyond the counter at the prescription counter, wishing I could access it and take some of the harder stuff but there was no way that was going to happen. I resorted to Tylenol and ibuprofen pills instead. The final item of medical necessity was a large bottle of Crown Royal. Hell, if it worked in the movies it would work here.

I went to the jewelry section and slowly rotated the turn-style display of necklaces draped over the miniature arms and found a pewter necklace with a double adjoined hearts. It was cheap but the necklace itself reflected a dull satin finish under the bright lights and looked strong.

The cashier gave me a puzzled look when I pulled out a hundred dollar bill with busted fingers and handed it to her, but nothing was said and I didn't offer. There were plenty of riff-raff floating around and drunken bums looking worse off than me so it was just business as usual for the cashier anyway.

I went back to the El Camino, took the necklace from the shopping bag, removed the two adjoined hearts of cheap pewter and tossed it. My mangled fingers made it difficult but I managed to slide the ring on and clasp the necklace back together. I poked my head through the loop and let it lay on my chest. At least I felt somewhat whole for the moment. I fired off the El Camino and took off to Gallup leaving the bad mojo further behind. I lamented the fact that only a small piece of Amy was coming along with me for this ride.

***

I steered the El Camino back on the highway and straight up US 491. It was still known by its original highway number, US 666 or the Devil's Highway. Many myths and legends grew around this part of New Mexico but it was nothing more than drunken tales spewed out over bottles of rotgut. It was a long and lonely stretch of highway rolling north into Colorado. I had to get clear of New Mexico.

I felt better the further I got from Moriarty. The twinges of pain in my arm and thighs were still evident and hitting the potholes in the rutted asphalt reminded me they were there. At least there was no evidence of infection at this point. I popped a couple of eight-hundred milligrams of ibuprofen with a swallow of coffee to help the horse pills down and cranked the radio up when a Rolling Stones song floated across the speakers.

Five grand could see me through but for a short time and I had to find a place to hole up. Who knew what was being said back in Moriarty and I was sure the site of the shootout was covered in a tangled web of crime scene tape and investigators trying to piece everything together. Who knew what the cops were thinking other than five shot-to-shit corpses and a house full of holes were staring them in the face with no motives or reasons. Thomas was MIA and who knew where that bastard was hiding at the present. For all I knew, the son-of-a-bitch was trailing behind me somewhere and itching for a chance to blow my head off. I knew if I saw him, I'd blow more than a few holes in his hide.

I rolled on through Shiprock and over the border into Colorado before hitting Cortez. Just past the DOT port, I spotted something I had forgotten all about up until then. I had no additional ammo for the .45 or the .38. There was some but not enough to sustain a prolonged siege should I happen upon Thomas or any Dixie Mafia affiliates. I rolled into the dirt parking lot of Rocky Mountain Gun and Tackle and limped in.

Pushing the door open, a small bell jingled over my head and an old man looked up from behind the glass counters up front. His face resembled a roadmap for all of life's experience. He stood up with the assistance of a cane.

"Help you?"

"Looking for some ammo."

"Which kinds? We got tons of bullets for a thousand different guns."

Short and to the point. I like that. ".45 and .38."

"A tall order." He turned slowly to look at the counter behind him, all stacked with boxes of ammunition of all types and brands. "Got .45 and .38."

"How many?"

"Got two boxes of PMC full metal jacket and a box of Federal Hydra-Shok for .45 and a couple boxes of lead wad-cutters in .38."

I made a twirling motion with the hand with the broken fingers. "I'll take all three .45 and the two boxes of .38. You got any speed loaders for a .38 and mags for a .45?"

The old man limped over and began setting the boxes on the counter. "You preparing for a war or what?"

"No, just can't trust the government." I lied.

"No, especially them damned liberals." He leaned over his cane and pointed to one of the walls. "We got a few mags for a Colt and I think we got some speed loaders over on the corner wall. What kinda .38? Smith, Colt or what?"

"Colt."

"Check the wall. I'm pretty sure there's one or two for a Colt."

I walked over, located the magazines and speed loaders. I took all five .45 magazines along with the only two speed loaders and set them on the counter along with the bullets. He took a pen from his overalls, licked the tip and began scribbling down a receipt. "No sir, can't trust liberals. You hear about the big firefight down in New Mexico?"

I felt an icy hand squeezing my heart. "No."

He pointed his pen. "It's crap like that mess that gets people thinking we need more laws on the books or even worse, get every law-abiding gun owner to turn in their guns."

"What about New Mexico?"

He tilted his head. "Big news. Even went national level like CNN and FOX, hell it's all everyone's squawking about. A big gun battle between rival gang or Mexican cartel guys, police don't know which or what the hell's going on. FBI is all in it too. Five people dead. Heard several thousand bullets went flying. I'm surprised you ain't heard none of it."

"I avoid the news, nothing but bad news."

"True on that." He went back to tallying the bill. "They also looking for a couple people. No names and such."

I was about to ask another question but the bell over the door jingled and looking back, an icy grip of fear threatened to rip my guts out. A sheriff's deputy walked in, uniform all pressed with razor-sharp creases and clean-cut. He took off his beige colored Stetson but the gold star mounted on it hit me like a laser. I had left both pistols in the car. I turned back to the old man. "How much?"

"Well, I reckon...let's see."

Oh for fuck's sake!

"Hollow points run twenty-six bucks, full metal will run fifteen, the .38's will be twelve..." His voice drifted to a whisper as he concentrated on the math like he was trying to break Einstein's $E=MC$ squared problem. "...tax...one-hundred fifty-two dollars and nineteen cents."

I pulled out a couple hundred dollar bills and laid them on the counter.

"Dave, you got any nine-mill pistols along the lines of a Beretta 92?" The deputy was looking over the pistols under the glass case next to me.

Dave scooped up the bills, looked at the deputy. "Henry, I think we got a shipment in but I ain't put it out yet. I think there's a couple new ones mixed in. If you give me a minute I can go see." He turned his attention back to me. "I gotta go in the back for your change. Give me a minute while I get it." He took up his cane and hobbled toward the back of the store leaving me with the deputy.

He smiled at me with clean teeth. "How you doing?"

I nodded. "Not too bad."

"Looks like you got beat up."

The icy knot grew. "Not too bad...car accident a few days back."

He leaned over the counter, looking back toward the door. "That your El Camino out there?"

"It is."

"They don't make them like that anymore. Everyone wants an arm and a leg for those cars now."

I started gathering up everything on the counter. Fuck the change. "True, it's been a good car."

"Notice it has New Mexico plates. Is that where you from?"

I remained silent. Some months ago, I traded in the Nevada plates and had registered the El Camino in New Mexico. "Yes."

"You hear about the shooting down there? Good Lord! I mean five people dead, and from the media footage, the house is being held together with splinters."

"Sounds bad."

"You ain't heard about it?"

"No, I avoid the news."

"They say they looking for a couple guys."

"No names?"

"Nope, not yet, but it'll all come through eventually." He leaned up against the counter and looked at me. "I doubt those guys they want so badly would come up here anyway."

"Let's hope not, sir."

"But if they did, it sounds like those two are a pair of mean hombres. We might end up with our hands full, which is why I need a better pistol than this old wheel gun I got." He slapped the holster with a heavy hand. The light gleamed off the blued finish of the .357 revolver.

"Let's hope they don't come here."

"I agree," he leaned over the counter. "Hey, Dave! You looking for that Beretta or did you fall down again?"

A muttered curse came from the back. I felt relieved to see Dave shuffling back to the counter and laying out the change. "Still looking for the pistol, give me a moment." He turned and shuffled to the back once again.

I gathered up the money and the ammo. "I'll see you around deputy. I got a doctor's appointment to get to." I started walking away slowly, carefully.

"Take care, sir." He focused in on the pistols under the glass countertop.

I left the store, tossed the boxes and magazines behind the seat, fired off the El Camino and left Cortez towards Durango on Highway 160.

TWENTY-FOUR

I couldn't go anymore. The pounding waves of fatigue washed over me and I was done. I pulled off the road outside of a town called Hesperus, spotted the motel, and drifted into the parking lot. I rose out of the El Camino and admired the noontime sun showering me with rays of warmth. Hesperus was nestled in a valley, surrounded by thick cloves of trees and rolling lands of green grass. It was far better to see green than the dusty brown colors of New Mexico.

The motel was overgrown and looked like it had been here for centuries but it would help cover up the El Camino. I hobbled into the motel lounge and checked in under the assumed name of James McMullen. It was as good a name as any and thankfully, the robust woman with the painted on make-up working the counter didn't ask for an ID of some kind. She just took my word for it, took the cash advance for a few days and handed over the key to a room. She looked me over in disgust and probably thought I had dove off into a stump grinder face first.

"Car accident," I said, hoping to deflect the curious look.

"You sure lost that one didn't you, sir?" she handed a receipt.

"I did."

She smiled. "At least you're alive. A lot of people don't wake up some mornings."

If only she knew. I went to the room, stopping once to grab my duffel bag.

I spent the next hour settling in and unpacking. I found the few photos of Amy and held them up into the light and wondered where or what she was doing. I started feeling like she had played me a fool since so many questions remained. I sat down on the edge of the bed and looked at the photos, remembering every fine detail. In a man's life, there is the one woman that makes memories last forever. Sometimes a man is fortunate to find their one true woman, while others long for one or had them at one point in life and then lost them with only memories to keep them company on long winter nights for the rest of life.

Memories were all I had left.

I took the .45 and set it in the bedside drawer and laid out the .45 mags and began loading them up with the Hydra-Shok rounds. I had two boxes left of .45 along with the .38, which was loaded with the wad-cutter rounds and the speed-loaders also loaded up. If anyone came looking for me, they were going to have to eat a wall of lead in getting to me. I fell back on the bed. My eyes stared at the ceiling for a few moments before sleep washed over me.

It was a door slamming that woke me up and I jumped for the .38. A wave of fear washed over every sense and I pointed the snub-nosed pistol at the door with shaking hands. After a few minutes, I lowered it and breathed out a sigh of relief. The room had grown darker and realized I had zoned out for a few hours and it was late afternoon.

Taking up a cigarette, I limped outside, lit up and leaned against the awning post, watching the dark, thin filaments of cirrus clouds tickling the distant red, blue skyline. Somewhere in America, Amy was watching the same sunset. I wasn't sure where, but she had to be or maybe it was just my wishful thinking.

***

Several days at the hotel was beginning to drive me batshit crazy. The only good thing was the glancing shots to the shoulder and leg were healing up but still seeped thin blood and other fluids. The skin had turned into a brown ragged map of torn tissue colored with patches of white globs. At least they weren't yellow and I had not run a fever. The only material left to help keep it clean was running water and antiseptic soap wrapped in gauze. It stung like a bitch with every rinsing but it did help.

The broken fingers were still taped firmly together and I had no intentions of undoing the bindings on the mangled digits until I could move and flex them.

Depression's claws were sinking deep into the cortex of my brain and thunderstorms of my own imagination were running rampant. I found myself sleeping with the .45 under the pillow or carrying it around the room or to the nearby convenience store. I was sure the Dixie Mafia or the armies of dirty cops were coming. I was a loose end that needed to be disposed of. There were times I awoke at the slightest sound from outside, or the slamming of nearby doors and quickly grabbed the pistol and waited for the inevitable when the door was going to be kicked in and shotgun welding hitmen came rushing into the room.

It didn't help with the news coverage of what was going on in New Mexico.

The television blared they were still looking for me. *Logan Pierce wanted for questioning in the High Hills shooting that has left five people dead…considered armed and dangerous. If seen, do not attempt to approach him. Thomas Hauser, the other suspect wanted in connection with the shooting, also remains at large. Details are still forthcoming but little is known in exactly what happened at Hauser's home…"*

A picture of my face loomed on the screen and I felt the icy knot of fear gripping my gut. I jumped up, pain shot through my shoulder and leg. I hobbled to the mirror. The photo they had was several years old already. I had a little less grey hair then as compared to now. The nose was still healing up but it had an unnatural curve. I thanked the Devil's Dog Pound for that added piece of cover. If I continued letting the beard grow, I would be just another faceless soul in the civilian world. I was going to have to take additional steps to conceal my appearance.

"James Hendricks, also a suspect in the shooting, was apprehended earlier this morning in the nearby town of Edgewood…" My attention snapped and glued to the television screen. There he was, sure as shit, being approached by several well-armed Torrance County deputies along with some FBI agents. He and Jill were walking out of the Walmart in Edgewood carrying several bags. He wore sunglasses and a baseball cap but it wasn't enough to conceal who he was. Someone recognized him. The cops held their pistols out, screaming for him to drop to the ground. He looked to Jill, mumbled something to her and they kissed quickly. She stepped back, anguish washed over her face as he held up his hands and slowly dropped to his knees. The cops ascended and quickly threw him to the ground and applied the handcuffs.

The news ended the segment and droned on to the next bit of news about some homeless woman trying to hold up a Walmart. I killed the television.

They got Hendricks. He must've taken refuge after his rumble with the Devil's Dog Pound to heal up instead of running. I felt a twinge of guilt knowing I had gotten away and he hadn't. Amy was nowhere to be seen and the news hadn't mentioned her at all. Thomas was still on the loose. Had he gotten to her? No, she would be smarter than that. Where was she then? I asked myself all kinds of questions and nothing viable came up from the voids of rational thought. The only thing I could do was keep running.

The first rule for going into hiding is to find the rock to hide under and keep digging down.

I ditched the normal t-shirt and jean look and went casual country. With flannel shirts, jeans and boots and a beat down Stetson hat from a nearby thrift store, I blended in a bit more into the mass of local humanity. I weighed my options on where to go next.

The city of Durango was an option. It was a college town mixed with old ranchers and farmers. Blending in would be fairly easy but I needed to wear clothes opposite than what I was usually accustomed to. I even went so far as to change my hair color to a darker shade of brown. The news media said I was driving a white El Camino. What to do there? I might as well have a neon sign flashing begging the cops to pull me over.

I resorted to covering the car in a tarp for the moment until something could be done with it. I couldn't begin to think I might end up having to part with it.

***

I drove the El Camino back towards Cortez along highway 160. Anger, along with a host of other mangled emotions, gripped me. I spotted a dusty, half-used trail, turned and drove down it. I had a single gallon of gasoline in the bed.

Farmers around the county were burning off the weeds and debris from their fields and were setting up for new crops. Driving for over an hour on State land, I found a cut out leading down to a rocky canyon trail. Steering the El Camino down to the bottom, I ground to a halt within a series of rock walls embedded under a clear, cold blue sky. It was a good day for a funeral. I took the .45 from the glove box and studied it.

End of the line...end of the road. Who would've thought everything would end at this moment?

The Colt stallion, worn from the years of use and abuse looked more like a worn down version of me. I stuffed it in the waistband of my trousers, cleared out the glove box and saw the business cards.

Sleepy Quinn. The elegant styled font leapt out at me. The other business card made me angry and bitter. It was the one from Richardson.

"As right as a virgin's virtue," the words drifted into memory.

Another guy I'd love to use for target practice. I stuffed it in the duffel bag and finished clearing everything out before stepping out into the open, feeling the gravel grind under pivoting boot heels.

I grabbed the gasoline, popped the top and began dousing the El Camino down in the fluid. The stench assailed my nostrils and signaled defeat for everything I had worked for. I had lost Amy, lost my toolbox, the money, and now, the El Camino.

I fumbled for a cigarette...and then the matches. I lit up, watched the flame reach my fingertips before dropping it into the bed of the El Camino. Nothing happened. The flame extinguished and I lit another, then another before the flames roared to life like a summoned Genie of Islamic folklore. The flames spread quickly and the El Camino's paint began to curl. Everything flashed up in a geyser of flame and the interior boiled off to a smoldering black cloud of smoke.

My heart sank.

The El Camino continued to burn. I grabbed the duffel bag, turned away and began the long, long trek back to the main road where

I managed to thumb a ride to Durango from a local farmer just before the setting sun.

***

I popped another penicillin pill along with a handful of Ibuprofen. I avoided the use of the OxyContin pills as much as possible. If I needed to run or fight, I needed all my wits about me. I had found another motel in Durango, near the outskirts of town and plunked down a weeks' worth of lodging. I figured I would be healed up enough to make my next move. I wasn't sure where but the key factor was to stay low.

I was feeling better and changed out the dressing for the wounds a couple times a day. The blood had stopped flowing and the body's own healing process was finally kicking in. I gently poked at the raw edges of the wounds and still felt sharp pin-pricks of pain. My mental health was beginning to suffer. I felt everyone outside these walls, were enemies to my life. I hobbled over to the window and slowly parted the curtain. Nothing was there and I let off a sigh of relief.

I had noticed them one morning while setting the trash out for pickup and instantly, the hairs on the back of my neck stood on end. I had moved the curtain over to reveal a small sliver of the outside world flood my vision and watched them.

There were two men sitting in the sedan. It was an older Crown Vic with a couple of small black antennas on the rear of the roof, tinted windows and just regular Colorado plates. I held the .45 in a sweaty left hand and my breathing was hard. The men wore sunglasses and open top shirts, hair close-cropped, clean cut and from what I could see, they were muscular and led to one conclusion: hard hitters from the Dixie Mafia.

Or cops?

How in the hell did they find me here?

My mind raced through the mental Rolodex of probabilities. Hendricks? No way. Big Mac, Cueball, the host of other names from the managers at Duggan's all the way down to the landlord. Did I leave something back at the old place, some vital piece of info that led them here? Nothing came to mind.

What to do now? I checked and found I had five magazines stuffed with 220-grain hollow points and a half box of shells. If they came in swinging, I was going to have to make do with what I had. Or should I go out blazing off the first rounds by going up to them? I nixed the later and decided to wait.

I watched for close to an hour before the Crown Vic fired up and slowly pulled out of the parking lot, made a left and moved off at a slow pace before disappearing from view. I waited for an hour before realizing a small thin, ragged line of blood from my aching shoulder had run down my forearm. I cleaned up the blood and continued watching, waiting but nothing came of it. The Crown Vic never returned.

Night time was the worse times. No sooner I'd fall asleep then images of men dying, gasping would invade the deep dark regions of slumber. Hobart would often come to me in these fitful nightmares holding his bloody brain in his hands screaming something I couldn't make out. Gunfire had set the house afire and flames licked at his ankles. Then Dwayne would appear blasting his cheap chrome pistol before collapsing to the ground with half his face blown off. Andrea was lying on the floor always naked and bloody.

I would awaken from these nightmares with a violent start and grab the .45, poking the shaking muzzle around the dark room. The bedsheets were a twisted, knotted mess wrapped around my torso. I was always covered in a thin sheen of sweat. I was glad I hadn't shot anyone.

I could hardly sleep and I had to make plans to keep running.

My thoughts were disjointed and I found it was hard to fall asleep. The demons were waiting for me if I did sleep so I avoided it as much as possible.

Find Thomas. That thought was wishful thinking.

If I could find Thomas, I knew I would kill him but we were in the midst of a shit storm. We had everyone looking for us. I was sure the Dixie Mafia, the army of cops all across the country, both good and bad and possibly the Mexican cartel were searching for me and neither one was a good prospect.

I wondered what Amy was going to tell me before Thomas crashed his way into my house. *I have to tell you something.* She had said but she never had a chance to. The words played over and over in my mind. I wondered what she was going to tell me. Was it another deep, dark secret she had withheld from me in the time we had been together or was it something to do with the money and guns? I had no idea what it could've been, and there was no way I could find out. All that was left was speculations.

The .45 weighed heavily in my hands and I leaned forward in the chair. The stifling heat circulating in the room bore down on me and gentle tickles of sweat rolled down the bridge of my nose. My paranoia was getting to me, scratching the edges of my mind. I didn't want to die, nor did I have any intentions of ending up in prison.

"Aw, fuck it," I whispered.

Run silent, run deep.

Wait for the bitter end to things and try to take out everyone I could before I got hammered dead in a wall of burning lead.

TWENTY-FIVE

I sat back in the booth seat at the local Denny's and took a sip of my coffee. The diner was dead and I was the only customer. A yellow Pete 379 rolled up in front and the air brakes set in an angry hiss. The flatbed, spread axle trailer was loaded heavy with one-ton bales of fresh hay. The machine was clean and the chrome glistened under the Durango sun. Something looked familiar, very familiar with that truck.

I looked down and eyed the dirty, tattered business card lying on the countertop. The elegantly cursive lines of *Sleepy Quinn* etched across the surface glared back up to me. I had called old man DuBois on a whim. It was a long shot if he would even hire me but I had to try something. I had to stay busy. The demons waited in the shadows of my sleep if I relaxed for a minute.

Old man DuBois, tall and thin, slinked his way across the parking lot and only took off his battered straw hat once he was inside.

He looked around, spotted the waitress. "Angela? A cup of coffee if you would?"

The waitress went to get a fresh cup from behind the long counter. He eyed me and smiled wide. "Logan?"

I started to rise up but the old man set a hand on my shoulder and he slid into the seat next to me. "DuBois." He held out his hand and I was surprised at the strength.

"I heard you may be looking for someone?" I asked.

He laughed softly. "Well, I had to admit, I am looking for a mechanic."

I looked out front and eyed the yellow Pete. "Nice rig."

He followed my gaze. "It is. It's been a fine machine for what it does."

"How's it running since the cam job last year?" I sipped my tea and took the gamble.

He looked surprised. "How you know about that?"

"I worked on it, sir."

"You worked on that rig out there?"

"Duggan's Truck Stop in Moriarty, New Mexico, last summer. The cam lobes were worn out."

He sat back in his seat and a wide smile cracked open. "Damn! That's right! I thought you looked familiar. You know that truck is a running machine now thanks to you. Not one lick of problem."

The waitress slid up silently to the table and placed a coffee mug down and filled it with the black gold that keeps truckers and mechanics alive. DuBois took a sip and looked back to me. "What in hell brings you up to Durango anyways? I thought you were making money and having a good time?"

"Economy. Fuel prices have about killed off the industry I think. Drifted up here and need a bit of money."

He grunted in agreement. "Damn right, I'm having to charge a fuel tax just to keep afloat. I thank God all my trucks are paid off, a lot of poor bastards ain't so lucky. So you need a job?"

"I do."

"You're in luck. I hired one fellow but he went on a drunk and ain't been seen since. I got a couple Pete's, one with a Cat and the other with a Cummins motor, both need in frames done. The Cat also needs a head. I bought all the parts and he tore 'em down but he ran off and made a mess of things. He put everything off in piles and I can't tell if it's Cat or Cummins parts."

The waitress returned and topped off our cups.

"Can you work on farm equipment and such?"

"I'm sure I can. It's just nuts and bolts."

"Now another thing. I know you're used to making big bucks. Pay is about fifteen bucks an hour average with this outfit."

I knew where he was going. "Pay doesn't matter. I'm looking for something to get back on my feet and I know I have to start at the bottom."

He took a swallow of his coffee and winced. "Where you living?"

"Motel at the end of town."

"That won't do. We got a bunkhouse on the farm for hired hands. You can stay there but you gotta get your own food, clothing and such things."

"Sounds fair." I was now interested in taking the job. A bunkhouse would help hide me a bit further away from everyone.

"Well, we got a few tractors, a few balers and a lot of equipment like water pumpers for the fields and stuff. Got a half-dozen Petes we run all over the place, some as far as the Dakotas. And I know you can work on ISX motors." He smiled wide.

I smiled and knew, felt it, I had the job in the bag.

***

I spent the better part of the summer months over at the Sleepy Quinn. The ranch was up north of Durango some twenty-five miles, nestled within the Animas rangelands. The work was easy enough and it gave me plenty of time to heal up for good. I worked on his equipment and as sure as he had said, paid me cash every other Friday. It wasn't much but I didn't care either. The idea here was to lay low. I had a roof over my head, a place to hole up quietly and I was still able to ply my craft.

During down times, I took up jogging. Amy had been concerned about my smoking and drinking and I decided to make the effort and quit. For a smoker, it's damn near impossible and difficult. The first few weeks were a bastard but as the days rolled on, the early morning jogs became easier. I lay off the cigarettes, narrowing them down to just five or so a day. The thick tar and chemical build up in the lungs were soon hacked up and clearing out but I still couldn't completely kick the habit. I figured if I had to run from the bronze shields or mafia boys, I would at least have a good chance at surviving.

Working within the Animas mountain ranges proved just the ticket to healing both physically and mentally. That didn't do away with the nightmares though. There were times I would awaken to find the sheets twisted and soaked in sweat and my hands on the .45 or the .38.

I thought Amy would've loved it here and there were times ghostly shadows of her danced along the tall grass and the stream banks. I wished my mind never left those places but business was business and old man DuBois was busy. He always paid in cash and I tucked it away, rarely leaving the ranch. When I did, it was usually to a restaurant or other eatery to grab a bite to eat or to the store to stock up on groceries. Over the following months though, I was finding all of it getting old fast.

I still carried a pistol. The other was kept in the center console of a mid-nineties Dodge Ram that looked like it had done a couple tours in Iraq. It was an old ranch truck and didn't have a straight panel on it anywhere. I couldn't complain though. It was secured for a few hundred bucks. I also managed to obtain a battered Winchester 97 twelve-gauge pump from one of the farm hands. I cut the barrel down and made the buttstock into a pistol grip. It was small and compact and would be good for close work if ever the need should arise.

Since having to abandon my old tool box back in Moriarty, I managed to buy another toolbox. It wasn't all that great but it was better than nothing and cost me a grand with some tools thrown in. I spent another easy grand buying more tools to do my profession justice, but I lamented the loss of my previous collection of tools. I had been king once and vowed to be one again.

Around mid-summer, DuBois bought in a crew of illegals from Mexico. I'm not sure how he got ahold of them but it was the same crew year after year who came and worked the fields and cattle. Most of them were good guys and hard working. You hear everyone in America crying how the illegals are stealing their jobs. I have yet to find anyone willing to break their backs on a farm, ranch or fruit field for minimum wage or less.

I also found some of the illegals had US driver's licenses, social security cards and such. How they managed to obtain them was beyond me but they had a toehold in getting their slice of the American dream and some were working to become American citizens someday.

I was wondering on how long the name Logan Pierce would hold up. So far, DuBois had taken my word for anything said even though it wasn't worth the breath it was told under anywhere else. In case the cops came around and I had to leave the Sleepy Quinn, I would need a job. A job usually required a social security card and a driver's license. I needed a backup, a new 'legal' identity that proved I was still a US citizen without the cops catching on.

I befriended a Mexican by the name of Julio. He was a young rocking roller with a flair for money, rooster fights, blaring Mariachi music and an Elvis styled hair-do. I was told he was the man who could get anything, including social security cards, birth certificates for new identities. It was just one of his many money-making sideline gigs. Some of the illegals paid the whole seasons worth of wages for these documents just to stay here on US soil.

I decided it was time to hit him up.

One of their past times was rooster fighting. It's illegal as all hell here in Colorado but it still goes on quietly. I was sure DuBois knew about it but said nothing on the matter. They were illegals after all and they were never really welcome when they rolled into Durango. They had this bad habit of clearing out bars in massive brawls for fun. So, they, along with the other illegals working the nearby ranches and farms, would roll on over to an abandoned ranch house and barn located on the far west corner of the Sleepy Quinn. Within the barn, they set up a make-shift *gallera* complete with bar and concession stand, and for a few hours, they bet their paychecks on rooster scraps.

I never bothered going to the fights in the past, but I knew Julio would be here throwing down his money. I saw him near the wooden walled arena, yelling at the top of his lungs along with the crowd around him. Two white roosters exploded in balls of feathered fury, each strapped with one and a quarter inch metal spurs called 'gaffs.' The roosters moved and pummeled each other with those metal spurs and within a matter of minutes, one of the rooster's feathers ran red with blood. The crowd went wild with joy or anguish. The next round, the bloody rooster faltered while its opponent pummeled, slashed and stabbed at its neck with its metal spur until the referee called an end to it.

Julio had lost and shouted his displeasure at the dying rooster.

I tugged him away from the crowd of spectators trading money and off to a dark corner. "Julio, I gotta ask a favor." I pulled out a roll of money and began unrolling each one hundred dollar bill at a time. "I'm going to help you recoup some of your present losses. I need a social security card. I know you get them for around a few hundred bucks."

He smiled and cocked his head. "You, *amigo*, need a social security card? Wh…" He caught himself, held up a hand. He knew better than to ask. The less he knew the better. "Sorry, yes a few hundred."

I handed him five hundred. "The rest of this is to stay quiet you dig?"

He furrowed his eyes in misunderstanding. *"Dig?* What does this mean? You mean with shovel dig? You want me to bury this money?"

I shook my head. "It's a term for 'understand', as in *do you understand? Comprende?"*

The lights went on upstairs. "Yes, of course…I *dig*! I love America and how they say these things."

A couple weeks later, I was staring up at the roof of my bunk, looking at pictures of Amy taped up to the ceiling. I had pretty much caught up with DuBois' fleet of trucks and knocked off early for a little afternoon siesta when shadows of booted feet came from under the door and a sharp rap followed.

I slid off the bunk and opened the door. Julio flashed his toothy grin and handed me an envelope. "This was hard to find and took me a little longer. I was trying to match up your size and age close as possible."

I opened the envelope and stared at the blue card within and my new name. "Manuel Santiago Ortega." I looked up at him like it was some sort of joke.

He shot me double thumbs up and a tooth-filled smile. "You

dig, yes?"

I gave a thin smile. "It'll do I reckon."

***

The following Monday, I rolled into Durango and got a duplicate birth certificate and then a driver's license. Even though I was a white boy with a Mexican name, I still managed to get them with no issue. Maybe a few raised eyebrows but nothing became of it.

The shooting down in New Mexico became nothing more than a distant memory. I had done my best to forget. The news focused on other things since five dead people from months ago were old news. I didn't hear anything for some time and kept my business busy on the ranch equipment until one day I got a hankering for some Heinekens and Crown Royal.

It was payday. And I calculated I had officially been a diesel mechanic for twenty years, and that called for a reason to celebrate. I was officially now part of the old breed of mechanics. Some of the illegals, along with Julio, were planning on rolling into town and catch up on knocking over a few bars. They insisted I come along for the fun.

I decided to tag along and we piled in the farm's battered '78 Ford truck and rolled into Durango. I promised myself a few drinks and no more.

I was lying to myself.

We stopped in at one of the local bars and got totally shit-faced on rounds of Crown and Coke when a busty blonde broad came sauntering up with painted on blue jeans and an open top blouse. She was looking for business and saw we had money by the fat stacks tossing it around. Some of the locals were none too happy and quietly griped among themselves. To make matters worse, some of the Mexicans had partnered up with some of the bar whores but this broad wouldn't leave me alone for anything.

Amy was at the forefront of my mind always. Even if she wasn't around, I still liked to think she was. I told this blonde broad I wasn't interested. I was feeling a good buzz and working on my fifth Heineken. I lost count of the Crown shots while minding my own business watching the television at the bar.

"C'mon, just one drink? Surely you can afford one?" she persisted, pressing in closer with her breasts.

I pushed the brim of my Stetson upwards. "Naw, dead broke," it was a nice way of saying fuck off.

"I can offer up something else if you want to play but a drink would be nice."

The local news faded in on the screen and even though I was drunk, I halted mid-sip. On the screen, cops had found the El Camino down in the canyon. There was no mistaking it. The burned rusted hull was being dragged up on a flat-bed tow truck.

I looked around. No one appeared to be interested in the news. I focused back in on the television and even though I couldn't hear it, I watched the images of cops talking on the screen and caught a glimpse of an FBI agent man walking under the crime scene tape.

"C'mon mister, a drink?"

"What part of 'fuck off' do you not understand?" I snapped.

Her eyes went wide. She slapped my arm, spilling my drink. "Fucker! Fuck you too bastard!"

I was concerned with my spilled drink. "You God-damned cunt!"

Somewhere off from the far corner a cowpuncher with a missing front tooth yelled out. "Hey, friend! How about you shut the hell up?"

I looked over. "You her pimp? How about you mind your own damned business?"

The bar whore slapped my face. I'd had enough. I grabbed her wrist when she reared back to take another hit. I squeezed hard and she winced and let out a yelp. Once she got the message, she began pleading for me to let go. I tossed her hand free and she stepped away.

Chairs shuffled and booted heels meandered over and began crowding me in up against the bar.

I stood up on rubbery legs, downed the remaining shot of Crown before slamming the shot glass down on the bar top. These were five of the ugliest sons of bitches anyone ever seen. Genuine cowboys that looked like they had been rolling around in cow shit all day.

The man with the missing tooth stepped forward. His breath reeked of cheap booze and rotten teeth. "You wanna say that again, mister?"

I wiped the liquor from the corner of my mouth. "Whoa....the honor guards here."

The man with the missing front tooth glared with wide eyes. "I think you owe Missy here an apology."

The bar room fell silent except for the music blaring in the background.

"Oh?" I belched.

"Oh yeah, you think you fuckers can just come in here, flash a few bucks around and take up the women and insult them?"

I was feeling the hard buzz kicking in. "Alright, you want an apology?" I signaled the bartender over. He slowly shuffled over with concern etched on his face. I indicated I wanted another shot.

"Alright, guys let's not get something started," he waved his bar towel at us like he was shooing away flies.

One of the cowboys leaned over and snatched the towel from his hand. "We'll tell you when it's over, Sparky."

Toothless' grin widened. "Apologize, fucker."

Well, I wasn't getting any more drink and that was a

disappointment. Amy had it right. I really needed to quit. "Alright, I'll apologize fellas." I turned to Missy. "Missy…that's your name right?"

She nodded and massaged her wrist. "It's alright, Buck, he's just drunk."

Buck held his toothless grin and his eyes bored into mine. "He's still going to apologize to you and everybody here."

I gave Missy a glance then looked to Buck. "Alright cowboy. I'm sorry, truly sorry Missy, you got to come in here, find one of these fine cowpunchers, and beg for a dick to suck that's probably been in the ass of a sheep at one point in the day, but…"

Buck's toothless grin vanished. He launched a hard right. Lights flashed and a flood of bouncing stars clouded my vision and I fell back. I dropped and rolled but I was up. Five against one wasn't good odds but I was going to make a hell of an effort. The sound of chairs being pushed back and heavy footfalls came up behind me. The illegals came running up with Julio leading the pack and throwing fists and feet into the crowd of cowboys. Missy and other women, and maybe a few men, screamed in sudden terror as chairs broke, glass shattered and men yelled and cursed.

Of course from that point on, drunk and disoriented, I fought back with what I had but it wasn't much. I kicked one cowboy in the balls before one of the Mexicans slammed a hard left against the side of his face. I grabbed Buck, flipped him over my hip where he slammed his head on the floor. I rained down the thunder on his face hoping to knock a few rotten teeth from his skull but a boot flew up and hit me hard in the jaw. The cops came rushing in at some point. How they got there so fast was beyond me. They joined the fray and began arresting and hosing the crowd with cans of mace.

Myself included.

I bailed out the following morning with a hangover hammering in my head. I had a few bumps and bruises and a swollen eye. I wasn't sure if I got most of those from the cowboys or the cops but I wasn't any worse for wear. I had a court date set for next Monday. Manuel Santiago Ortega wasn't going to be there and as sure as the sun rose in the mornings, he was going to have an arrest warrant issued.

The biggest concern was the Law had found the El Camino. I hadn't found out any further details but I knew the FBI was involved. Now every cop in fifty states would be looking for me.

Not to mention my damned booking photo and fingerprints were now in the system. It wasn't going to take a rocket scientist to add two and two. I reached into my jacket, took out the last remaining cigarette and lit up.

It was obvious there was only one choice. The last few months had floated by easily enough and there had been no more talk on the television about the shooting up until now. The main question was who else was coming to Durango? It was a matter of time before the State cops from New Mexico, or hit men from the Dixie Mafia, came flooding into town like an avalanche. They were sure to be packing every conceivable type of gun, bullet and explosive.

Either way, my sanctuary in Colorado was at an end due to my own drunken stupidity. I crumpled the cigarette package and tossed it. I pulled the battered Stetson down over my eyes and began the long walk back to the ranch.

I loaded up everything and told old man DuBois I had to leave. I gave the excuse my parents up in Idaho had called and needed me to go back home as one of them was sick.

DuBois understood and offered his hand. "Anytime you need a job young fella, you come on back here. You're a helluva hand."

I bid farewell and took off in the battered Dodge and headed east towards Kansas.

TWENTY-SIX

For several months, I drifted from Colorado and into Kansas before pushing through Missouri and Iowa before hitting the end of the road in Minnesota. I bled out the last of the money and destroyed a few vehicles getting this far.

The Dodge lost a transmission in Wichita and I bought an early nineties Chevy truck only to have it blow a motor in Iowa. I sold it for scrap and sold the bottom half of the toolbox minus the tools. I tossed the top box and tools in a battered Jeep Cherokee I bought from a junkyard. I hit the road before the money run out in Clearwater, Minnesota. I took a job as a mechanic at the local truck stop to make some cash before pushing off to other parts unknown. The season was in the firm grips of an early winter squall. The ground was crusted over with several inches of snow and ice.

There wasn't any news coming out of New Mexico for some

time. The last bit of news was weeks old. The news said I was still a wanted man and to notify the FBI if spotted. There was also a five thousand dollar reward for information leading up to my arrest.

During these past few months, I took steps to cover up my identity. I grew a beard and mustache and began working out as much as I could. Besides the possible fight or flight scenario, it added some bulk to my frame should either occasion arise.

I had stolen a driver's license and social security card from some drunk at a homeless shelter in Iowa. I carefully altered it with my own photo. I was now known as Sam Highborn. I figured if I kept moving, anyone looking was going to have a hard time pinning me down. Even if I was discovered, whoever did, might not like what they found. I carried the .45 everywhere and had the Winchester pump in the Jeep.

Being a man of limited options, places to hide were becoming nonexistent. Even the idea of Canada was ruled out. If I was caught there the authorities would toss my ass in prison and eventually extradite back to the states anyway. Everywhere I looked, enemies of my freedom and my life were looking for me. The walls were slowly closing in. I felt the growing pressure mounting from one day to the next. I was sure the Dixie Mafia were top contenders in looking under every rock right along with the army of bad cops down in New Mexico.

It was a question of who would find me first, and most importantly, it was when and how it would finish.

I zipped up the Ike jacket, hiked the small backpack up higher on the shoulder, wincing when it hit the wrong spot from injuries of old. A cold blast of winter wind sent my balls crawling up further inside my gut as I pushed the door open outside. I tugged the beanie cap over my ears. A ripple of goosebumps shot over my legs and I cursed the thin polyester trousers and the lack of thermals.

The Jeep was parked up front. Company rules stated all

employees had to park up front. I jogged across the parking lot, moving between the masses of parked semis as the snow began falling in thick sheets and swirling around in the wind like an angry wraith.

The evening skies were streaked with dark clouds blotting out the distant horizon. These clouds were heavily laden with snow being pushed along by the cold winds gusting through the truck stop. It was only a matter of time before they let loose of their burden and the earth would be covered in what was being said to be eight inches or better. Another storm was chasing the heels of this one and was projected to dump another ten inches.

The last twelve hours had been busy and brutal. Most of the local trucking companies were outfitting themselves for the storm with extra maintenance and snow chains. Other trucks were looking for a hole to park in to wait out the worst the weather. Most of the truckers had all coasted off the road and huddled together in the massive parking lot like a herd of cattle seeking warmth off one another. The cold air was thick with vapor exhaust and reeked of burnt diesel fuel and oil.

Through all the noise, something didn't feel right. I slowed my pace and looked side to side. After all these months on the run, I had developed a sixth, seventh and eighth sense. Once I felt a threat, I was off and running, but this time, I was out of money and payday was several days off yet.

I approached the Jeep. The snow picked up in tempo, blurring my vision but I stopped just yards away. Something was off, nothing felt right. I looked off to the right. Several drivers were crossing the lot, huddled up in bulky jackets. They looked ahead, paused and stopped, muttering something I couldn't make out. Looking straight at the Jeep, I saw the shadows shift through the flurry of snow and grey mist. A couple of Chevy Yukons were stacked behind each other, blocking the Jeep in.

A couple of shadows moved from behind the first Yukon and one man stopped in his tracks. He wore black tactical gear, his face covered by a black mask, his eyes locked in on my own. But it was the rifle he held that spoke volumes. The M4 was evil, lethal-looking, the barrel rose up. A couple other shadows shifted off to my left, guns came up. One of them had no hat. The glow from the overhead lights reflected off his bald head and set off my sixth and seventh senses.

Richardson.

Nope, not getting shot again. I bolted.

"Halt! U.S. Marshals!"

I kept running, ditching behind a line of parked semis. Did New Mexico State Police even have jurisdiction in another state? The question roared through my brain. I caught gears and landed one foot in front of the other. Anyone could claim to be a Fed. The M4s told me they were the dirty cops from New Mexico. I unslung my pack and fumbled for the .45, tossed the bag and kept a steady pace over the ice-impacted asphalt. Whoever it was, they were going to have hell trying to kill me off.

Alaska…damn it! I should've gone there.

Running, sides heaving, the cold stabbing my lungs, the .45 shook in my hand. The cops, if that was who they were, looked pretty determined to get me. They were going to find out I was too stubborn to just give up or wait to get shot. The trucks were packed in tight. I disappeared in between two trailers and kept going. A driver popped a door open on a Kenworth and started to get out when he saw me charging through. He yelped in surprise and jumped back inside the cab. I hit the open between the truck lanes. Another gunman came into view off to my left. The shadow yelled out "Halt! Get down on the ground!"

"Drop the gun!" another deeper voiced screamed.

I slid on my toes trying to stop, flailing my arms. I hooked an abrupt right and made for the next line of parked trucks. I kept going like a freight train towing the pursuers along through the truck stop parking lot. I took a chance and looked back and counted eight shadows within the misty blinding snows. I was leading a good pace. For once I was thankful for starting the running regimen months ago. I hunched over and slid between two trailers, rolled under one and moved to the front line of idling trucks. I slowed and knelt down by the bumper of a Freightliner, gasping for breath. For the moment I had lost sight of the hunters.

The snow picked up in tempo and everything blurred. The hazy yellow lights from the overhead light poles reflected off the snowfall. I could see the dark shadows of the tree line a couple rows in front of me. If I made it to that point there was a good chance of melting away into the dark forest. What I would do afterward would be debated on later. Right now it was survival. Several shadows popped up behind me. I launched myself forward.

I hit the open and a green Volvo laid on the air horn as I ran out in front of the blinding headlights and kept going. The men stalled a moment as the semi rolled on by buying precious seconds. I melted away and hid low between a low boy trailer hauling a D9 cat front loader and a car hauler piled high with Dodge Chargers.

"Logan Pierce!" The voice drifted across the grey gloom. "There's nowhere for you to run!"

I stayed silent.

The voice carried on. "Throw down your gun and come out with your hands up!"

Looking up cautiously between the framework of the car hauler, I counted eight men and all carried pistols, shotguns or M4s. The man I thought to be Richardson looked much older and the hair was a lighter shade of black with grey streaks. I wasn't sure. It had to be him. He held his pistol out in front of him but it was pointed down.

He called out again.

I heard the snow crunching behind me and I whirled. A driver stood with a wooden club raised up over his head. His mouth formed a quick o shape when the .45 leveled on him. "Get the fuck moving, hero!" I whispered harshly.

He took a look up.

I snapped a look back, saw several men raise their weapons up. Red laser dots bounced across the snow and car hauler frame. I bolted forward, knocking the trucker over. He swung his club but it only impacted the frame on the car hauler. Off to the right, several men ran hard, armed with pistols. They were trying to get in front of me, cut me off. I slipped behind a trailer, jogging down between several trucks and knelt down again. The last row of trucks was before me. I could smell my freedom waiting in the woods beyond.

Looking left, then right, I took a deep breath. My teeth chattered in fear. Any second shots were going to be fired. I didn't want to be shot again. The adrenaline coursing through my veins gave me the strength to keep running. The cold air bit deep into my lungs. I was sweating like a pig in the summertime. Shadows moved in the grey haze, headlights reflected off the gloom but the hunters were out there, waiting to take their shot. Without another thought, I threw myself forward out in the open fast and hard. The snow was coming down fast and thick.

A truck driver materialized out of the blinding white sheet. I hit him hard. Both of us spilled out over the parking lot. The driver rose up to his knees cursing. "Mother fucker...." He paused, eyed the .45 in my grip, saw several men running up armed to the teeth. He quickly scrambled to his feet and ran for cover.

I lifted myself up and felt a sharp pain echo up through the right ankle joint. I stumbled, fell and rose up again just as the eight men faded into view. I limped away fast-paced, falling and leaning up against the cattle catcher mounted on the front of an International. I steadied myself, rolled away and tried running but the ankle wasn't working. I tried running but slipped and fell. The .45 scattered away from my grip and disappeared in the soft, cold snow.

I rolled over just in time to see several men flying up and landing on top of me knocking the wind out of my lungs.

A dog pile ensued along with a few grunts, kicks, knees to the face, my arms twisted, and a solid punch to the side of my face. I fought back with everything I had. If I was going out they were going to have to work for it. They rolled me over on my face. I was yelling in pain from the suffocating weight on my back. A knee slammed my face into the ice-packed asphalt. I felt the cold metallic clasps clamping around the wrists and the ratcheting sound of handcuffs being applied tight and firm. I huffed out a mouthful of dirty snow.

Okay...maybe they were cops after all. They had to understand that the reach of the Dixie Mafia stretched far and wide. Then you take into consideration the dirty cops and Mexican Cartel might also be looking? How in the hell was I supposed to know these guys were real cops? You can get a badge out of a box of Cracker Jacks and any kind of tactical gear you desired off the computer. You can't take anyone's word for shit anymore.

A Chevy Yukon rolled up, red and blue lights flashing. Several SUV type vehicles including a few local PD units followed behind it. I was hoisted up to my feet and then slammed against the hood, my face pressed against the warm metallic surface. I moaned and rested my forehead against it. The beanie was slapped off my head. A pair of hands went through my pockets and clothes. Everything of value was tossed up on the hood and gone through. The necklace with Amy's ring laid there within inches. Several men wore bullet-proof vests with the words US Marshals etched in thick yellow letters stamped on the black fabric. Looking around at the others, they also had the same tactical gear and yellow lettering. One of them had found the .45, held it up, and ejected the magazine into the palm of his hand.

A mobile news van materialized out of nowhere. A blonde in a long overcoat hopped out the passenger side holding a microphone. Her two assistants quickly set up the camera. Somehow the bastards knew about the operation the Feds were pulling and hitched along. The camera lights flared to life and the anchorwoman began a hard-edged dialog on the operation to nab one of New Mexico's most wanted.

One of the agents walked up holding a camera. "Stand up straight and look into the camera." The camera flashed. The handcuffs were undone long enough to get fingerprints before being clamped back into place. With camera and fingerprints, the deputy slid into the passenger seat of the Yukon where a computer screen illuminated his face.

A man wandered up. He'd been the man I thought was Richardson. "Logan Pierce, my, my, you are a hard man to find."

I gave a muffled reply. "You got the wrong guy."

He held up a large photograph. "Funny, you sure look like him. You still want to play games?"

"I look like lots of people," I snapped back.

The agent finished punching on his computer, leaned his head out the window. "We got a positive ID."

Damn it.

"Another of New Mexico's most wanted finally captured," he stabbed a finger at what little belongings laid out on the hood. He held up the driver's license and read the name. "Sam Highborn?"

"That's what it says."

He fingered the edge and peeled away the clear laminate. "Such a cheap job, and to think you actually got a job here using this." He shook his head. He peeled the laminate away before tearing off my photograph. He held up the driver license showing the real Highborn. "You don't look like Sam Highborn."

I didn't say anything.

"So, what happened back in New Mexico?" he pressed.

"What the hell you talking about?" I whispered.

"Don't insult my intelligence, Logan. You remember the shootings?" He didn't wait for an answer. "Of course you do. Five dead, a house shot full of holes. There were a couple survivors....you were one of them."

I didn't say anything.

"I'm Agent Williams with the FBI, Logan. Everyone's looking forward to hearing about your part in New Mexico." He leaned over the hood, eyeing the necklace. He picked it up, looked at the ring dangling from the cold grey links and rolled his eyes over to mine. "Amy said you'd have this on you."

"Amy?" I whispered.

He smiled, took me by the elbow, popped the back door on the Yukon and placed me in the back seat. Another deputy slid in beside me. They weren't taking any chances.

Leaning in, his breath smelled of onions. "I hope you decide to make the right decision, Logan. You better get ready to explain what happened back in New Mexico. These games you're playing are over." The doors slammed shut.

There wasn't any more running, no more looking over the shoulder, just the lingering cold hard knowledge I was going to prison for the rest of my life.

The thing that stuck in my brain was his comment. *Amy said you'd have this on you...*

How the hell would he know that?

TWENTY-SEVEN

The sounds of locks opening and closing sounded like thunder in the hollow lime-green painted halls. I was escorted through a series of man traps, one door buzzing and clicking then opening while the ones we passed through slammed shut and locked. A couple of Marshal Deputies held onto my elbows, pulling me deeper down into the bowels of Hell and forgotten oblivion and dreams of forlorn anguish.

When we arrived in booking, I was photographed, fingerprinted and told to strip *au natural* by an unconcerned officer. He was heavy-set, with thick jowls that shook every time he spoke or rotated his melon-sized head. He'd probably been doing this job for years and had seen more ass than an army of porn stars. He snapped on a pair of blue nitrile gloves over thick hands. He picked up my grease soaked uniform and began searching the fabric for hidden contraband before turning his attention to me.

"Turn and face the wall, sir...now squat and cough."

I turned, squatted and coughed.

"Again, cough harder please."

I did then stood up.

"Again."

I did it again.

"Turn and face me."

I turned.

"Run your fingers through your hair."

I raked them through.

"The beard...run your fingers through."

I clawed my fingers through the beard several times.

"Open your mouth wide."

I had hoped my breath would've killed the bastard when he looked inside.

"Lift your arms."

I did and he looked under the armpits.

"Show me your hands....spread your fingers out."

I held out my hands and spread the fingers.

"Lift your sack."

I lifted my ball sack while he looked for any hidden contraband.

"Left foot up...let me see the bottoms."

I lifted the left foot.

"Spread the toes."

I spread the toes out while he leaned over to look between the digits. The thought crossed my mind to kick him in the face but I suppressed the urge.

"Right foot," he motioned.

I repeated the process with the right foot.

"Okay, step over to the bench sir and grab your uniform."

The 'uniform' consisted of white paper-thin cotton issue

prisoner duds and a pair of foam slippers. My clothes and anything else I had on me was bagged and tagged and tossed into a cardboard box signed with my name and carted off to another part of booking I assumed was the storage area. 537929. That was my inmate number as it was scrawled all across the box in tight neat writing.

"Scars?" asked the woman processing the paperwork. She was detailing possible evidence into a report.

"Some."

"Gunshots?" She held up the paper. "It says here you were possibly shot earlier this year."

"I was."

"Where?"

"Shoulder and legs."

"Show me please."

I took off my shirt revealing the healed-over scars from where Thomas had given me his parting gift.

She took up a small digital camera from her desk and shot a few pictures. "Looks painful."

I didn't say anything.

She picked up her pen. "What doctor did you go see for that?"

"None," I said

She paused, looked at the scar then went back to writing. She shook her head in disbelief. "Your legs? Show me those also."

I stood, dropped my cotton pants and showed the pinkish hued rumble strip scars. More flashing of pictures from the digital camera.

"Pull up your pants. Tattoos?"

I put my shirt back on. "Did you see any? Or do I need to strip again?"

"Attorney?" She ignored the remark.

I snorted. "What for?"

"There's a court date coming up soon. I recommend you get

one or we'll appoint one for you."

"Not interested."

She shook her head and scribbled on the paper again. "If you do not have money for an attorney, we will appoint one for you."

"Go ahead and appoint one. I don't give a shit and I won't be telling him or her shit either."

"Suit yourself, Mr. Pierce." She focused in on her report, scribbling a few notations.

Once the paperwork was finished, she motioned a guard over. He instructed me to rise and face the wall and place my hands behind my back. He flipped on a set of handcuffs and cinched them tight. Grabbing my elbow, we went out of the booking department, through several doors, down a long, wide and well-lit hallway. He held my elbow and steered me in the direction we were going until we came to a door off to the right side.

He paused, keyed his mike. "Central, be advised one for Six Delta."

After several minutes, the door clicked and buzzed. He opened it and guided me through before letting the door slam shut behind us. We found ourselves standing in a large pod chamber containing some twenty cells. There were ten on the bottom floor and ten more on the second level. The walkways were lined with chain link fence and gates. It was a prison within a prison and meant no further freedoms were allowed beyond this point.

The guard handed over the paperwork to one of several guards who resembled linebackers. He nodded and my personal guard left the pod. The four of us looked each other up. None of them looked in the mood to play. A fourth guard sat at a desk, scribbling away on a notepad. He looked up once and went back to writing.

The silence was deafening.

"Mr. Pierce!" The voice boomed across the pod and grabbed

my attention. "I'm Lieutenant Haines, I'm in charge of solitary confinement." He held out his hands. "Welcome to my house. You just missed dinner. I can arrange for a plate to be bought to you if you're hungry?"

I shook my head. I was just too damned tired to worry about eating.

"Alright," he paused looking me over. "Breakfast will be at six, lunch at noon and dinner at five. The counselor will be by later to drop off toiletries and anything else you might need. Do you need anything in particular?"

I held out my hands. The chain links rattled. "How about a hacksaw? Maybe a torch set?"

No one smiled.

He looked at me with a deadpan expression and ignored my comment. "You will be allowed to shower in the morning. Inmates are not allowed to mingle with others in this section. You will be under constant monitoring, checks every half hour, maybe more often if you show signs of depression. You are allowed to make phone calls only if you have money for a pre-paid card."

He rambled on about the standing rules and policies for several minutes before signaling to the trio of guards to take me away. The three weren't taking any chances. A couple grabbed my elbows while the third walked behind us.

I slowly hobbled across the pod floor and up the stairs. The ankle still hurt but it wasn't broken. We reached the top of the stairs and the gate buzzed and then clicked open. We walked down the corridor passed several cells. The inmates inside had their faces pressed against the glass watching the procession pass by.

The guard behind us called out to stop. We stopped in front of a cell. One of the guards keyed his mike requesting cell Bravo two-seven to be opened. The cell door buzzed and was opened while two of the guards undid the shackles but kept a firm grip on my wrists. Once the shackles were removed, I was then instructed to walk into the cell.

The cell door slammed shut and signaled the finality of my situation. I felt like this was the lowest depths a man could go in this hell of a life. The only good thing about all of this was there was no cellmate waiting for me. I liked the idea of being by myself.

The CO's wandered off, checking the other cells in the pod as they left. Every now and then voices echoed out across the pod from the other inmates. Several called out to me but I ignored them. I was lost in my own thoughts.

I saw the window and climbed up on the bunk and looked outside through the thick shatterproof window. Snow kept falling at a steady pace, blanketing everything in a thick layer of white. The lights from the city cast a yellowed haze over the fresh blanket of snow.

I felt the sudden loss of my freedom and realized the Marshals were dead-assed serious but also, they had to understand, I was just as serious about staying alive. I wanted to know if Amy was okay, perhaps even see her. No one was saying anything and I refused to volunteer any info. Hell, I had lost everything in waiting and it was the last hand to play.

In a few hours, the world would be awake, people would be walking to work on the streets below and here I was locked away. Rolling back on the bunk, I found the mattress less than desirable. The one-inch thick foam covered in pinstriped fabric seemed to melt into the cold metal bunk. Voices hissed and whispered throughout the pod. The neighbor next door began calling out to me and by his tone, I knew he was Spanish.

"Hey, *esse*…the new guy…neighbor."

I rolled over in my bunk. *Do Mexicans actually live this far north?* "You talking to me?" My voice echoed off the cold grey walls.

"Yeah, what's *cho* name? You look like that guy on TV...the news."

I had been on the run for so long and never felt secure in anything these long past five months. Life on the edge had taken a toll on my ability to sleep regularly. I felt at any moment, the Dixie Mafia or the dirty cops were going to kill me at anywhere or anytime, and that always had kept me on edge. In here though, I felt a sense of safety even if my freedoms had been stripped away. The Mafia would have to climb a twenty-foot chain-link fence, then over rolled razor wire, surveillance cameras and a horde of correctional officers.

"What guy?" I muttered softly and closed my heavy eyelids.

"That guy from *Nuevo Mexico* they caught....you him?"

But before I could answer, the heavy tentacles of fatigue dragged me under into an ocean of deep sleep.

TWENTY-EIGHT

The following morning, I was escorted from my cell in full dress shackles and escorted by several guards. I don't know if somebody messed up the paperwork but they were claiming I was a flight risk. Maybe I was but where the hell was I going to run off to? The library? The rec yard? The other prisoners could be heard howling, yelling or trying to play the role of bad-ass.

We went through booking where the same guard with the thick jowls gave another quick search and pat down. I thanked God I didn't have to strip down and have him staring up my ass again. We exited the side doors where a van idled in the snow-covered parking lot. The snow floated silently in the air. It felt good to feel it tickling the nerves on my face. It felt like freedom.

From there, I was transported in the van along the city roads serving as arteries throughout St. Paul and into a massive white granite building that had 'Federal' written all over it. The van interior grew dark as it nosed down into an underground parking lot. We came to a stop at a dock area. When the side door slid open, several Marshal Deputies stood there with deep frowns etched across their faces.

The guard unlocked the shackle lock-down and assisted me out to the concrete floor.

The leg shackles sucked. They only allowed me to shuffle my feet for so many inches and there was absolutely no chance of me bolting and running. I was taken down a series of well-lit hallways through remote controlled bared gates and eventually up to an elevator.

The ride up the elevator was silent. The Marshal guys didn't say a word inch wise and kept a wary eye on me. The only sounds were the elevator sliding up on its rails or a soft cough and sniffling from one of the Marshal Deputies.

The elevator glided to a stop on the fifth floor, the doors rolled open and instead of bright white walls, we were greeted with grey walls and well-polished granite flooring. I shuffled forward, the chains rattling as we exited. One of the marshals pointed which way to go and we shuffled off in that direction until we reached a door at the far end of the hallway. One of the Deputies rapped on it and it opened.

It was Williams who answered. "Well, Mr. Pierce, step inside please."

I moved slowly inside the room. The only sounds were the rattling of my chains.

Williams indicated for the Deputies to undo the shackles. As they undid the handcuffs and shackles, Williams watched me intently, studying an adversary. With the shackles finally removed, he indicated for me to take a seat. I took a moment to rub the circulation back into the sore wrists. The room was small. The white paint glared under the lights. Nothing hung on the walls, not a calendar, no photos, nothing, save for a single large framed-in tinted window on the one wall to my left. Everything was going to be recorded and people were watching from behind it. I slowly seated myself, leaned over the table, exhaled and rested my forehead in my hands. The chair pulled out across from me and Williams sat down and smiled. "We figured you would like to change your tune."

"I need a damned cigarette."

"Sorry, I don't smoke." He opened the folder and began laying out photos between us. One was of Hobart sprawled out in a bloody pool next to the nephews. A few were close up headshots. All were dead. The only photograph I didn't recognize was a distant shot of a man hanging from a tree. Under the dangling corpse, were a few crumpled papers and a ragged green backpack.

I looked away suddenly feeling sick.

Williams noted my reaction, smiled and leaned back in his chair. The door opened again and another man, dressed in black khakis and a tan long-sleeve shirt stepped in, also carrying a folder and a writing pad. He closed the door, sighed, and took up the remaining seat in the room.

Williams broke the silence. "Logan, this is Steven Kirkpatrick from the FBI branch here in Saint Paul. He is in charge of this investigation."

Kirkpatrick nodded. "You were a hard man to find, Logan."

"I didn't want to be found."

"It's obvious why we had to call in the big guns, the U.S. Marshals, they always find their man."

Williams looked over, nodded then looked back to me while breaking out a pen and laying out a notepad. "So, I think we all know why we're here." He flicked his pen and rested the point on the notepad. "Let's start with the events that happened in New Mexico, Logan."

"Should I lawyer up?" I asked.

Williams shrugged. "It's up to you. We can stop this interview and wait for your lawyer, sure. Is that what you want?"

I shrugged. What difference would it make? "I'm not sure on anything."

Kirkpatrick leaned forward and got to the point. "We could go that way but then the process slows down. We would have to stop, take you back to jail where you get to eat prison food and stay in your cell for twenty-three hours a day while we find a lawyer to take your case. That could take a couple of days. Or we can talk. We just need to know a few things. That's all. What happened in New Mexico? What was your association with the Dixie Mafia?"

"Wait up now, I am not in any way *'associated'* with the Dixie Mafia."

He held his hands open. "We beg to differ. You were at Thomas' house when five people were killed and also we know about your on-going affair with Amy Hauser. You worked at Duggan's Truck Stop, with known members of the Dixie Mafia, we could go on and on, so yes, you are connected."

"I don't know shit about the Dixie Mafia. Yes...me and Amy...we had our thing but that was it. The rest is a coincidence."

"So, you knew Amy was married to a mobster?" Williams asked.

"Yes...well, no, not until later."

"You knew about Duggan's being a front for the Dixie Mafia?"

"A front?"

"A business set up to take in dirty money and make it clean."

"I didn't know." I leaned in. "I just needed a damned job to fix my car and go to Texas."

"To another Duggan's location?"

I flinched. "No, find a job in the oil fields. I don't know shit about the Dixie Mafia. How many times have I got to say it?"

Kirkpatrick cleared his throat and Williams took his cue. He slid over several photographs. Hobart's dead eyes looked into my soul. "New Mexico, the night of the shooting, what happened? You were there when five Dixie Mafia members were shot." He slid another photograph forward. Dwayne with a bullet hole in his check and the back of his head blown out, brains and blood glistened in the flash of the camera.

I turned away. "It's not what you think."

Kirkpatrick leaned back in his chair. "Enlighten us."

"I really, really need a cigarette for God's sake."

Kirkpatrick and Williams looked at each other and Williams nodded. Kirkpatrick fumbled in his shirt pocket and produced a pack of Camels. He tapped one out, handed it to me and then lit it with his lighter.

"Where is Amy?" I whispered.

Williams replied. "Safe."

"I would like to talk to her."

"Out of the question, Logan, you're in no position to negotiate anything."

"No way at all?"

Williams shook his head. "Everything has gone too far to turn back now. Sorry kid, but when you went on the run, it changed everything."

"Meaning?"

"You should've surrendered to authorities a long time ago."

Kirkpatrick cleared his throat. "Logan, look, I don't want to keep beating around the bush here. Here's what's going to happen. You tell us everything, and I mean everything on what happened and we can throw you a lifeline. Or we can go all the way through the legal process and you'll end up in prison for twenty to life."

"I didn't do a damn thing, nothing I'm ashamed of nor did I

break any laws."

Williams shuffled through the stack of folders and pulled one out and flipped it open. "Let's see, we have accessory to murder, five counts, that's about twenty years per charge, then possession of a destructive device..."

I cut him off. "I didn't *have* a bomb."

"A sawed-off Winchester twelve gauge pump was recovered from your Jeep," Kirkpatrick quipped.

Before I could answer, Williams continued. "That's ten years off your life. Let's see...fugitive from justice across state lines is about another five years, engaging in monetary transactions in property derived from unlawful activities, that's another ten years. The charges go on and on and on, Logan. Should I continue?"

"Not to mention your fleeing and assault on federal officers at the truck stop back in Clearwater *and* the State of New Mexico and Torrance County law officials who are lining up their charges against you as we speak," Kirkpatrick added.

"Alright, alright...I get the point. What's this lifeline?"

Williams spoke low, so low that his voice rumbled in the room. "WITSEC."

"I'm not following."

Kirkpatrick frowned. "Witness protection, it's a program run by the U.S. Marshals."

Williams leaned forward. "Essentially, you cooperate with us on everything, and I mean everything, and we'll look at placing you in the program. That means a new start in life." He paused, watching my expression. "But, if you withhold even the slightest detail, we'll throw your sorry butt in prison to rot."

"Witness Protection?"

Williams held his hands open. "It's all you got left."

"Hendricks?"

"What about him?" William's expression went flat, unreadable.

"Did he take this offer?"

Kirkpatrick shifted his weight. "It's none of your concern and not relevant to your current situation."

I figured they had Hendricks stuffed away in this program, but they weren't giving up any information about him either. I plied my next question. "Amy?"

"You should've quit running a long time ago."

"I don't get why and I don't feel like talking unless I get to see her."

Williams shook his head. "We'll play a game, Logan; let us start by giving you a little bit of info. Then you give us something in return."

I sighed. If this was poker, I was losing. "Go ahead."

Kirkpatrick frowned. "Here's what happened."

Amy had gotten away the night of the shootings. Instead of going after the money hidden in the well house, she had run towards the main road. She had run across the field, down to Martinez Road and hid within a cluster of juniper trees. She called her point of contact with the FBI.

I held up a hand. "Wait…FBI?"

Williams looked hard into my eyes. "She had been working with us for over a year prior to your involvement with the night in question."

I looked down in thought and swore silently. I remembered the times where she was collecting and going through those files in the back storage room, and the thumb drives. I had thought Johnson had wanted her to go through the files. She had been collecting and giving material all along to the Feds. She had gone to school for accounting, so she knew what to look for. Then those phone calls in the middle of the night. I had thought it was Thomas but it was the Feds. "Why?"

"When her sister was murdered, she came to us with information about Dave Musgrave's homicide and other items of interest."

"Murdered? I thought it was an accident? She told me it was a fire."

"Lorraine was shot several times before the fire was deliberately set to her house. Her sister was an assistant district attorney in Biloxi. Her homicide has been linked back to the Dixie Mafia."

"Attorney?" I rubbed my forehead. "Assistant DA? So all of this is about her sister's death?"

"When she came to us she was a mess, but she agreed with helping us out in exchange for a few things. I honestly had my doubts she could pull it off due to her drug habit but we got what we needed." Williams pointed out.

Kirkpatrick leaned forward. "As well as Thomas Hauser's involvement. It was all over embezzled money from Duggan's Truck Stop and the guns, of which were stolen from several military installations, then transported by some low-key trucking outfits. These guns and explosives were then dropped off at Duggan's in Moriarty. Dave Musgrave then took control and stored them where they were ultimately destined to be sold to his contact within the *Cráneos Muertos* Cartel in Mexico."

I sighed in disbelief. "I thought the cartel was the same thing."

"There's numerous gangs and cartels in Mexico. Musgrave initially sold them to the *Cráneos Muertos* faction. Arturo, whose loyalty's lie with another rival group known as *La Familia Beltran*, had already paid the Dixie Mafia for them."

"You guys...put her in danger."

"She had to get us the evidence we needed to move forward with the case and she had no problem with it. We had set precautions in place for her safety."

"Precautions? What the hell were those?"

Kirkpatrick drummed his fingers on the table. "It's immaterial at this point isn't it?"

I didn't. After everything I had been through, I wanted to know. My mind went through all the scenarios and people working at the truck stop, eventually settling on the fact the FBI had to have planted one of their own inside of Duggan's. It made sense. I leaned over and saw the picture of the man hanging from a tree. The one item that stuck out was the green backpack lying on the ground under the man's feet. It dawned on me who the man was hanging from the tree like rotten fruit.

"Derek..." I whispered. His mysterious suicide had captured the local news for a few days and then faded away into oblivion. The green backpack, I should've seen it sooner. Amy would collect the information then pass the pack off to Derek. I didn't know how much he had divulged in those last minutes on earth. I was sure he had told Thomas and his cousins about Amy and me. He was the only rational explanation.

"Are you done?" Williams spoke.

"Am I right?"

Kirkpatrick cleared his throat. "Logan, Derek was an alias and yes...he was working undercover," he cleared his throat. "We'll come back to this matter at a later time.

"He had a wonderful wife and two daughters in case you wanted to know," Williams added. He looked over to Kirkpatrick. "Let's continue."

Kirkpatrick continued.

They came running and picked her up from Martinez Road. She explained everything that was going on and the Feds realized they had to get me and Amy out of a precarious dilemma.

They called Torrance County and also additional back up from the Albuquerque FBI branch. They had to wait a long time for back up to arrive. With only the two agents it would have been suicide going in. Amy was beside herself in the waiting. Eventually, the cavalry arrived but it was too late. When everybody went to the house, no one was there and soon law enforcement officials began to assume the worst had happened to me.

A call came across the radio that a large amount of gunfire was coming from Juan Thomas Road. An unusual amount and then the cops from three different counties arrived on scene at Thomas' house but they were greeted with five corpses. Two plus two equals I had been there and they figured Thomas had taken me as a hostage. From there, they looked. They had put out a BOLO, or a Be-On-the-Look-Out on me and Thomas.

Thomas was found a few days later in Texas. I didn't know about this fact. He had been found in some farmhouse banging some broad he knew. A small firefight broke out and the lady caught a bullet to the face and Thomas caught one in the gut but he was still among the living. Everyone thought he had killed me off but then the El Camino shows up as a burned wreck outside Durango and everyone realized I was on the run.

"Needless to say, Amy has been worried sick since you disappeared. No one expected you to run," Williams said.

Kirkpatrick nodded. "Or for this long."

I listened to the story and swore.

"So, we've explained our side of things a bit. Now..." Williams took up his pen and rested the point on the notepad. "New Mexico, what happened?"

I finished my smoke and smashed out the butt in the ashtray. A beer would be nice right about now but I didn't think they would give me one. I exhaled, wiped my face with both hands and sighed. I explained everything. I began my story with the El Camino breaking down, my employment at Duggan's Truck Stop, the affair with Amy minus the explicit details on the subject. I explained in depth how Hendricks and I had found the money, the guns and all the events leading up to the night of the shooting and the events involved. I told them about the men who had done the shooting from outside Thomas' house and murdered everyone. The bombshell dropped when I mentioned Richardson and Nguyen being State cops.

Williams eyed me. "You sure they were cops?"

"They didn't show badges or politely knock on the front door asking for the money, but yeah, I'm positive."

"State cops?" Kirkpatrick asked, his eyebrows knitted in concern.

"That's what I said. State cops."

They looked at each other.

"Let me guess, you didn't know."

"You've heard of Arturo? He's also a State cop." Williams jotted down notes on his notepad.

I nodded I had.

Kirkpatrick leaned in. "We knew he had other men on the force working around him but we didn't know any names. It raises some concerns and answers a lot of questions."

"You said there were five men. We have Arturo, Richardson and Nguyen. Who were the other two?"

"I don't know their names."

"Can you ID the other two men?"

I nodded that I could. I felt the urge to press in with my request. "Amy."

Williams leaned back in his chair, sighed and began tapping his fingers on the table.

I leaned in over the table. "Williams, for God's sake, I'm asking please," I held my hands open. "I've lost everything but this one last sliver of hope. This one thing I'm asking…begging for. I don't care about what I've lost already. I just need to know, please, can I see her? It's all I got left is this one strand of hope."

The room fell silent with the exception of the heater cycling in and out as warm air was being pushed through the vent.

Williams frowned. "I'm going to say, you two have this uncanny sense about each other, some weird psychic connection. I can't put a finger on it but she knows you've been found, Logan. It's been all over the news obviously, and the moment the story broke, she was calling wanting…demanding to see you."

I felt a surge of hope.

Williams looked over to Kirkpatrick while he unwrapped a stick of gum. He popped it in his maw. "I don't see an issue. We still have more questions but I think we got a good witness to events and a solid case. We have to move on this right away though. We got other guys to grab."

Williams looked into my face for some time. I knew he was assessing, digesting the information I had given him. These guys were trained to look for minor deviations in tone, facial expressions, whether I looked away, blinked my eyes too much, anything that hinted I was lying. I held my gaze straight with his. Finally, he looked over to the tinted glass, nodded and waved a hand.

Minutes passed and the sound of the clock on the wall sounded like salvo shots from a battleship with each passing second.

The door cracked open slowly.

She stood there, tears and something was spoken that I couldn't make out. I rose quickly from my seat.

She rushed over and we embraced, her tears soaked through the jumpsuit and I felt my own tears roll. So many months of not knowing and finally, she was here. I found a measure of hope swell from the deepest regions of my heart. "My God…Amy."

"Logan…" she whispered.

"I missed you," she placed her hand on my chest, looked up into my eyes. "It's okay. It's over, Logan." She touched my face. "God, you're a mess. That beard makes you look like a homeless guy that got run over. And the hair…baby, what have you done to yourself?" I could see the look of concern etched in those deep green eyes and her voice tone cracked.

I wanted to choke but surprisingly, my tone was firm. "It helps…with the winter winds."

"You looked better with shorter hair."

"God…you're beautiful, I thought about you every day, wondered where you were, wondering about why…everything."

"I thought about you too. It's all over now baby, seriously, it's over," she looked over to Williams, then back to me. "It's okay. We're together again."

I cried and I was glad to hear her say it was over. After losing everything, I had finally found the one thing that mattered in this life. It was Amy. It was all that mattered. I felt the sudden release from the dark pits of hell. I was climbing out of it, back up to the land of the living, back into the warmth of her light.

Williams placed a briefcase on the table and popped the metal clasps. "Alright, Logan," he pulled out a folder. "We have a lot of paperwork to go through and it starts with this one. In exchange for your testimony against Arturo, Richardson, Nguyen and two other yet to be named State police officers; you will need to sign this," he slid over a single piece of paper.

I picked it up. "What's this?"

He rested his fingers together in a church steeple. "Your start to a new life."

Kirkpatrick leaned back in his seat and popped his gum.

EPILOGUE

It's been a year since the Marshal Services dumped us off in Montana. Several weeks before our exodus from Washington DC, they showed us a video and an assortment of photographs of our new house along with the town we would relocate to. The house was a small two-story affair and had been built around 1929 with a large backyard of plush green and several trees. Finding a job shouldn't be too hard. Eastern Montana was claiming the title of being home to the Bakkan oil fields. It wasn't Texas but it would do.

We flew to Billings and were whisked away east on a vast open highway in a rented Dodge Durango. We had a couple of WITSEC guys with us who acted as councilors. They tagged along to ensure our first weeks in the real world would be a positive transition. I was just glad to finally see the countryside for the first time in over a year. Life inside the fortress was beginning to drive both of us nuts.

For the last year, we had been pigeon-holed in some fortified complex in Washington DC. Everyone referred to this place as the 'fortress' which was a suitable nickname. It was bomb proof, had an army of armed security, and every steel plated door was locked at all times. If someone wanted in to get to anyone inside, it was going to take a small army, a battalion of Abrams tanks, and a squad of B-52's to make the smallest of dents. The place was large enough for twelve families and I had seen plenty of people come and go. We weren't allowed to converse with the other tenants, which had been fine with me. Most of those guys were genuine Italian mob or ostracized gang members who had done a shit-ton of bad things.

During our stay at the fortress, we had learned our new names: Larry and Ava Williams. Along with new birth certificates and social security numbers, we also received a marriage license. I guess that made it official minus the honeymoon, of which, I promised we would take once the storms of our old lives had finished washing away. We were drilled on our new identities, our backgrounds and how to avoid talking with other people about our past.

I can tell you I was born in Virginia, moved to Utah to some back-wood community, dropped out of high school and received a GED instead of a diploma. This made it easier to avoid having people look up high school yearbook photos. I had been a mechanic since 1989 (not too far off in truth since I had started in 1988), I was never married before I met Ava on a vacation trip to Mexico (drop the 'New' and thank God I never had to talk about the ex…ever), we married several months later in Vegas by an Elvis impersonator, we wanted a simpler life and moved to Montana. We had been married for several years now.

For Ava, it was a bit more difficult since she still had a southern twang in her tones. She was born in Oklahoma, moved to Alabama, and also had dropped out of school and received a GED, she went to work as an accountant for a law firm before heading to Mexico where we met and later married. She also had never been married prior.

Both of our parents were deceased, we had no siblings, and any relatives living were estranged. Friends were few and far between and past employers were trucking or lawyer outfits that had gone under or were bought out. A lot of effort was placed into securing our identities.

In exchange for our new lives, we both gave our testimonies over the course of a year. The last I heard, Thomas was looking at spending the rest of his life behind bars. Along with Amy's damning words and the mountain of physical evidence, a bunch of other Dixie mob guys landed behind bars along with a few judges, lawyers, and one congressman. The tainted tentacles of corruption ran deep, deeper than I had thought and it all boiled down to illegal gun running, prostitution, extortion, drugs, and murder.

New Mexico was in turmoil with the breaking news about the scandal involving the State troopers. The five men had smeared shit across the image of the State Police and for those sins, the five men would be meted out justice to the fullest.

I put the finger on the four men sitting in the courtroom and explained my part in the testimony. I wished Richardson had been there. When the arrest warrants were issued, he had decided it was better to eat a .40 caliber bullet from his service pistol than go to prison.

With the physical evidence and my words, they were looking at life behind bars. The four cut a deal and managed to get light sentences but they were still looking at spending forty plus years up in Santa Fe even when they gave up information dealing with the cartels down in Mexico. They would be lucky to get out and collect Social Security.

The last I saw of the remaining four men, was them being led out of the courtroom in chains. I identified all four as being the men I had seen outside Thomas' house making it into a pile of toothpicks. But it was a former stripper girlfriend of Richardson who shined a dim light on the whereabouts of the missing money. She had made a deal with the DA and agreed to tell everything. She took the stand and when cross-examined about the location of the money, she stated Officer Richardson was the only one who knew of its whereabouts. They, the five officers, had all agreed that after they had taken the money on the night of the shootings, Richardson had hidden said money at an undisclosed location. After a specified amount of time had passed, he would've handed out everyone's cut.

To date, the money is still missing.

I was just glad to place the whole shit-sandwich road behind me…us. We could start to live a life. Although I had lost everything, I had Ava with me. That in itself was worth everything I had gone through.

I had thought about shifting careers but thought better of it. I had the opportunity to start down a different career path but nixed it. At least the Marshals had granted me that single thread of life. Being a mechanic was all I knew and understood. I had looked into being an aircraft technician. The thought of being an A and P mechanic, or working on aircraft did have some appeal to it and would've paid better but being a diesel mechanic was all I knew or understood.

I couldn't get my old toolbox back. WITSEC stated it was too much of an identifier. God only knew if the toolbox was even still around. I had to resign myself to the fact that the shop crew back in Moriarty had already helped themselves to my tools and they were long gone. WITSEC officials did manage to get me an old Snap-On triple bay loaded down with tools they had dug up from some government surplus warehouse. The government and military liked to toss away tools and toolboxes by the truckload so it was a simple request on their part. All of it was small potatoes compared to what I had originally, but it would kick-start my career back into motion. I took up busting wrenches at a nearby truck dealership.

Ava took a job as an assistant for a local accounting firm.

We made a few new friends and we were known to keep our personal lives private. I liked it that way. The best part was never having to worry about paying alimony to the ex-wife anymore. I was sure she was howling in rage at not having all the extra cash from my broken back.

On the money side, the WITSEC guys made sure we had some money, not a whole lot as some might think, but it was enough to start out again. We were given six months to get back on our feet before the funds were cut off. In the first month in Montana, we bought an old Jeep Cherokee I had found on a local Internet site. For a few hundred bucks, and a head gasket later, we had wheels. The following month we bought an older Chevy pickup for around five hundred bucks supposedly had a bad transmission. It turned out to be only a bad clutch. So far, we had done well getting back up on life within a few months.

Life rolled on and soon we were making and banking some of our earnings. Once the Marshals saw we were self-sufficient enough, they cut off the money tap and we were truly on our own.

The nightmares subsided. It was getting rare I would wake up with the sheets clutched in a bundle while clawing for the .45 that wasn't there. Ava did her best to soothe me during these moments of terror. I had also quit the drink and very seldom smoked. It was rare when I had a beer, a Heineken for old time's sake, but that went unfinished and Ava dumped the remaining flat brew down the sink. I stayed away from the hard stuff.

But as in all things, a person adapts to a different vice. This time I took up the computer and discovered Facebook.

I started up an account and took measures to secure my identity. The WITSEC guys had warned us from the beginning to avoid any kind of social media. Maybe I should've known better but this was a small town and the winters were long. I made up a place where I was at, made a few friends from work and started looking around. The internet age is sometimes a wondrous thing but it is also a place full of pitfalls and folly.

One night, I had a friend's request.

I hit the link.

George Olsen....who is this?

I clicked on the profile but it revealed not much of anything. He was located in Palm Springs, California and I didn't know anyone living there. I hit the message tab and typed a response.

Who is this?

A half hour floated by before I got another message in the form of a picture. There within grease-stained hands was the key with the letters NNRR stamped across the end.

My heart froze and my jaw dropped. Did I dare answer?

I typed out a slow response with numbed fingers. *What is that?*

Money. The reply came.

What money?

Don't be stupid, I know where it's at...Paleface.

You got to be joking was my first thought. I didn't answer. I shut down Facebook and the computer. The computer whined to a halt and I looked around the dark living room. My heart was beating hard, my throat pulsing with fear.

I was sure it was Hendricks. He was still scheming on things about the missing money. I wondered just how in the hell he had figured out how to track me down on Facebook. Had someone within the Marshals service told him? Maybe he picked up on an accidental slip of the lip. Hendricks was good at finding out information even from the smallest of details and then knitting all of those tiny tidbits into a bigger picture. What if it was a Marshals deputy pretending to be Hendricks just to scare the hell out of me and force me off of social media? Maybe it was a test? I was sure they were looking for the money also.

What if the money was in easy reach though? I couldn't remember if I had given the key back to Hendricks when we found the money. For the life of me and as many times as I thought it over, I just couldn't remember.

The main question running through my mind was how Hendricks had figured out where Richardson hid all the money. As far as the money went, both his and my cuts were still missing. Not to mention the additional monies that was hoarded at Thomas' house. I had seen Dwayne lift those two duffel packs from the floor during the night of the shooting. Who knew how much was in those large bags he had carried out of the room. I figured maybe a cool million easy on top of our original cuts. The money was said to be earned through extortion, prostitution rings and other criminal ventures the Dixie Mafia had invested into. Richardson though had made certain no one would find the money when he committed to eating a .40 caliber sandwich.

I wasn't sure what happened to Hendricks once the mess in New Mexico settled. I knew Williams had said he had spoken to him and his girlfriend Jill but had they also shoved them into the WITSEC program? No one volunteered any information on him or his whereabouts and I concluded that they had. Hendricks had been in the thick of it as much as I had but he got away lightly compared to the ass beatings I received out of it.

Should I contact my WITSEC POC, or point of contact, and tell him about this? That meant calling in and giving a code, then waiting for the POC guy to come on the line where you explain things, then you might get an ass-chewing for being stupid, then he would tell me and Ava to pack up and get ready to be shuffled off to another location. The whole thought of moving again was stressful. I had a good life, Ava was happy with the low-key existence we had and I had no intentions of disrupting that.

But we could sure use more money.

Shit.

I shook it off. Even if it was Hendricks, I didn't want any part of the money. Screw that mess. I'd lost my El Camino, my toolbox and my old .45. I'd gotten two busted fingers, a broken nose, damn near went to prison for life, and almost lost Ava forever. The cold Montana winter winds would often caress the rippled scars on my shoulder and legs to remind me of those wasted efforts.

I slid silently out of bed a few mornings later so as to not disturb Ava and went to the kitchen and began making a fresh pot of coffee. While the coffee was brewing, I fired up the computer and logged onto Facebook. The message appeared to be from Hendricks. I was sure of it. I clicked on the message and tapped a few keys. *"I think you have the wrong guy, but good luck, stranger."*

I deleted my Facebook account, noting there was no response. I had no intentions of waiting for one. Hendricks, or Olsen or whoever it was, was going to have to ride solo if they wanted the money. No damned way was I going back into that mess. I silently wished Hendricks well in his future endeavors.

To hell with that money.

Ava had awakened, sliding one foot in front of the other, shaking her hair with a delicate hand as she moved silently into the kitchen. She smiled, bid me morning and poured herself a cup of coffee. She was dressed in nothing more than a pair of silk panties and a halter top. Sexy was all I could think. We had plans to go hiking and camping over at Glacier National Park for the weekend.

I looked at Ava, admiring her curves.

She gave that smile and wink. That same smile and wink she always did without realizing it.

I shut the computer down, walked into the kitchen, and poured a cup of coffee. I stroked her honey-blonde hair and she smiled, leaned in and we kissed.

No further thoughts of the money came to mind.

I had other things going.

About the Author

John L. Thompson currently lives in New Mexico with his wife of twenty-six years. He has been working in the trucking industry for the better part of twenty five years as a diesel technician. When he is not searching the badlands for remnants of the old west, he can be found working on novel and short story scripts. He is also an editor for Dead Guns Press.

He has had stories published in Shotgun Honey, Yellow Mama, Out of the Gutter, Runeright and Science Fiction Trails to name a few.

Truck Stop is his first novel.

Acknowledgments

There are plenty of people who had an encouraging hand in the writing of this book. It's only fair to give them some of the lime-light.

First off, a hat off to the proof readers, James Nollet, Marc Thompson, Christopher Davis, Michael Dean, M. Leon Smith, and especially my wife, Katherine Thompson, who took time out of their busy schedules to read over the script and made valuable recommendations.

Also to the TA shop crew in Moriarty, New Mexico from 2005 until 2011. You know who you are. There are too many friends to list here. Our time might've passed but the memories remain.